The Tycoon and the Texan

The Tycoon and the Texan

Phyliss Miranda

KENSINGTON
Kensington Publishing Corp.
www.kensingtonbooks.com

KENSINGTON BOOKS are published by

Kensington Publishing Corp.
119 West 40th Street
New York, NY 10018

All Kensington titles, imprints, and distributed lines are available at special quantity discounts for bulk purchases for sales promotions, premiums, fundraising, educational, or institutional use. Special book excerpts or customized printings can also be created to fit specific needs. For details, write or phone the office of the Kensington special sales manager: Kensington Publishing Corp., 119 West 40th Street, New York, NY 10018, attn: Special Sales Department; phone 1-800-221-2647.

KENSINGTON and the k logo are Reg. U.S. Pat. & TM Off.

First electronic edition: September 2013

ISBN-13: 978-1-60183-119-4
ISBN-10: 1-60183-119-6

First print edition: September 2013

ISBN-13: 978-1-60183-133-0
ISBN-10: 1-60183-133-1

Printed in the United States of America

To my longtime friends, Harold and Patricia Rasche,
whom I love dearly.
Thanks for being such important people in my husband's and my lives
and giving me the idea for the bachelorette auction.
But more important, for allowing me to use your names in my story.

Chapter One

Staring out the fifteenth-floor window of the Los Angeles Elliott Towers, McCall Johnson tried to ignore Nicodemus Dartmouth's presence. He filled the impressive, finely appointed boardroom, reminding her of a Texas Blue Norther, blustery, wild, and unpredictable.

Dying down long enough to catch his second wind, Nick left no doubt that he knew exactly where he was headed. "Mother, you know I really don't give a rusty rat's ass what decorations you use for tonight's benefit." His words were tinged with exasperation as he took his favorite Mr. Clean stance. Offering McCall a sly, irresistible grin, he surveyed the boardroom table covered with vases and flowers.

McCall closed her eyes and took a deep breath. She knew he thought one of his smiles would make things bearable, but it didn't. She'd prefer to fight a forest fire with a water gun rather than witness another Dartmouth family scrimmage, but she had no choice. After four nail-biting years as administrative assistant with the prestigious Elliott-Dartmouth Foundation, not even counting the years spent as Nick's personal secretary in his construction business, she'd heard the same old arguments, the same old positions, and the same old battle of wills more times than she could count.

Okay, so scrubbing toilets could be worse. Although she was paid well, in order to keep her independence in the current economy, not to mention saving money for her mother's headstone, she figured she had to accept her Costco lifestyle and suck it up big-time. Someday, once her parents' estate was settled, maybe she'd find financial security. For now, her job had to remain top priority.

She looked up at Nick, an intense and focused man. The few times he'd let down his guard, McCall had seen a gentle, flirtatious, even lovable man behind his façade. But, she hadn't seen that side of him for a while.

Nick folded his arms across his chest and leveled a stare at the purple and white flowers floating aimlessly in a rose bowl.

As if seeing Nick for the first time, breathless, McCall's free hand moved to her neck, and her gaze settled on the physique of the hard-fisted hunk of testosterone. As hard as she'd tried to disguise it, Nick had always made her weak in the knees; and she could bet her bottom dollar he knew it, too.

Nick's raggedy, sleeveless jersey showcased taut muscles bulging beneath rock-hard shoulders. Tight fitting baseball pants stretched like a thin coat of latex over narrow hips and emphasized his ironclad build.

A tear in the right pant knee allowed a full view of bloody road rash. Apparently, he'd had an altercation with home plate. She suspected he lost, something the man didn't do well.

How could the CEO of one of the largest construction companies on the West Coast, not to mention the owner of a Double A baseball farm team, run around looking like a Salvation Army reject? And why did this sudden change of appearance intrigue her, making her absolutely giddy? Maybe those irresistible smiles had worked better than she realized.

Nick ripped off his ball cap, slapped it against a thigh, and sent dust flying before plopping it back on his head. "I don't care what you call them, Mother, those stupid decorations aren't suitable for a roadside memorial."

"You might not take this seriously. However, darling, I do," aristocratic Madeline Elliott-Dartmouth sparred. "I need your honest opinion."

"So, you called me away from one hell of a good baseball workout for my opinion?" Like summer lightning, his dark eyes flashed. "If it's an *honest* opinion you want, then that's what you'll get. They look like someone took a leak in a jar and stuffed weeds down its throat. They're crap."

"Please refrain from using such despicable language, my dear. We are not running a construction crew. We're holding a gala for the crème de la crème of Orange County."

"Creamy mint or not, they're still crap!" he boomed.

"Now, Nicodemus—"

"Nick, Mother, Nick . . . N-I-C-K—"

"I should know your name. After all, I named you. *Nicodemus,* you are being most unreasonable."

"Unreasonable? I'll show you unreasonable—"

"Darling, you must remember this is a charitable foundation, not one of your—"

"What? One of my uncouth construction crews? Or one of my sweaty baseball players?" Nick placed his hands behind his back and took a stance that reeked of unbridled energy and unwavering zest for life. He gave a sideways glance at McCall and raised an eyebrow.

"If you would put as much effort into this event as you do your monkeys—"

"If you're referring to my baseball club, they are the Gorillas, Mother, Gorillas—"

"An ape is an ape." Madeline waved her hands in a gesture of dismissal.

Nick shook his head. "I don't know why in the hell I agreed to this."

"Because, one of these days you will inherit all of *this.*" She swept the room with her arms. "And you need experience in the charitable side of our businesses."

"Bullshit!" Nick's well-honed body moved around the conference room with the grace of a skilled prizefighter. Floating, agile, wearing away his opponent one jab at a time.

McCall's back stiffened. She'd heard enough. It was time for her to slow Nick down a bit. "Nick, listen to your mother. You're being totally disrespectful—" Interrupted by the soft ring of the telephone in the distance, she closed her notepad and headed for the doorway. "You should be happy to have a mother who loves you and cares about your opinion."

In a well-bred Southern voice, Josephine Sawyer, the Foundation's Executive Director and resident mother hen, took charge. "She's right. Why don't you listen to Madeline for once?"

Reaching the outer office, McCall snatched up the phone and settled into her chair. After being asked to hold by the caller's secretary, McCall keep a surveillant eye on the doorway.

Nick removed his hat, ran his hands through his hair, and glared at his mother before turning to Josie. "You two are teaming up on me, and I damn well know it."

After a brief conversation, McCall hung up. So far, it had been one heck of a day and a sure bet it was about to get worse. From the inception of the idea for the gala, she had fretted that tonight's charity event would be nothing but a disaster hunting a home. If the argument over the decorations wasn't enough, she now had to go back into the boardroom and deliver more bad news.

"Hellfire and brimstone, Mr. Impatience is going to get his co-jones twisted in a wad over this one," she muttered under her breath, hoping to relieve some of her frustration. "But, he'll survive. He always does."

McCall marched back into the raging storm. "Excuse me—"

"What?" Nick and Madeline's responses rippled into one volcanic chorus.

"That was Colleen Overton. She specifically asked me to give Nick a message." McCall clenched her jaw, expecting an outburst. She didn't have long to wait.

"What in the hell did she want?" Nick spun to face McCall. Sharp, unfathomable eyes of a wild mustang stampeded hers. "To make sure we ordered enough Dom Pérignon?"

"No, Nick, she wanted—"

"Caviar? No, cream puffs. Is that soft enough for you, Mother?" Nick called over his shoulder.

His stare lingered on McCall, bored into her, unnerving her. If only his captivating presence didn't exude such virility. His ruggedness unsettled her.

She took a deep breath, determined to deliver the message without giving either of the Dartmouths the opportunity to launch another assault. "Miss Overton has the flu and can't attend tonight." McCall, a true-blue born and bred Texan with a decade in California under her belt, knew her thick West Texas drawl still showed up in every word that came out of her mouth.

Ignoring their strange expressions, she took her seat and opened her notebook. Under the heading *NICK* she added a mark and studied Mrs. Dartmouth's column. So far, Madeline Dartmouth remained three wins ahead of her son. McCall wondered if she should add a heading for the normally neutral executive director who suddenly seemed entrenched in the argument.

Staring at the score sheet, McCall gnawed on her lower lip. A strange feeling knotted tight in her gut.

Something wasn't right.

When she delivered the message about Colleen, Nick seemed truly caught off guard and infuriated, but then anything not going according to plan frustrated the bigger-than-life man.

Yet, the look Mrs. Dartmouth exchanged with the strange and suddenly quiet Josephine Sawyer wouldn't have gone unnoticed by a blind man. The two women accepted the bad news as though they'd been informed that crescent rolls would replace croissants on the evening's menu.

For all the years McCall had served as administrative assistant to the Elliott-Dartmouth Foundation, coupled with her time working for Nick at Dartmouth Construction, she had been privy to arguments about everything from major expenditures to whether fennel was a spice or a vegetable. This skirmish was definitely different.

Maybe Nick was right. Josie and Madeline had teamed up against him. Mrs. Dartmouth opposing her son was nothing out of the ordinary, but why the executive director's sudden interest in this battle?

A new wave of chaos ignited.

"Nicodemus, you are being rude. And, for your information, we are serving *pâte á chou* and caviar," Madeline said.

Not wavering, Nick continued. "I warned you from the start that even for charity the whole damn idea of auctioning off bachelorettes for dates was asinine. This proves it—"

"It proves nothing except you are the one who is being, as you so delicately called it, asinine." Madeline punctuated each word with her best boarding school English.

"Why doesn't everyone settle down?" Josie's words pierced the air. "Madeline. Nicodemus. Both of you, listen to me. We're not getting anywhere by arguing."

Silence engulfed the room. Only a low hum could be detected from the air-conditioning duct. It seemed almost as if Josie had blown a whistle and sent the quarrelsome twosome scurrying to the penalty box for time-out.

"Then by damn—" Nick's deep-timbred voice was that of a man determined to remain in control.

"Nicodemus!" Madeline warned.

"Josie's right. We've got bigger problems than those jerkass flowers. In less than eight hours the benefit begins, and we're short one woman."

"We can auction off only nineteen—" Josie spoke up.

"No!" In unison, Nick and Madeline responded.

Nick took charge. "We advertised twenty women, and by damn— sorry Mother—by damn—crap—I meant, oh hell, we're going to have twenty. Not nineteen, not eighteen, but twenty. One. Two. Three." Nick spoke with depth and authority that impacted the room in the same manner as his six-foot-three-inch frame.

"We can count," his mother retorted.

"Just make sure that we have twenty women on that catwalk by eight o'clock. We're in LA, and the last time I checked, this town's overrun with beautiful women. So I don't give a damn where you get her. Just make it happen," Nick stormed.

"Why don't you call that gold-digger Lauren, dear? If you can find her, I am sure she would be more than willing to come to your aid," his mother said in a crisp emphatic tone.

"If I recall, you made certain that she'd never speak to me again, much less do me *or you* a favor," Nick's voice cracked like a bull-whip. He grabbed a bottle of Penta from an ice bucket. "Is anyone else thirsty?" He addressed the room, but only looked at McCall. A slight smile curved at the corner of his mouth.

All three women shook their heads.

Nick snapped off the cap in one twist of his long, strong fingers, lifted the water to his lips, and drank. Oh, Nick didn't just take a drink; he took pleasure in the whole process.

McCall took pleasure in watching him.

Like a field of bone-dry wildflowers, the man accustomed to

getting what he wanted drank until sated and tossed the empty bottle in the trash.

McCall wondered if making such a production was nothing but a way to give him time to think or possibly linger on pleasant thoughts. Considering his silence after the mention of Lauren, it must have been the latter.

Regardless, McCall could never understand why he seemed to place the blame for his many failed relationships squarely on his mother. In McCall's estimation, Lucifer himself probably couldn't live with the unpredictable but devilishly handsome son-of-a-biscuit-eater.

"If we're through, I'll go back to my desk." McCall closed her notepad.

"Go ahead. I'm sure you can dredge up more bad news." Nick's smile was without malice, almost apologetic. "I'm out of here."

"Nicodemus, I'm not finished. And, as far as Lauren is concerned, I did you a favor." Madeline continued. "When are you going to stop protecting the underdog and learn if you sleep with dogs you will get fleas?"

"Never, Mother. Hopefully, never."

McCall retreated to her desk outside the boardroom and rested her head in her hands. She heard footsteps and looked up to see Nick standing in the doorway. Windswept and sun-bronzed skin that would make the most avid California surfer jealous peeked from above the gaping neckline of his jersey. A smile, which deepened the cleft in his chin, could melt iron.

Not that McCall noticed.

From inside the boardroom, Madeline's steely words drew McCall back to the matters at hand. "Nicodemus, I have made a decision. As Chairwoman of the Board, I do not wish you to return to the Foundation until you take some time off to take a long, hard look at yourself and get an attitude adjustment." She seemed to regroup for her final assault. "I simply will not tolerate it. Take a vacation." There was no doubt in her voice she wasn't making a suggestion, rather issuing an order. She then added, "Of course, after tonight's gala."

Nick groaned. Being out of his mother's sight, he shrugged, and made an animated frowny-face for McCall's benefit.

To fight off a smile, she glared at him and raised a questioning eyebrow. Actually, she agreed. A little self-evaluation was just what the dark-haired hunk needed.

"She's incorrigible." His lips parted in a dazzling display of perfect white teeth against the most kissable mouth McCall had ever seen.

Not that she had given it a thought.

"And you aren't?" A blush warmed her cheeks and settled over her bosom. She glanced down to avoid his rich, luscious, chocolate eyes, but like a magnet, she found herself drawn to him. "But Nick, she's right."

"I've heard blushing is good for the circulation."

No doubt Nick was aware of her discomfort. His mischievous smile said as much.

"What's the count?" he asked.

McCall scanned her notepad. "You won four, and with Josie's help, your mother took ten. I lost count after that." She offered him a quick, sheepish smile, enjoying the long-standing game they played.

"Round two." Nick shot her a lazy grin, winked, and casually leaned back to stick his head into the boardroom. "Bye, girls. See you at eight, and I expect one of you out there on the stage if you can't come up with someone . . . *darlings!*"

Patrician Madeline Elliott-Dartmouth, the epitome of sophistication, strolled from the boardroom as though she had just dismissed court. Brushing by Nick, she nodded and smiled sweetly at McCall. Adjusting the brim of her cardinal-red hat, the monarch walked toward the front door, never taking a sideways glance at her son. "I'll do nothing of the sort." She pulled on a glove. "McCall, I see no reason why you are not one of the bachelorettes." Squaring her shoulders, she waltzed out.

Nick turned to Josie. "At least Mother and I agree on something. Using Mac is a good idea unless you're concerned she'll put *your* choices to shame?"

Josie let out an audible breath, accentuating her frustration. "You need to be on a leash!" She stormed to her office.

"I'm not a rabid dog," Nick called to her.

Josie's foot kicked the door.

McCall and Nick made eye contact, sharing an amused exchange. Throwing up his hands, he lifted his shoulders in mock resignation. "She's gonna break her foot one of these days, and I'm not paying her medical bills."

Long, Viking legs carried him toward McCall. He reached out and moved her stapler next to her telephone, then turned her desk calendar over to the correct date. April 6th.

Placing one hand on each side of her desk, he leaned close enough that she felt the movement of his words, and whispered, "Take the gig. You won't be sorry. I'll see to it."

Strangely flattered by his attention, McCall tilted back her head and tucked strands of mahogany hair behind her ears. His gaze branded her as quickly as hot coals seared raw meat.

She grabbed her coffee cup and took a sip of the bitter liquid that tasted as strong as Goliath and as cold as ice.

So the fancy son-of-a-gun thinks a flashy smile and his quick wit will get him whatever he wants? Think again, Dartmouth, think again, McCall thought.

Nick frowned. "Still drinking that battery acid?"

"Yeah." She took another swig just for the heck of it and resisted asking what business was it of his?

As if reading her mind, he said, "I'm telling you, it's bad for you." With casual ease, he pulled upright and stood like a towering oak tree. "See ya . . ."

And then he was gone.

Damnation! Nicodemus did funny things to her. Things that bad boys shouldn't do to good girls. Hell's bells, damn his rich-boy hide for toying with her. Isn't that a game playboys enjoy?

But she had to admit that she enjoyed his flirtatious ways and their inside jokes.

McCall went to the break room and refreshed her coffee. She had never thought of herself as a bachelorette. A strong-willed, leveled-headed, single woman, yes, but certainly not attractive enough for some rich guy to pay good money at a charity for a date.

She tugged at the hem of her bulky cardigan and pulled the lapels tight across her breasts. She was too tall for most men. In high school, fourteen years before, her friends described her as willowy, and nicknamed her Leafeater. That was just a nice way of saying she resembled a giraffe with her long legs. Even in flat-heeled shoes she still towered over the majority of men. Too much hip, legs stronger than most marathon runners, and breasts a tad too small for many men's liking all hid beneath her long skirt, loose-fitting blouse, and baggy sweater.

Five years of ministering to her sick mother had provided her with little time and even less desire to take an interest in her appearance. Maybe her wardrobe and hairstyle needed updating, but at the moment she saw no reason to put forth the effort. Attracting a man and dating were at the bottom of her priorities, right below doing windows and scrubbing the bathtub.

Maybe God hadn't given her an eye for fashion, so she had settled for strength and old-fashioned grit.

McCall's thoughts vacillated between Nick and his mother's tenuous relationship and her own feelings for her dead mother. If Nick only knew how it felt to be an orphan, not having anyone to seek advice from, maybe he'd see Madeline differently. McCall saw it, so why couldn't he?

What could she do to make him see the light?

Her musing served to dredge up feelings she tried to keep hidden deep inside.

Since her mother's death four months before, McCall only cared about the necessities to make it through the day . . . be neat, clean, and unnoticed. She blended in like crown molding on a wall and avoided mirrors, thus steering clear of the reality that she could exist outside the memories of her mother.

She blew on her coffee to cool it before taking a sip. "He's right. This crap isn't fit to drink." She added a package of pink sweetener.

If she hadn't known Nick better, she would be insulted by his brazen comments about being one of the bachelorettes, figuring he didn't give a flying fig whether he embarrassed her or not. Nick wasn't like that. No matter how perturbed she got with him, underneath it all she pegged him as an old-fashioned heartthrob with a deep festering wound that needed soothing. But first a woman would have to crack his crustacean armor, an impossible feat. A task she certainly had no desire to take on.

Nick's unpredictability and nasty moods didn't come with her job description. But for some reason, when Mrs. Dartmouth's and Josie's patience floundered, they turned to her to deal with the obsessive, hard-nosed rascal. Particularly when he was in the midst of a new business deal. His most recent testy attitude could probably be attributed to his negotiations on a stalled business venture.

McCall bit her lip. As in the past, she'd help the man who was accustomed to getting what he wanted through his newest "whim-wham" as his mother liked to refer to his deals.

She'd do it one more time . . . somehow. It was the Texas thing to do.

Chapter Two

McCall made her way back to her desk, moved her stapler to its original place, and rebooted her laptop. While she waited, her mind wandered back to Nick, but analyzing the man that irritated her so, while making her heart flutter with a wink or an easy smile, didn't resolve anything.

She tried to get some work done, but after wasting an hour or more, she logged off and sat there staring at the large aquarium taking up the whole side of one wall.

Watching an orange-and-white-striped clownfish ease through the water, she reflected on her mother's illness and eventual death. Thoughts of taking care of her during her lengthy illness once again surfaced. No matter how hard McCall tried, she couldn't block them from taking over when least expected. But in some ways they comforted her. She'd done the right thing and didn't regret putting her life on hold to take care of her mother.

Day after day, McCall's routine had been the same. After grueling hours at the office and fighting the LA traffic, she'd arrive home barely in time to relieve the day nurse. McCall prepared dinner, not that Mama would eat, and sat by her mother's bedside for hours talking and reading. When she got too restless, McCall turned on their favorite George Strait CD and watched the frail woman fall into a fretful drug-induced slumber.

Around midnight, McCall showered and returned to the sickroom, where she slumped onto the chaise lounge. Eventually, out of sheer exhaustion, she fell into her own restless sleep.

Each night, between a mixture of dreams and reality, strong arms pulled her against the chest of a wonderfully muscular man. A man with no name. A man whose face she couldn't see clearly. A man who gave her the comfort needed to face another day. He held and protected McCall from the hurt, preparing her for the eventual grief that came. He made tending to her ailing mother more tolerable.

Then too soon, the time would come for the dark-haired handsome man to leave. Each night, with a devil-may-care smile and a kiss to her temple, the man would fade from her dreams. Waving from the doorway, he'd say, "See ya, Angel."

And, he was gone.

Sometime before dawn, McCall would wake and face the reality that her dying mother lay only three feet away, and the man in her dreams was as unattainable as. . . .

She jarred out of her musing.

Jumpin' Jehoshaphat! Why in the blue blazes did her knight in shining armor always have to remind her of Nicodemus Dartmouth?

The sound of Josie's door opening startled McCall back to the present. She looked up to see her boss standing barefooted, unwrapping a Hershey bar.

"Well, have you found Colleen's replacement?" Josie broke off a square of chocolate.

"No, not yet."

"No need now. It's resolved."

"Great." McCall exhaled. Thank goodness the Dartmouths' insane idea was moot.

"It's resolved, but you aren't going to like it."

McCall became instantly alert. "Anything would be better than my being Colleen's replacement."

"I called nearly every woman in my contact list and they seem to be avoiding me like I'm asking them to dine with the devil."

"What do you expect? It's Saturday afternoon, and it's not enough notice for most of those hobnobby old goats to—"

"It doesn't matter, McCall, because Madeline called."

"I guess she's still in a snit?"

"You might say that. She gave me a directive . . . more of an ultimatum." Josie leaned against the doorframe and licked chocolate from her finger.

"An ultimatum?"

"She said that you *will* take Colleen's place."

"Ohhh, no." McCall rounded her desk. "I can't." She planted her hands on her hips. "I'm not the right person." Taking a deep breath, she willed her heart to slow down a bit. Images of her being paraded around like a competitor in the Westminster Dog Show flashed before her.

"Let me put it this way. When Mrs. Dartmouth says 'jump,' I simply prepare the measuring stick. Get the picture?"

"It would be embarrassing. I'd be the only girl up there without a single bid. Who's gonna bid on me? You?" McCall plopped on the corner of her desk and raised her chin in defiance. More images of her tripping on her gown and falling head over teakettle in front of several hundred people flashed before her eyes.

Josie tossed another square of chocolate in her mouth. "That isn't the issue. Madeline's so angry with Nick and his attitude that she's threatening to cancel the gala if we don't have the twentieth bachelorette right now."

"It's too late for her to do that."

"If she's set on it, she will do it. I don't have to remind you that Madeline Elliott-Dartmouth signs our paychecks."

"I can't do it, Josie. Honestly, I simply can't." McCall rubbed her sweaty palms together.

"Hey, I know you're kinda shy, and—"

"Kinda? I turn my back when I think the fish need privacy."

"Oh you're not all that shy, but it's either that or she will cancel the affair. When we don't meet our donor-based budget, *you* can explain it to her son, Mr. Congeniality, on our way to the unemployment office."

"I'm too tall and flat chested." McCall stopped to regroup. "And I don't have a dress that's appropriate."

"A dress isn't a problem. You'll put them all to shame. McCall, why do you think we ordered canapés topped with Kibbles 'n Bits?"

"I'll bite."

"For the 'dogs' who are coming." Josie made quotation marks in the air. "Nick's right about that. Plus, Maddi's on her way back to the office and said she's taken care of everything. Hairstylist, a beauty consultant. The works."

"Oh, damn! That's great."

"I've never heard you say a real cussword." Josie frowned.

"I don't have to. Nick says enough for us all." McCall had heard enough. She turned back to her desk and clicked on her computer mouse. The black screen flashed into hues of moss green and sky blue. McCall had made a decision. A very difficult one.

"What are you doing?"

"Writing my letter of resignation."

Josie tossed her candy wrapper in the trashcan. "Then who's going to pay the remainder of your mother's medical bills, huh?" She closed the lid on the laptop. "Do you have a rich grandmother I haven't heard about or something?"

"Certainly not a *something*. I pay my own way. A *something* sounds like a sugar daddy"

"Could be worse things." Josie shrugged.

Tempted to resort to one of Nick's tantrums, McCall hesitated, then peered up through gritty eyes. "Take my place, please. Mrs. Dartmouth won't care, as long as we have someone up there."

"Can't. I'm the auctioneer." Josie folded her arms.

The front door burst open and Nicodemus bolted in. "Hello, ladies. Any luck?"

"I thought they took you to the pound," Josie said dryly.

"You only wish. I've been sitting in the parking garage talking, rather listening, to Mother on the phone. I need an update."

"Well, there's now a fly in the ointment," Josie said.

"Son of a bitch, and Mother's on a rampage."

"The fly *is* your mother," McCall retorted tartly.

Nick rubbed a thumb along his chiseled jawline, obviously contemplating her boldness. The twinkle in his eye incited McCall's sizzling temper.

"Uh, your mother called and is demanding that McCall take Colleen's place, but—"

"I'll tell him, Josie. *But, I can't.*"

"Why not?" He sternly asked.

"I don't have a dress for one and—"

"McCall, Mother wants you there, and by damn, you'll do it or . . . or I'll fire you." Nick folded thick arms over his chest.

"You can't. I work for your mother." McCall grabbed for her purse.

Nick's strong fingers caught her by the wrist. "Hell if I can't. I originally hired you, remember?" He released her hand.

"Both of you stop squabbling," Josie barked. "We've had enough of that for one day."

Frowning, Nick whirled to her. Turning back to McCall, he said, "I don't intend to fire you, but I know who might." His voice softened. "Hey, Mac, just do it." His eyes changed from hard to gentle, understanding. "If for no other reason than to save your job."

Reaching across her desk, he picked up her stapler.

"Don't move that again." McCall's hand shot out in protection.

Long, warm, calloused fingers covered hers, searing her skin in the same fashion as his shocked expression. "Okay."

Unconsciously, she moistened her dry lips with her tongue before she realized that his thumb had curled beneath hers and lifted trembling fingers. "You've got strong hands." He released them. "See ya."

And, he was gone, leaving behind the clear, crisp smell of expensive cologne and one pounding heart.

McCall watched as the door closed. For a moment, she'd thought he was about to kiss her. Her hand, that is. She swung around facing Josie. "What kind of a burr does he have under his saddle today? And, don't try to tell me it's the gala. I know him too well not to know that there's more to it than meets the eye."

"It's that new land acquisition he's been talking about."

"The one that I haven't been paying any attention to?"

"And which Maddi calls one of his pipedreams. It's not going well. You know how relentless he is when he wants something. Then add his mother to the mix. She's about as enthusiastic about it as when he bought his baseball franchise."

"All I know is that he's been looking at some investment property. A farm maybe, but I didn't realize his mother was involved."

"Well, she was until he told her to butt out. She's kinda PO'd at him, but then what else is new? Back to what we were talking about. Don't try to change the subject. I'm still waiting on your answer about who's going to pay off your mom's medical bills if you lose your job."

"I'm nearly finished with them."

"Then who's going to replenish your savings and pay that damnable blood-sucking lawyer? Put up that headstone you are so desperately saving for?"

"That's dirty pool and you know it," McCall flared.

"Why don't you probate your parents' wills? Until you do, you won't have a good picture of your finances."

"I'm afraid of what I'll find. The medical bills and funeral have already drained me." McCall rubbed her neck.

"You said your dad had made a hefty investment, so look into it."

"My lawyer's doing that. Biggest problem is that Daddy invested heavily in a business venture out here in California, and we can't locate the other investors. The attorney is placing a creditor's notice in the newspaper, hoping to flush out who owes Daddy the money, but that can take months, even years, and we may never find them." She stopped and considered whether she wanted to say more, then added, "If there is truly an investment to be found."

"What are you really afraid of?"

"I don't know. Maybe that he did most of his investing up at Chumash Casino, and he just told Mama he'd committed it else-where. Daddy was a good man, but a rogue. Rough. He worked for the oil companies, a tough-as-nails Texan."

McCall's fingers moved to her arms and rubbed away little goose bumps. "Back to the gala. As I've already told you, I can't do the benefit because I don't even own an evening gown. I'm not exactly Naomi Campbell who can pick up something off the rack and look good. I'm just a lanky Texan. Mrs. Dartmouth has put me in an impossible position."

"Look, we don't have much time. It only took Maddi a little over an hour to arrange for her dress shop to send over an assortment of gowns and she's on her way back. You're a beautiful person, McCall, and not just inside, but outside, too. You've got to let go and begin living again." Josie grabbed her by the shoulders. "You can't continue to lug around memories of your mother like a tombstone. Why not reinvent yourself? Let today be the beginning of a new life by making you as sassy and daring outside as you are inside."

"Thanks, but you're throwing me to the barracudas."

"No, I'm not. Sweetheart, someday you'll thank me."

"I don't know." McCall inhaled. She glanced at the clock. Time wasn't on her side. "It looks like if I want to keep my job, I don't have any choice. I'll do it, but on one condition."

"You got it." The relief on Josie's face spoke for itself.

"That Russell bids on me—"

"My boyfriend?" Josie stuttered a bit on her words.

"Yeah. He won't have to take me out, just win the bid. I'll repay him the money from my income tax refund. No one will be the wiser."

"One problem. Everyone knows Russell and I are an item." Josie stepped away. "But I have an idea. Remember his friend Anson?"

"That blond hunka-hunka? The model?"

"Yeah, a real looker, but a gigolo."

"An honest-to-goodness real-life gigolo?"

"Oh yeah, a conceited pretty boy. Just remember the words *honest* and *gigolo* can't be used in the same sentence. Anson's attending the gala, and I'll get him to be your escort and bid on you. He'd do it just so he can brag that he went out with the Kasota Springs Cotton-patch Queen."

"Kasota Springs Oilpatch Princess!" McCall corrected. "And it was because I was the only senior who didn't already have a title. Are you sure he'll do it?"

"Oh yeah. He owes me big-time. And thanks. You'll be saving another gal a lot of grief." Josie pursed her lips, obviously giving the whole issue some thought. "I've got to call Anson, plus fill Russell in on the deal. Madeline and her troupe will be here any minute, so get yourself in the executive bathroom and start, uh, doing something." Josie flung her arms through the air. "Whatever you think you should do to prepare for your unsuspecting knight in shining armor."

McCall whirled to face her. "What'd you say?"

Josie stopped as though hobbled. "Oh, uh, we have to get you ready for . . . for your special night with a smiling admirer."

Chapter Three

Three hours later, Nick slammed down his Scotch glass. Resting his elbows on the bar behind him, he surveyed the room.

"Another Ambassador, Mr. Dartmouth?" the bartender asked over Nick's shoulder.

"Make it neat, Tony." Nick pulled back his dinner jacket and hooked his thumb beneath the cummerbund. "I wonder what in the hell she's trying to prove."

"Miss Johnson?" Tony set down the Scotch. "She's sure a show-stopper."

"You might say that." Nick downed the drink and slid the empty glass on the bar behind him. "Make this one a double."

Nick couldn't take his eyes off McCall, who stood at the entrance to the ballroom escorted by a blond Adonis. Incandescent light seemed to radiate around her. Tall and regal with shimmery brunette hair swept into a stylish coiffure, she wore a beaded ivory evening gown that showed off her curves in places where a woman should have curves. She was setting the room abuzz.

He halted his probing gaze on her necklace. Eloquent, extravagant, and clinging perfectly to her bosom. He shook off a feeling of possessiveness. Intimacy.

"She looks like a million dollars." Tony whistled softly.

"Yeah." Why in the world would her being there and looking so angelic affect Nick so? The room was packed with beautiful women, some tucked, others chiseled, and most implanted, and so blue-blooded that a pedigree registration was required for an invitation.

But only the lady on the arm of the sun-baked, sock-in-his-pants dumb ass bothered Nick.

"Better slow down on the rotgut or you'll end up in the dog pound for sure." Josie eased onto the stool next to him.

"It couldn't be any worse than sitting around with one of your overly Botoxed bimbos." He ran his finger around the inside of his collar.

"I hear tell orange is the fashion trend in the hoosegow, and it isn't your color. Gonna offer a lady a drink?"

"The bar's free. Tell Tony over there." He motioned toward the end of the bar.

She gave Nick a benign smile as if dealing with a temperamental adolescent, reached over, and picked up his drink. "Do you have to work at being nasty or does it come naturally?" She took a swallow. "Private stock, huh?"

He nodded.

Josie motioned to Tony. "I'll have what he's having."

The bartender raised a questioning eyebrow to Nick.

He shrugged his shoulders in a give-the-lady-what-she-wants way, but kept his stare fixed on McCall and the yo-yo attached to her arm.

Josie turned to Nick. "She cleaned up nicely, didn't she?"

"Who in the hell is *she*?"

"You know who in the hell *she* is . . ."

"Where is Mother?"

"Right here, darling." Madeline Dartmouth strolled up. "A Chambord splash, please," she said to Tony.

Josie picked up her cocktail glass. "Time to go to work. Auction's about to begin." She slipped off the stool and flipped an outrageous teal blue and silver boa around her neck. "Thanks for the drink, darling."

Under his breath, Nick muttered a profanity, hopefully not loud enough for his mother to hear exactly what he said.

"I heard that." His mother accepted a flute of champagne with a splash of Chambord. "Where were you all afternoon? You didn't answer your cell phone."

"Nope. Went back, finished ball practice, then to the gym. After your ass-chewing I figured I needed to work off some steam."

"I see you've noticed McCall. Such a lovely, regal assistant we have, don't you think?" She kept her gaze fixed on her son.

"Yeah Mom, she looks great." He wanted to say that she looked better than great . . . breathtaking, sexy, and sassy, but for his mother's benefit "great" worked just fine.

"I believe she will fetch an astronomically outrageous donation. Or at least, if Anson has anything to do with it."

"So, Mac finally caved?" Not waiting for a response, he continued. "And who in the hell is Anson? That degenerate that's hanging onto her like he's afraid she'll bolt if he lets go of her hand?"

"Darling, he's Anson Cargill," Madeline said, as if knowing his last name would make a difference. "Is he not absolutely the most luscious man you have ever seen? You know, he's a model."

"No, and I don't see anything luscious about him." Nick snickered. "It doesn't take a brain surgeon to see that he's a pec-implanted buffoon." He turned back to the bar. "An idiot—" He broke off. "And he doesn't have any business manhandling McCall that way, either."

"I believe the green monster is rearing its ugly head."

Nick clenched his jaw. *Jealous, huh!* What would she know about green monsters? He tried to act nonchalant. On the inside, his gut was tied in knots. He didn't know why the thought of McCall being auctioned off bothered him. He had been a party to pushing her into it.

They had always had an easygoing relationship, but maybe he was too much a buffoon himself to step it up a notch and see where it might take them.

There was one thing for sure. McCall had succeeded in getting something awfully uncomfortable stuck in Nick's craw. He didn't like it one iota. "She agreed to be a bachelorette?"

"Yes, and *I* couldn't be more pleased. Darling, there's Bambi or Buffy. I can never remember her name, but you know, Judge Armstrong's daughter. And she seems headed your way." Madeline whisked up the hem of her ball gown. "I selected guests to join us at our table who know you and recognize you're under a lot of pressure—those who can tolerate your sometimes indelicate mood. I am hopeful you'll be on your best behavior." The diamonds around Madeline's neck flashed like a mirrored ball in sunlight.

Nick groaned. "Why aren't you wearing Grandmother's necklace like you always do to a soiree like this?"

"I decided to showcase it on a beautiful, much younger lady. No doubt you approve?" She glanced in the direction of McCall before strolling away.

Nick didn't have a chance to take another look at McCall because a ball of fire-engine-red taffeta with a head protruding out of the top rushed his way. Grabbing a fresh drink, he headed in the opposite direction. Judge's daughter or not, he wasn't about to wait around in hopes of remembering whether her name was Bambi, Fifi, or Pipi.

Feeling like a piece of USDA Grade A beef, Nick hit the door to the men's room, downing the last of the Scotch as he went. He handed the glass off to the surprised attendant. "LeRoy, get the fire extinguisher, there's a rolling ball of fire coming our way."

"You weren't trying to avoid me—" a female voice chided.

"Miss Armstrong, unless you have a healthy set of cojones beneath that lovely red gown, I think you made a wrong turn." Nick opened the door and tapped the brass plate. GENTLEMEN.

"I-I, uh, oh dear." The startled woman backed away, turned, and fled.

Nick leaned on the counter. *What next?* All he wanted was space so he could think. Decide what he should do about Mr. Raging Testosterone. McCall was way too naïve for the likes of such a man. Huh, hell, more like a gigolo. There were a lot of them around. Male whores.

And he's with the woman who Nick . . . what? Thought a lot of? Was grateful to have as a friend? Fantasized about?

Damn it! Just because on occasion he woke with a rather rigid indication of an optimistic fantasy didn't necessarily mean it included McCall.

"Son of a bitch!" He needed another drink.

Just as the door burst open, the attendant shot him a questioning look.

Mr. Hormones and a man Nick recognized as Josie's boyfriend Russell entered, stopping in front of him.

"Hi, Nick. You know Anson Cargill?"

Nick stretched to his full height. Towering over the two men, he extended his chest much in the same manner as a rooster about to let the newbie in the chicken coop know who was the cock-of-the-walk. "Don't believe I do . . ." He punctuated it with a silent, *and I don't give a rusty rat's ass that he's a model.* Tentatively, he accepted the blond man's extended hand. His handshake reminded Nick of a glob of gooey gelatin.

Russell slapped Anson on the back. "I'm sure you know McCall is Anson's date. And Nick, ol' sport, not in your wildest fantasy could you imagine what plans he has for her once he wins her in the auction."

Anson licked his lips. "She is hot." He adjusted his crotch. "I can hardly wait to—"

"Shut your trap, golden boy! You don't have a right to talk about her like that." Anger singed Nick's words as he clenched his fist, knowing he could wax the floor with one man under each arm if he wanted.

Nick flexed his fingers. *This might get his attention!* Deciding the effort it'd take to knock the smug smile off the jerkass's face wasn't worth it, Nick relaxed his hand.

On second thought, this could be interesting!

"Well, Russell, ol' sport, you better hurry into the john because I think Anson here might need you to hold the sock stuffed in his pants while he takes a leak."

Before he could see their reactions, Nick left.

Safely back in the ballroom, fury consumed him. "That bastard better not touch her, or he'll have me to deal with." He stormed to the VIP table and took his seat.

"Nick, darling, I ordered you an Ambassador because I figured you could use one by now." His mother nodded to Josie. "Let the games begin," she cooed.

Although preferring a hardhat to a monkey suit, Nick knew how to dress appropriately when the occasion called for it. *I didn't think McCall had an appropriate dress. Wasn't that her excuse? She certainly found one quick enough for Mr. Full of Himself!*

"What is this?" Nick picked up a glittery decorated fan.

"That's your number, so Josie will know who you are when you place your bid," Madeline said.

"She knows who I am."

Ignoring her son, Madeline turned and drew the man next to her into conversation.

"I'll buy a woman when a frog doesn't bump his ass every time he jumps," Nick grumbled. "You know I've already made my donation."

Madeline turned in her son's direction. "A generous one, I might add. Thank you, my dear."

Absentmindedly, he tapped the fan on his open palm. He had no need for a number because he had no intention of bidding on any woman. He'd never had to pay for a date in his life and he certainly wasn't about to begin now. He thought the whole idea of getting a woman at an auction a bit unsavory for anyone except a desperate and probably homely person. Besides, the only one he was interested in obviously was making her preference known. Not that he would bid on her anyway, except to protect her—to keep her out of the clutches of some gigolo like the Mr. Way Too Much Testosterone.

Nick slammed down the numbered fan. *Damn it sideways.* And he forced her to do it, too. He stiffened at the pressure of a feminine hand on his shoulder.

"You are so uptight, Nicky."

Lavish, sickly sweet perfume filled the space around him as the woman he knew only as Judge Armstrong's daughter leaned forward.

"Finally, I have a chance to speak with you," she purred more than spoke the words. "If you bid on me, Nicky, I'll see that you have an evening you'll never forget."

Twisting in his chair slightly, he came within inches of overly collagened ruby-red lips and enormous muddied eyes that made him think of two cow patties in the snow. He leaned back and whispered, "You look lovely tonight, Miss Armstrong." He resisted adding that he wasn't likely to forget that face anytime soon.

Her hand slid from his shoulder, down his spine, stopping short of seizing a handful of butt. "Thank you." And she droned away.

Oh, crap! Nick grabbed his glass of water and drank until it was empty. Over the rim, he caught his mother's frown.

"I see you've already made your selection," his mother chided.

"This isn't like scouting for a first baseman." He reached for her water goblet and leaned in toward his mother. "Besides, I'm not going to give you a chance to run off another woman like you did Lauren."

"Pish-posh! She was not right for you, Nicodemus!"

"Maddi—" he growled.

"Don't call me by my nickname!" Madeline growled in hushed tones.

"Then call me Nick."

"Lower your voice, *Nick!* And Lauren wasn't right for you."

"That was my choice. Just because she wasn't a New York debutante doesn't mean that she wasn't *right* for me."

"Trust me, Nico . . . Nick, she was all wrong for you."

Nick didn't try to disguise his anger meant only for his mother as he exhaled and rolled his eyes.

"Very unbecoming. You must trust me. If you are not too pig-headed to realize it, you will know when the right woman comes along."

The sound of a spoon on crystal pinged through the air. Josie called the partygoers to attention and gave a welcome that ended when Nick and Madeline stood, accepting accolades for their unselfish dedication to the geriatric community.

"Now, on to what this benefit is all about," Josie said.

"To get deeper into our pockets," roared a robust man in his seventies.

Heads turned and laughter filled the air.

"Of course, Mr. Senator. We used our fine state's tax department as our example," Josie said in her honey-edged drawl, and waited for the laughter to subside before continuing. "The rules are as in the past. All bids must be in increments of one hundred dollars for the men. However, we've decided to sweeten the pot."

A whir of surprise filled the air as the crowd buzzed amongst themselves.

"Piqued your interest? This year, a woman can overbid that special man of hers by one dollar." She waited for the applause to stop. "I'm sure the bachelorettes are amenable to doing windows or mowing the lawn." The auctioneer took a drink of water, preparing to continue. "For our first lady . . ."

"Well, if it isn't Miss Put-Your-Hands-Down-My-Pants." Nick groaned under his breath, and laid his salad fork across the plate. He scanned the room trying to locate McCall, but she had disappeared. *Probably being wowed by Mr. Testosterone!*

Josie's slow Southern drawl drew out the bid into what seemed like an eternity. "We'll start the bid on Miss Bunny Armstrong at two hundred dollars. Two hundred, two hundred." She waved toward the center. "Harold Rasche bid two hundred. Is there three? Three hundred—"

"Three hundred? That's ridiculous. I might as well get another Scotch." Nick raised his hand and motioned Tony in his direction.

"Three hundred to Nick Dartmouth. Do we have—" The auctioneer cried.

"Five hundred!" Madeline shouted matter-of-factly, before lowering her velvety voice. "Nick, darling, *put* your hand down. You nearly bought Buffy or whatever her name is."

"Son of a . . ." Nick glanced in the direction of his mother, then mentally finished his expletive.

"Six hundred." A man's voice called from across the room.

"Six hundred and one," barked the woman to his side.

"Going, once. Going, twice. Sold to Mrs. Harold Rasche for six hundred and one dollars." The gavel came down.

With each bachelorette, the bidding got more intense. Josie landed the gavel and called a halt to the bidding on yet another woman. Beatrice Kemp overbid her husband by one dollar and quickly added an additional two thousand dollars before donating the sum to the charity.

Where in the hell was McCall? Time had come for Nick to find out.

Placing his napkin on the table, he leaned into his mother. "I've had all of this happy horseshit I can take. See ya."

Madeline Dartmouth grabbed his arm and lowered her voice. "No! You *will* sit here until we are finished, *by damn.*" She tossed her head back, squared her shoulders, obviously pleased for being so gritty.

Nick slumped forward. "Blessed. I've got better things to do."

Mrs. Dartmouth shot him a frown.

Josie's words drew his attention back to the stage. "For our last lady this evening"—she glided her arm in the direction of the side entrance—"Miss McCall Johnson."

The house lights lowered and two spotlights roamed across McCall. Gasps hummed in the air as Anson escorted her to the stage, bowed, and returned to his table. He glared directly at Nick, picked up his fan, and saluted before beginning the bidding. "Two hundred dollars."

"Three," came a bid across the room.

The senator bellowed, "Make it five."

The blond Adonis, "Six."

"Six, we have six. Seven?" Josie called.

Nick twisted in his seat and slammed his shin on a table leg, sending a sharp pain through his body. "Son of a . . ." He grabbed for his knee with one hand, while raising his numbered fan with the other.

"We have seven. Eight? Eight . . ."

"Eleven hundred," Mr. Hormonal declared.

"Eleven hundred and one," Madeline said.

"Two thousand," Anson responded.

"Two thousand, one," Madeline bid.

"Five thousand," bellowed Harold Rasche.

"Hush up, you fool. You don't have a dog in this fight," Mrs. Rasche shrieked.

Josie took up the slack. "Bid withdrawn. Two thousand and one dollars to Madeline Dartmouth." She raised her gavel. "Going once, going—"

"Three thousand," Anson called out.

Someone had to stop this foolishness.

"Hell's bells. Three thousand dollars a day," Nick ground out as though he had made a two-dollar bid at the racetrack. "for one week minimum."

Josie's mouth dropped open and the gavel hit the podium. "Sold! I guess." Obviously rattled, she sputtered, "Sold to Nick Dartmouth for, uh, twe-twenty-one thousand dollars?"

Nick nodded before moving his gaze to McCall. Her piercing eyes were a storm of fury.

His knee hurt like crazy, but he'd been hurt worse sliding into home. Pushing back from the table, he limped toward the stage— toward an icy stare masking the most captivatingly beautiful woman he'd ever seen in his life. And she seemed completely unaware of her desirability.

A volunteer handed Nick a bouquet of long-stemmed yellow roses cushioned against white baby's breath.

He made a princely bow and extended the flowers to McCall.

McCall returned a shallow curtsey, squared her shoulders, and tossed back her head as Madeline had instructed earlier in the day when she gave McCall her tips.

Speaking softly to the devilishly handsome rogue whose eyes she would prefer to scratch out because he had been so patronizing with his bid, McCall said, "Thank you for your generosity, Mr. Dartmouth."

A rakish smile crossed his lips. "No. Thank you, ma'am."

Hurrying off the stage, McCall's trembling legs carried her to the exit. Somewhere in the distance she heard the roar of the crowd as Josie called the auction closed, announcing that the benefit had exceeded their expectations.

All McCall could think was *don't let Nick see me cry*. Regardless of how her heart raced or how difficult it became to breathe or how close to buckling her legs felt, she would not cry. Torment gnawed at her insides.

"McCall, wait." Nick called from behind.

She increased her pace. Her face burned with embarrassment. Rich people acting like spoiled brats and using her as their pawn hurt and hurt badly. No doubt, she served as the laughingstock of the gala.

Nearing the exit, McCall dropped the roses in a trash can and hit the double doors. They flew wide open, and she rushed down the hall toward the stairwell.

Faster and faster.

Farther and farther.

Nick overtook her, and she found herself whirled around and pulled against his rock-hard chest. Molding his full length to her, he pinned her against the wall.

"Let me go," she spat. Her heart pounded and her face grew hot with humiliation. She bit back tears.

"McCall, what's wrong?"

"You're a cad, Nicodemus! A heartless, cold, nasty cad." As he pressed closer, she felt his erratic heartbeat, upsetting her balance.

"I didn't mean to be." His brown eyes blazed with his love of combat.

"But, you were . . . you are." Through a veil of near tears, she fought for control. "I hate you." Fists pounded against a wall of pure muscle. Pushing, she struggled to get free.

"You aren't capable of hating anybody." Nick cuffed her wrists with one strong hand and held them to his chest.

"Maybe *hate* is too strong of a word, but you embarrassed me. I can see the headlines now: 'Millionaires duke it out at auction until playboy pays a ridiculously vulgar amount for poor displaced Texan.'"

"I'm sorry. I didn't mean to embarrass you. I know how much you dreaded the whole ordeal tonight and thought I'd help you by making sure you weren't forced into a date with someone who doesn't know or appreciate you."

"Don't think that you know how I feel because you don't!"

Tucking a wayward strand of hair behind her ear, he whispered, "I'm just a lost ship adrift at sea in a raging storm." He brought his hard mouth down on her parted lips and staked his claim.

She did not return his kiss, only went rigid at the intimacy of his action.

He pulled back and stared deep in her eyes, but held her close.

Struggling free, she faced him furiously, only to find herself back in his arms. "Nick, you always know where you're headed."

"My head does, but my heart does funny things without asking me." His breath burned on her cheek.

McCall swallowed the emotion caught in her throat, but no matter how hard she tried, she couldn't pull her gaze from Nick's suntanned face.

Deep inside, he made a primitive groan and reclaimed her lips, pulling her tightly against him.

McCall tried to twist out of his grip, only to have him increase the pressure on her mouth, his probing tongue making his desires crystal clear. His tempo increased.

Her emotions swam through a maze of feelings and spiraled out of control. Yet, his lips were more persuasive than she cared to admit, and she found herself swallowed up in his slow, drugging kisses.

Like a life preserver, rationality towed McCall out of the moment and back to reality. She was in the arms of the man she had just professed to hate. She eased out of his grip. He let her go.

Eyes as dark and powerful as he was pierced her own. His forehead furrowed and a panicked expression crossed his face. "I'm so sorry, Mac." Nick ran his finger along her trembling lips, then stepped back. "I got caught up in the moment. I've always known you were a beauty, but I've never seen you look as stunning as you do right now."

Her heart refused to accept his explanation. More furious at herself for responding than at him, in one stalwart motion, she struck him across the face. In disbelief, her fingers shot up to her throbbing lips.

"I deserved that." His fingers rustled through his hair.

"Nicodemus Dartmouth, you need to learn you don't get everything you want. Some things have to be earned, not bought."

Chapter Four

McCall sat in the dinky living room of her terra-cotta bungalow on Hollywood Way in Burbank, barefoot, wearing a white, ribbed T-shirt, boxer shorts, and the stunning, several-hundred-thousand-dollar diamond necklace.

The Dartmouths' chauffeur had escorted her back to her house not far from MGM Studios. She'd hung the borrowed ball gown on the back of the bedroom door and taken a moment to touch the delicate beading. Even Cinderella had to return to the real world, a world without champagne, beef Wellington, or a constant flood of beautiful people dripping in costly jewels and furs.

Tomorrow, her fantasy would vanish. Mrs. Dartmouth's valet would pick up the ball gown and necklace, leaving behind only McCall's memories of the night she went to heaven and back.

Absentmindedly, she brought her fingertips to her lips, remembering Nick's ravishing kiss. She wasn't angry that he'd kissed her, only at the way he'd gone about it . . . and the physical power he had over her. There had been a demand, a forceful urgency in his kiss, but no violence. She had felt his need. If only he had kissed her because he wanted to, not to make a point that he could take what he wanted without asking.

Dropping her hand to the jewels around her neck, she let her mind wander back to earlier in the day.

After McCall's miracle transformation, Madeline had stepped back and admired her creation before handing McCall a wine-colored velvet box containing a Dartmouth family heirloom—Madeline's mother's diamond necklace. After placing the jewel around McCall's neck, Madeline had simply said, "This has never been worn by anyone outside my family. May you find your knight in shining armor."

Banging on the front door brought McCall back to reality. Not just knocking, but banging with purpose like a policeman demanding immediate access.

"By damn, McCall, let me in." Nick's strong voice rang in the crisp night air.

"Go to hell!"

"We've got to talk."

"We don't have anything to talk about." McCall rested her chin in her hands. Dern, if they didn't have plenty to discuss, but no doubt letting him in was a very bad idea.

"I'll stay out here all night and sleep on your porch if you don't let me in."

"I'll call the police and report an intruder." She took a deep breath. "Or better yet, I'll shoot you and drag your body inside."

"You wouldn't dare."

"Don't bet the ranch on it."

An eerie silence hid in the night.

McCall threw her quilt aside and stomped to the door. She looked through the small beveled window. She couldn't see him, yet his Jaguar was parked at the curb. She marched back to her chair, flipped off the television, and cocooned herself in the quilt. "Hell's bells, that man can make me use language I didn't even know I had in me. He's such a jerk. Jerkass." She snickered, using one of his favorite phrases.

Only an occasional vehicle driving down Hollywood Way disturbed the night.

"He's too quiet. Not good." She walked to the window and pulled back the curtain for a peep.

The Jaguar remained by the curb.

Returning to her chair, she pulled the blanket under her arms. "What is that no-good scoundrel up to?" She folded her arms across her chest and chastised herself out loud. "Why do I care? After all, he owes his own foundation the money, so it'll be easy for him to go back on his word."

As much as she hated to admit it, she was relieved Anson hadn't won the bid because he had gotten way out of line. Not only had he gone berserk and bid over the agreed amount, but during the evening he'd seemed to feel that he deserved privileges she had no intentions of dishing out.

Rap! Six taps in cadence, then a pause followed with two evenly spaced taps resonated from somewhere near the bottom of the door.

Dragging the blanket behind, McCall opened the door to find Nick's beautifully proportioned body spread out on the concrete porch. In the dim light, propped up by one elbow, the rich outline of his shoulders strained against the fabric of his black tuxedo.

"What are you doing?" Every fiber in her body warned her not to ask, but she did.

"Got a blanket? I'm cold." An easy smile played at the corners of his mouth.

She threw the quilt at him. "You're nuts." Slamming the door, she yanked a pillow off the couch, opened the door a second time, and tossed the throw cushion on top of the quilt. "I don't want you to be uncomfortable."

McCall turned off the porch light, latched the chain, and plopped down on the sofa. Pulling her knees to her chin, she hugged them.

Although she chided herself that she was supposed to be angry with the big man, for some reason, her heart didn't feel the same. She couldn't deny the spark of excitement his presence sent through her. How in the heck could she stay angry with a man who possessed so much charisma? She would.

Tap! Ding! Tap!

Tiny pebbles of gravel bounced off the window.

"Enough is enough." She stormed to the door and yanked it open as far as the security chain would allow. "Nick, go home. I don't want to argue with you."

"Please, Mac. I'm freezing and need to go to the uh, you know, use your little boy's room."

"No! Go away. Plus, I don't even have a little boy's room." Inwardly, she smiled.

"Then I'll water your geraniums. Might fertilize your petunias while I'm at it—"

"Get in here," she yelled in resignation as she yanked the chain loose and ripped the door wide open.

"Thanks." He handed her the quilt and pillow and shot her his finest schoolboy grin. "I think I'm warm enough now."

"You ought to be. It's seventy degrees and my powder room is back that way." McCall threw the bedding on the sofa and pointed to the second door on the left.

"Could I bother you for a drink?" His smile was intimate as a kiss. Leaving behind the musky-citrus scent of expensive cologne, he sauntered in the direction of the powder room. "I'd like it neat, please."

"Don't dawdle." She turned toward the kitchen.

Surely she could trust him to take care of his business and get on his way. Even a dying man gets a final request. She couldn't deny a thirsty guy a drink, could she?

With legs spread apart and hands on her hips, McCall stared into her cupboard. A bottle of inexpensive, no, just a plain cheap wine she'd bought, cooking sherry, and one shot of tequila. Maybe she ought to down a shooter before he got finished, uh, powdering his nose.

Send him home thirsty. Her heart and brain fought with one another. *Don't let him out of the doghouse until he's proven he knows the error of his ways. Hello therapy of some sort.*

Nick cleared his throat and she whirled around to find him filling the doorframe, black tie hung loosely down either side of a gaping white ruffled shirt. Not just gaping, but at least three buttons unfastened exposing a mass of manly dark hair. Her gaze trailed down the front of his shirt, imagining where the triangle of masculine curls ended.

She swallowed hard. "Not much of a selection. Don't guess I could interest you in some Kool-Aid? It's fruit punch."

"Toss the wine and a corkscrew my way."

"Do I look like a corkscrew type gal? Trust me, you won't need one." She picked up the bottle by its neck. "Just take it with you."

"You don't want me to drink and drive, do you? So pitch it to me."

Before she realized what was happening, she literally tossed the bottle to him.

With lightning speed, he caught the wine with the ease of a honed first baseman. "I'm glad I didn't say throw."

"Just wanted to see how good you are, Slugger."

"And?" He checked the label and wagged a questioning brow, but made no move to leave.

"You're a good catcher." She turned to the cabinet and opened a cupboard door. No doubt he planned to stay for a drink. "Guess you're expecting wineglasses, too?"

"If I've got to catch 'em and juggle this bottle at the same time, I'll pass." With one strong twist he loosened and removed the metal cap. "I can drink straight from the bottle. What are you going to have?"

Damn! Here he goes again. Smooth, easy, confident. *What am I going to have?* What she wanted and what she was going to get were entirely two different things.

With glasses in hand, McCall slipped past him, avoiding the faint glint of humor in his eyes, and set the glasses on the coffee table before moving the bedding to the chair. "Cheese glasses," she announced, as though they were Waterford crystal.

Nick followed her to the front room and poured two fingers of the rosy smelling wine in each glass.

"Ah, Two Buck Chuck?"

"Yeah, it was on sale."

"Don't believe I've ever drank wine that costs less than a large Coke with a woman in men's underwear and a zillion dollars' worth of diamonds around her neck. Were you planning to sleep in them?" Nick handed her a glass.

"Underwear or the necklace?" She grabbed the drink and ducked her head. Did she really ask that?

"Either, or."

Conscious of his scrutiny, she felt an unwelcome blush creep into her cheeks. She had forgotten she still wore the gems. "Well, I-I guess so. I didn't know what to do. I couldn't very well leave them on the nightstand."

"They are beautiful on you. You looked great tonight." He paused then added, "You didn't just look great, you looked beautiful and very sexy."

Although enjoying his flattery, she had no intention of letting the sweet-talking tycoon back into her graces so easily. "Thank you.

Tonight was glitzy and exciting, like a Christmas present all wrapped up in beautiful beads and ribbons. But Nick, beneath all the dazzle, I'm still the same old, plain-Jane McCall." She took a sip of wine.

"You're anything but plain, and you proved it tonight." Not waiting for a reply, he quickly continued. "I'm sorry that I hurt you." He gently touched her lip with his fingertip. "I'm not sorry that I kissed you, just sorry the way I went about it. McCall, I didn't have any right to take what I wanted. I should have asked first. I was just trying to console you, but guess I went about it the wrong way."

A newly awakened sense of life made it easy for her to say, "You're lucky I didn't make your cojones scream for a paramedic." She ran her middle finger around the lip of her glass. Once. Twice . . . three times. "So, you think I would have given you a kiss just for the asking?"

"I don't know. I do know I acted like an idiot, but I couldn't stand to watch"—he hesitated, apparently gathering his thoughts—"that, that booty-grabbing so-called model schmooze around on you." Nick's dark eyes pierced the distance between them. "There just wasn't something right about your, uh, date. He was up to no good."

McCall chewed on her lip. She needed to clear the air, let him know that Anson was not her date, only part of a scheme to get out of having to go out with a stranger, but she enjoyed the devilishly handsome man's groveling way too much to confess.

Get serious! Nick didn't deserve an explanation. After all she had seen him walk away from his mother and had watched as Miss Floozy Armstrong followed him to the restroom. Even when she asked Anson about what happened in the men's room, he simply responded that she didn't want to know what was going on when he walked in on Nick and the woman.

She wasn't sure she believed the whole story, but when Nick bid on the brazen gal, the tale seemed plausible.

McCall's thoughts flashed back to Nick's apology. She'd known him too long not to realize that the big man didn't offer up a helping of I'm sorries very often, so she should partake. "What?"

"That Anson was up to no good."

"I'm a big girl. I've been through the hoops and know how men can be."

"Then you forgive me?"

McCall refused to give in. "Where are the roses?" Her hands automatically touched the diamonds around her neck.

"In the car. I'll go get them."

"No. They've lost their appeal. One question—"

"Shoot."

"Nick, you didn't plan to pay for a date with me, did you?"

"Hell if I didn't." He reached in his lapel pocket, pulled out a slip of paper and handed it to her.

She stared at the zeros on the copy of a cashier's check. "It's for thirty-thousand dollars."

"Yeah. It's my donation. I got the draft the day before the gala. I had no intention of buying any bachelorette unless someone special came along. I gave the original to Josie yesterday."

"You were serious about paying this much money for a date?"

"Twice that if it'd keep Mr. Testosterone away from you."

She gulped.

Now, she really couldn't tell him the truth about the plan for Anson to bid on her, especially since Josie was involved, not to mention that his mother had become privy to the ploy.

"It's my turn. Let me ask you something personal." He lifted her chin with his thumb, running his finger across her lip.

"If it's not too personal." The caress of his finger felt oddly comforting.

"It is. You've been hurt really bad, haven't you?"

"Way too personal." Oh glory, if he only knew how the coarseness in his kiss brought back painful memories. Memories no woman should endure. The difference, Nick didn't intentionally plan to hurt her and hated that he had. But the rough and ready man in her past had only done what men do, as her Mother had explained.

But if Granny had known, all hell would have broken loose.

She studied Nick's face and choked back tears. No one had seen her cry since she'd been a child. Even at her mother's funeral she'd stood strong and saved the tears for the privacy of her bedroom.

By the look on Nick's face, he'd seen the hurt in her eyes. The question obviously threw up as many roadblocks as a dragnet.

"Fair enough. But Mac, if you ever want to talk about it, I'll be here."

"I won't." She bit into her lip and felt the blood seep to the surface, much like the question had reopened the wound in her heart.

No, she'd never turn to a man for comfort, because she had long since quit asking for help. Early in her life, McCall had learned that the only person she could depend on was herself. Except, of course, for her dear, sweet, crusty old Granny, who gave her unconditional love. Someday, maybe—just maybe—she would find a man she could confide in, but then she'd probably run him off like she had everyone and everything else in her life.

Nick's words broke into her musing.

"The offer remains. If you ever need to talk, I'll be here. You know, McCall, it'd take an idiot not to recognize that we come from different worlds, but we can enjoy the best of both and have a good time truly getting to know one another—"

"We already know each other." She puckered her lips thoughtfully. "It'd be like two bulls raking the ground, sizing one another up. We'd be miserable, even for a few hours."

"Mother is making me take a vacation, remember?" His thumb moved to her cheek and slowly made tiny circles, easing away her uncertainty. "We don't have to fight. Plus, I made a commitment and I don't welsh on deals."

Great! So, now I'm a deal? But, she did like the word *commitment*, not that she believed such a thing existed for someone like Nick. In business, yes, but never in his personal life. Commitment and Nicodemus Dartmouth constituted profanity.

"Don't you see, Nick? I'm the wide-open prairie of Texas and you're the glitz and glamour of Hollywood. It's just a bad idea. Even for only one date."

He dropped his hand and picked up the wine, taking a swallow and making a face. Maybe Kool-Aid would have been better. Shuddering, he said, "We aren't that different. I'll show you." He set down the glass. "I'll say a word and you give me your immediate response."

"Sounds fair enough." She tucked her legs under her bottom and faced the gorgeous sun-drenched man sitting on her couch. Even in the dim lamplight, his tan looked natural, not a fake spray-tan color, but one that resulted from hours in the sun. His lips were full, kissable, his chest rock solid, stomach flat, thighs firm and hard, and his . . . Oh my, was he ever . . . !

"No fair hitting below the belt." His gaze dropped from her eyes, to her shoulders, and stopped at her breasts. "Here goes. Ready?"

McCall shot him a meek smile, having a good idea where his thoughts had wandered.

She nodded. *Twenty questions? This is going to be easy.* She'd show him how few things they held in common, and at the same time keep her eyes above the belt.

"Ambassador Twenty-Five," he said.

"Mad Dog 20/20," she answered.

An endless list followed. Metropolitan Opera. Grand Ol' Opry.

Eggs Benedict. Huevos Rancheros.

Calamari. Catfish.

Chambord Martini. Boones Farm Strawberry Hill.

Tea and scones. Orange Crush and Fritos.

"Caviar—"

"Got you on this one." McCall pushed back on the couch, letting her gaze fall back to his lap, but quickly redirected her focus to his exposed chest. "Texas caviar." Unintentionally, she licked her lips. And resisted the impulse to fan her face to cool off the flush she felt deepen.

"I think you're cheating, but I'll give you that one. Oysters Rock-efeller." He expanded his chest, probably not expecting her to have a rapid-fire response.

"Rocky Mountain oysters." She folded over in laughter and eased back up to see him watching her. "See what I mean? You prefer to deep-sea fish in the Pacific while I'm happy to fish in the pond at Granny's house in Texas, drink Lone Star beer and dance the Cotton-Eyed Joe at the Texas Moon Palace, eat homemade ice cream on the stoop, and enjoy a West Texas sunset. We are almost from two different planets."

"Ever heard of Mar-a-Lago in Palm Beach, Florida?"

"I've heard of Palm Beach."

"It's an exclusive members-only club that Mother belongs to.

Want to go there for dinner?" he said, as though asking her to join him for a Value Meal at McDonald's.

"All the way to Florida? Don't think I'd be back in time to deliver my Meals on Wheels."

"You're a hard nut to crack." Nick rested his arm on the back of the couch. "If you could go anywhere, where would you go?"

"Anywhere? Let's see." She pursed her lips and arched an eyebrow mischievously. "Okay, someplace where it'll be raining and the sun is shining with nary a cloud in the sky."

"Huh, making it a challenge? Let's see." With his free hand, he rubbed his thumb along his roughened jawline. "I guess you want it to be in a foreign country, maybe the rainforest?"

She would put a stop to his tomfoolery. He couldn't buy her by offering a luxurious incredible once-in-a-lifetime date. "No. It has to be in the United States"—she watched the glimmer in his eye increase, as though saying he had just the place in mind—"and I have to be able to walk to a foreign country."

His eyes sparkled and a Cheshire grin encompassed his face, making the shallow cleft in his chin deepen.

Before he could respond, she quickly added, "And not Old Mexico either!" Yeah, she had him now.

His grin deflated. She had outwitted him and felt good about it. Now, the charade could end.

"Since that might be hard, ever done any boating?" Nick asked.

"No, but I've been told it's wonderfully relaxing—"

"See, that's something we agree upon."

"Where is all of this going, Nick?"

"I wish I knew. Maybe nowhere, maybe somewhere. We'll just have to see." Nick rose to his full height and pulled her to her feet. Slipping his hand behind her back, he whispered. "But, I do know that I want us to go on our date and enjoy ourselves. Let nature take its course." He touched her lips. "I wish I could take back that kiss and do it right. But if you'll forgive me, I promise never to touch you again unless you give me permission."

"But, you're touching me now." She looked into chocolate eyes, flecked and ringed with copper.

"And, I think you're letting me," he said in a hoarse voice, slowly removing one hairpin after another until her dark tresses tumbled to her shoulders. He tucked the thin pieces of metal in his pocket.

Hell's bells was she ever letting him touch her! Afraid to pull her any closer, determined to keep his word, Nick shifted slightly only to have the tips of her breasts rub against his chest. The thin ribbed T-shirt did little to hide her nearness and drove him crazy. He should get the hell out of Dodge before she got a good feel of his growing masculinity, but he enjoyed how the rise and fall of her chest against him ignited his senses.

"You have beautiful hair." He weaved his fingers through her curls, fluffed them lightly, and slid his hand back to her waist. "Very beautiful."

Dern if he wasn't enjoying a woman in his arms that fit him like a piece of a jigsaw puzzle.

Eye to eye.

Shoulder to shoulder.

Heart to heart, and . . . holy cow!

Holy cow was right!

"I don't know if this is a good idea." She made no effort to pull away, but lightly ran her fingers through the turf of curly hair beneath his gaping stark-white shirt.

"I'm not particularly known for my best ideas when it comes to my personal life, so I guess I'll have to come up with a way to convince you that I'm sincere." Nick eased away, afraid to stand close much longer. "Since we finally agreed upon something, I'll have my driver here at ten in the morning. Bring an overnight bag in case you want to freshen up. Dress comfortably, and I'll provide bathing suits. We'll go out on my boat, okay?"

Apparently afraid to speak, she nodded.

Kissing her nonchalantly on the temple, he said, "No matter where we're headed, I promise from this moment forth, I'll never kiss you again without asking permission."

He gazed into violet-blue eyes that danced with azure fire and sealed the promise with a light tap on the nose. "See ya, Angel Eyes."

And he left.

Chapter Five

Nick stood on the deck of the *Belle Poule Princess* and watched the road leading to the harbor. How much damage had he done to the trust he'd built with McCall over their eight-year friendship? Most likely he'd destroyed it with one foolish, reckless, and completely irresponsible kiss.

Glancing at his watch, he grimaced. Over an hour ago, the limousine driver had confirmed he had picked up McCall and was driving toward the wharf.

Since glitz did not impress her, Nick hoped the massive boat wouldn't deter her from enjoying their day. That is, if she didn't make his driver take her back home.

Maybe he should have scheduled a whale-watching cruise. Even sailing might be better. Well, this was a sailboat of sorts. Commissioned as a replica of an 1834 French frigate, it was as stately as the royalty the original ship carried more than a century and a half ago.

What in the hell kind of a jam had he gotten into? All he wanted was to do right by McCall and keep her out of the clutches of Mr. Wrong.

But if he backed out on their date or didn't keep his promise not to kiss her, he'd only prove her accusation. He would not allow that to happen. Not after realizing the hurt she'd obviously been harboring for years. He'd fulfill his obligation—show her an enjoyable day on his boat, maybe even a night on his private island watching the stars—and return to friend status.

One major stumbling block surfaced. After holding her, feeling her softness, and wanting her with every ounce of his soul, he was not sure he could go back to only friendship. Keeping his promise not to kiss her might be more of a challenge than he first thought.

"Master Dart, the galley is prepared," Nick's valet called from behind.

"Thanks. I'll be down in a minute." Nick leaned against the railing and watched the waves wash against the pier. "Stanley, I'm up to my ass in alligators and don't even remember why I wanted to drain the swamp in the first place. And it's a mess of my own making."

The portly gentleman who had nearly raised Nick stood as a sentry, wearing a petrous face. A diminutive smile crept from the corners of his mouth.

"It appears you have, sir." He turned to leave, then suddenly turned back to Nick. "Mrs. Dartmouth telephoned again."

"Did she leave another message?"

"Yes, sir, same as before. Anything else, Master Dart?"

Nick leaned farther out over the rail. If he had a plank, he would walk it. Anything to get out of his misery.

Three calls from his mother before breakfast had sent him into a much deserved lather. While he worked though his new and rather complex feelings for McCall, he didn't need his mother's interference. Plus, he still waited for his answer to what ulterior motive his mother had in loaning McCall his grandmother's diamond necklace.

"Did Mother ask for the tenth time whether McCall was joining me today?" He stuck his thumb in the waistband of his Dockers.

"Yes, sir. If I am not needed, I will wait in the galley."

"I'll be down shortly." Nick turned back to the rail.

Striking his unsolicited kiss from last night's list of atrocities, the first thing that went wrong was his intention. Not planning to buy a date, he'd meant to give the thirty thousand dollars only as a donation. That went awry, so why did he tell McCall he brought the cashier's check in case he found someone interesting at the auction? Who was he trying to fool? McCall or himself?

Feelings that had been hidden for more years than Nick wished to recognize had taken on an existence of their own and bitten him in the butt. Even deep-seated memories of Lauren, who he tried to keep out of his mind, had resurfaced.

Why in the hell does Mother have to keep reminding me of my failures of the heart?

The last thing he wanted was to add McCall to his list of failed relationships.

But his mother was right. Nick had to admit that his track record wasn't the best. Hell, it wasn't even acceptable, but like any red-blooded man he enjoyed female attention. Knowing a gal's last name and her favorite drink normally qualified as a meaningful relationship. Heaven only knew why he considered the word *commitment* a vulgarity. Maybe he felt comfortable with McCall because she wasn't looking for permanency—an arrangement he could live with.

Then, without warning, Cupid had come along, tapped him on the shoulder, and pointed out what he'd been too blind to see . . . he cared for McCall. Hell, he might as well ink a tattoo on his forehead saying as much.

After arriving back at his Beverly Park home the night before, Nick hadn't slept and instead floundered around in his bed, thinking about firm breasts drilling into his chest. The scent of her hair. Those kissable lips. Her mahogany tresses slipping through his finger. Visions of how beautiful she'd looked sashaying around in men's underwear with diamonds blanketing the valley between her breasts kept him aroused in a way a man shouldn't be when in bed alone.

After hours of staring at the bedroom ceiling trying to analyze the situation, he'd thrown back the covers, taken a cold shower, and had begun making plans for the day.

A sure cure for his predicament—let nature take her course. Mother was right. *Sometimes I'm a pigheaded nincompoop.*

Nick trudged below deck. Funny in a sordid sense, but the closest person to a father Nick had ever known still called him Master.

Stanley withdrew a toothpick from a savory dish in the oven, and read it like a thermometer. "Perfect, Master Dart."

"Stanley, I'm thirty-six, so let's drop the *Master*. Is everything ready?"

"As you wish, sir. The cook left explicit instructions. But, if I may inquire, why that ghastly Mogen David 20/20 with such a fine lunch?"

"I've decided to try something new." Nick picked up a butcher knife and tested the blade for sharpness.

Stanley raised an eyebrow. "Try something new? That in itself is something new, sir."

"Yeah." Nick chuckled, thinking back to the night before and the game he had played with McCall. "What did I prepare for lunch?" He hiked a hip on the corner of the table.

"Tofu and shiitake mushrooms in oyster sauce, artichokes with Gruyère, a watercress, and chickweed salad with raspberry vinaigrette, and an exquisite soup of tru-ear mushrooms and lily buds."

"Damn, that's foo-foo-ish." He slid the knife toward the cutting board. "Too late to change?"

"Yes, sir. But they are healthy dishes you enjoy."

"I guess it'll have to do, but McCall's too smart for me to pull this off. Go ahead and show me again exactly what magical tricks I need to impress her."

Stanley retrieved the knife. "Watch carefully." With the ease of a samurai warrior he sliced what Nick presumed to be watercress or chickweed. With a flourish, the older man raked the greenery up with the knife blade and dropped them into a bowl on top of something that looked like the cuttings from a freshly mowed lawn. Weeds and all. "See how easy it is, sir?"

"I've got it. So all I have to do is finish chopping these weeds, put them on top of the grass, and accept accolades for slaving all morning cooking for my lady? That's it?" Nick folded his arms across his chest. It looked easy enough.

"Sir, I do believe I would also pray that she makes no inquiry into your culinary skills."

"Got it. And, Stanley"—Nick slapped the older man on the shoulder—"Thanks. You are sure this will make her believe I'm a regular old-fashioned guy that cooks?"

"Maybe I should add a prayer, too, sir. I will be in my quarters preparing to return to town."

"Just make sure that the captain is clear on what I want. No slipups. We want to be left alone until I tell you otherwise. Understand?"

"Yes, sir. You want total privacy once you and your friend reach your private island. If we see the campfire has gone out, then we'll know to send a rowboat; otherwise, come sundown the captain will move the boat back to the dock and return for you and your friend in the morning. Good day, sir." Stanley retreated toward the stairs.

Nick ran his fingers through his hair. What did his mother always say? "What a wicked web we weave when first we practice to deceive."

The chance of being able to spend the night on the island with McCall was about as good as him receiving the Nobel Prize for Peace, but he wanted to be prepared just in case.

Maybe he should just confess his inadequacies and quit acting like he was sixteen and trying to impress the prom queen.

Three dozen long-stemmed yellow roses had arrived at McCall's bungalow shortly after breakfast, with a note. *Angel Eyes, please let me show you how sorry I am for being so insensitive to your feelings.* She knew the flowers and card were meant to disarm, but not until the chauffeur knocked did she realize it had done the job.

She had made her decision. Go boating. It was an outing, not a date, and certainly not a vow.

McCall had spent much of the night reliving the events of the prior evening. Although intrigued with Nick, not to mention her body's refusal to stop reminding her of his powerful physique and that chest of dark curly hair to die for, being alone with him was dangerous . . . very dangerous, indeed.

For hours, she had rolled and tumbled in bed formulating plan after plan, only to come to one conclusion. She had to get Nick to break his promise and kiss her. Then she would have a reason to challenge him about keeping his word. His obligation for the date would be over and they would both save face. A very simple plan had formed. If only it worked.

Madeline's chauffeur lowered the glass between him and McCall, jarring her back to the moment. "Miss Johnson, there's a call for you."

"Thank you." She searched the multitude of icons on the screen until she found the one indicating it was for the phone. Touching the screen, she answered.

"McCall, this is Josie!"

"Josie, your name came up on the screen, so I know who you are, but what's wrong?" McCall said with a tad of urgency.

"O-oh, I just wanted to, uh, to check on you."

"You know I'm in the Dartmouths' limo, so what's going on?"

"Nothing. Uh, Mrs. Dartmouth is giving you a . . . vacation."

McCall fought for a plausible explanation, but the nagging in the back of her mind jumped to conclusions. "She's firing me, isn't she?"

"She just wants you to take a few days off."

"And without pay, I presume." McCall laid her head back on the kid-glove leather and let the mellow music calm her jumbled thoughts.

After last night, she wouldn't have been surprised to lose her job. Although her finances would be tight, she'd live. It was Josie's flim-flamming that irritated McCall much like a cocklebur rubbing against a bull's butt.

"No. She distinctly said vacation. You know she isn't going to fire you, but just do as she says, okay?"

Letting Josie babble on, McCall's mind wandered.

She shuddered at the thought of what she had done. Madeline had every reason to fire her. After all, McCall had became insubordinate to both founders, not to mention her direct superior, Josie. As if McCall hadn't done enough damage, she'd ended up pulling on a concrete overcoat by slapping the living daylights out of Nick.

It sounded like Josie and Madeline had forgiven her and she would have a job when she returned.

McCall stared out the window as Josie droned on. "Now that this is all settled, have fun. Don't worry. Be happy and don't call me. I'll call you."

The telephone went dead.

Oh sure, Josie was only relaying information about the sudden decision for time off, but what was she not telling her?

McCall's thoughts returned to her original position with the Dart-mouths. To another time when decisions were made on her behalf without her input.

After working as Nick's secretary at the construction firm for years and at the first sign of a budding friendship, without warning he had transferred her to the foundation as an administrative assis-tant. In desperate need of money for her dwindling bank account due to her mother's lengthy illness, and certainly too proud to let anyone know she needed financial help, McCall had been thankful for any job and didn't ask questions. She enjoyed her work at the foundation and presumed Nick had his reasons for the transfer. To her surprise, her relationship with him improved once he was no longer her direct superior.

But even today, she still had no idea what she had done wrong to be so abruptly transferred without any explanations. It had taken Nick weeks to replace her.

A glimpse of the distant harbor drew McCall's attention back to the sun-laden morning. Wondering which boat belonged to Nick, she spied an ornate silhouette with three lofty masts that looked like a pirate's ship direct from a movie. Exactly like the one she had imagined a man with Nick's means would own.

"Okay, so this is the deal, McCall," she said under her breath, thankful for the glass divider between her and the driver. "It's a simple day of boating with no emotional involvement. Except you have to get him to kiss you. The sooner the better, understand?" She half expected to hear herself answer, *You can make all the deals you want with the devil, but I still don't trust you, McCall Elise Johnson.*

The driver pulled alongside the pier, whisked open the door, and escorted her toward the boat that looked as bold as its owner.

McCall pushed a strand of wayward hair behind her ear, tucked it under the red grosgrain headband, and smoothed the front of her cherry-red tank top with her hands. She tugged at the hem of her khaki shorts, and glanced down at a black scuff mark on one of her white Keds before spying Nick.

One glimpse of him and suddenly she wanted to turn skirt and run to escape his disturbing presence. But she couldn't lose sight of her goal. Get him to break his promise, so she'd have a reason to cancel their date. If all worked in her favor, she'd be home in time to catch the midday weather report.

Nick stood at the end of the pier, khaki Dockers turned up to his calves, boat shoes with no socks, a baby-blue shirt opened to his waist, and a smile that closed the distance between them. The mid-morning sun, coupled with the reflection from the water, made every ounce of his muscular frame look crisp and refreshing.

Increasingly uneasy with his perusal, she looked away.

It's a tough job, but someone has to do it.

"Mac, this way," Nick hailed. "I'm glad you came. Let me have that." He reached for her bag and tugged it off her shoulder. Slipping one hand on the small of her back, he led her toward the stairs. "Watch your step."

After a quick tour of the lavish boat, he settled her on a barstool in the galley and poured two goblets of wine.

Knowing the kitchen was called a galley exhausted her knowledge of boating.

"I have lunch about ready, and afterward we can do whatever you want. We can swim, do some exploring, or just relax and enjoy a beautiful day. It's your call, McCall."

"An adventurer, a cook, and a poet. What more could a woman want?" She smiled with an air of pleasure. "Better than what I had to offer." She took a sip of the familiar tasting wine. Peering over the rim of her glass, she eased into a deliberate shy schoolgirlish smile.

"Not to insult you, but vinegar would be better." Nick whacked on the greens laid out on a chopping board like he was trying to cut down an oak tree with a Bush Hog.

"Can I help?" She watched his intensity as he chased a sprig of chickweed, trying to behead it. "I mean, since you worked all morning preparing such a lovely lunch. Can I help by making some iced tea?"

"Sure. That would be refreshing."

McCall filled the kettle and turned on the heat. She slid against the counter, watching Nick as he scraped together a sampling of leaves and twice tried to transfer them on the flat edge of his knife.

"I'm just about finished." Nick made a final stab at gathering the greens.

Thud! The knife hit the cutting board.

Vegetables splattered on the counter.

A string of profanity slipped through Nick's lips. He clamped his mouth over a bloody hand.

McCall rushed to his side, led him to the sink, and held the wound under the faucet. Cold water blended with the red, making it look as though a pint of blood whirled toward the drain. In reality, if she used a magnifying glass maybe—just maybe—she could detect the actual wound.

"Hold still," she directed.

"But I'm gushing blood."

"You're not going to die. Nick, I've seen you come off a job site with blood all over you like you'd had a run-in with a pit bull and never complain. It's just a little cut." She lifted his hand. "See, it's almost stopped. A clean cut will make you bleed like a stuffed pig, but it isn't serious." She wrapped a paper towel around his hand and looked up into his pallid face. "Nick, you look peaked."

"I just don't like blood."

"Sit down a minute." She slid a chair under him and patted his hand like a school nurse.

Seeing that his color returned and the bleeding had subsided, she turned to the stove and lifted the lid on a pot of soup. "Smells good. What's in it?"

"Well, it's a family recipe, but it has"—he shot her a confident smile and tossed the bloody towel in the trashcan—"Uh, lily pads in it."

"Lily pads?" McCall wasn't a wiz at gourmet foods, but she was no slouch in the kitchen. She'd heard of using lily *buds* in Chinese cooking, but never lily *pads*. Oh well, the rich enjoyed exotic spices. "May I taste it?"

"Sure." Nick crossed the room, slid next to her, and handed her a spoon.

Standing so close that she felt the heat from his thigh pressed against hers, he boxed her in as he reached for a clean paper towel and dabbed away some blood seeping from the wound.

She spooned out a little of the soup. The salty liquid burned her lip and reminded her of Nick's kiss. But if she wanted to make her point, she had to forget and pretend the kiss had never happened. In reality, she silently prayed for another one.

"Very good." She kept a steamy gaze locked on his face, while suggestively flickering her tongue over the warm stainless steel. "Want a taste?"

"Sure."

She took a clean utensil, dipped up some broth, and blew to cool the liquid. Leaning forward, his fingers closed over hers to steady the spoon and he accepted a taste. "Ummm, it's, well, uh good. Really good."

"You sound surprised. Aren't you confident with your own cooking?" She smiled, lifted a questioning eyebrow, and sensually ran her tongue along the back of the spoon then tossed it in the sink.

His expression changed. Seriousness clouded his brow. "There's something I need to tell you." Nick tossed the second towel in the trash basket.

Carrying two plates of salad, she swaggered to the table, surrounded by Cocobolo rosewood captain's chairs. "Shucks, Nick, there's nothing that can't wait until we've eaten."

Nick's surprise at the success of his soup, along with his sudden need for confession, sealed his fate. An experienced chef could never prepare such a scrumptious soup without tasting. Then along came the vaudeville act in preparing the salad, definitely orchestrated by an inexperienced man's hand.

McCall watched him fumble with a box of tea until he succeeded in unwrapping and depositing several bags into a crockery teapot. Maybe she should let up on the pressure. Make way for him to admit he wasn't the chef. But she had become intrigued with the idea of him groveling.

Damn. No way was she that intrigued with the man. Maybe a bit inquisitive, a little captivated with a touch of charm, but never, never intrigued.

Come to think of it, she was so not into Nick that a little bit of flirting couldn't hurt. Besides, she had to fill her time while she waited for him to kiss her. She might even hasten the kiss to break their deal. And all for the right reasons; certainly not for pleasure.

She couldn't help but watch Nick. God, did he ever exude masculinity. Simply sexy and steamy hot.

The teakettle whistled. A bellow of mist hovered overhead.

Hot and steamy like Brad Pit in *Troy*.

Hot and steamy like a hot tub at a spa.

Hot and steamy like the visions traipsing around in McCall's head.

Purely business, girlfriend, she reminded herself. *Purely business.*

Chapter Six

As the harbor disappeared behind the *Belle Poule Princess,* McCall stretched out in the lounge chair. "Nick, the lunch was really nice. Thank you."

"You're welcome. I enjoyed doing it for you," he basically lied. Well, he had done *some* of the preparation.

Nick settled back on his chaise lounge across from her and nursed a bottle of Penta. He took a deep breath as she lifted a leg, squirted suntan lotion in her hands, and ran them up and down her calf. His gaze slipped slowly up her body, while his mouth felt like he'd taken a drink of sand.

The boat eased to a stop. Waves lapped against the hull.

Nick redirected his attention toward the sky and imagined which bathing suit would glove her body best. It would definitely be animal print, one of the requirements he had made when he called the boutique and placed his order for bathing suits, all two-piece or bikinis. He swallowed hard and drew his attention back to her face. Turning toward the ocean, he shut out the smoldering flame in her eyes.

McCall was definitely an animal print type woman. Just as dangerous, agile, and exciting as a wild lioness in a jungle. Anson had pegged one part of her body correctly. Strong, sexy legs that went all the way up to her . . . at least as far up as Nick could see beneath the flimsy zebra striped coverall.

McCall broke the silence. "Thank you for a lovely day."

"You're welcome, but you didn't eat much." He watched a seagull dip, tilt, and soar upward toward a bank of clouds.

"It was wonderfully delicious, but I wasn't all that hungry . . . for lunch," she said in a low, silky-smooth voice.

"Next time, I'll see that it's more to your liking."

"I didn't realize you'd gone totally vegetarian."

"I haven't. Just like to eat healthy. Have you ever seen what your aorta looks like clogged with grease?" Enough! He better steer away from anything having to do with food before she asked questions about his cooking that he couldn't answer.

"Look off to the north. That's what I've been waiting to show you," he said.

Nick took a quick glimpse at McCall, strolled farther down the deck, and pointed toward an exquisitely manicured island hunching out of the ocean like the back of a beautiful tortoise. In the distance, beyond mesmerizing aquamarine waters, palm trees shaded a beach enveloped by mounds of ivory sand dunes. Red and violet vines laced the tree line.

"Oh Nick, it's beautiful." She came up behind him and locked her arms around his waist. "Absolutely breathtaking." Her sultry words lingered against his neck.

Nick took in her smell of melon and citrus flowers, mixed with the crisp salty ocean breeze. Covering her hands with his, he tried to swallow the hot ache in his throat before it added to the already out-of-control throbbing way down south. He wished he hadn't changed into his swimming suit. No doubt, if he turned around there'd be no hiding his interest.

"The island belongs to my family. When I was young, my mother's servants would take me out here to play pirates of the Caribbean, complete with swords, an eye-patch, skull-and-crossbones flag, and even a gangplank. Stanley would be the sea wolf, and I'd walk him down the plank. Then we'd change roles and he'd chase me around the deck until I jumped overboard to escape." Nick took a deep breath. The heat from her hands and the rise and fall of her breast against his back became torture.

Resisting the urge to drag her into his arms and kiss her luscious mouth was a lot harder than he first thought. He dug deep inside for control. Moving her hands away, he stepped aside. "It's pretty lousy when your mother sends the hired help to play with you," he said, hoping she didn't detect the sadness that came with the memories.

McCall leaned her hip against the railing. "Can we go over to the island and play?"

"Auh, only if I can be the swashbuckling pirate and make you walk the gangplank." He grinned, thinking how much more fun she'd be to play with than Stanley. Maybe he would capture the wench, rip off her bodice, and torture her. Hell, it wouldn't be much different than what she was doing to him!

"What if I jump overboard to escape your evil, tortuous ways?" A mischievous look returned to her violet-blue eyes, and sparkled like gems in a treasure chest.

"It's a long swim, so I think you'd better wait until we're closer to the island."

McCall pulled her cover-up over her head. Dropping the gauze tunic on the deck, she lowered her eyes in the direction of his black swimming trunks. "Still like to play pirates, Slugger?"

She must have read his mind, or what was left of it. The prolonged anticipation from the time she lifted her arms above her head to remove her shirt to her standing before him barefoot, dark hair whipped by the wind, and a body as perfect as he had imagined in a zebra-print, two-piece bathing suit was almost unbearable. The idea of her lack of inhibitions and zest for life excited him. Why had he never noticed before?

"Mutineer?" He exchanged a smile with her and shook his head in amusement.

"You can torture me, but you'll have to capture me first, Black-beard!" She shimmied to the side of the boat, stepped over the rail, and twisted back in his direction. A sensual, daredevil gleam came to her eyes.

Nick lunged forward, missing her by a breath.

McCall dove overboard with the grace of a seasoned synchronized swimmer.

"Dooon't!" He screamed, ripped off his shirt, and dove in behind her.

Surfacing, he shook water from his hair and hissed. "Son of a bitch, she'll never make it to shore."

Chapter Seven

McCall hit the water headfirst, fought her way to the top, and heard Nick plunge in after her. By the time he resurfaced, she had gained a respectable distance on him. He yelled something, but the roar of the surf drowned out his words. She swam like a damsel fleeing a ruthless buccaneer.

Intending only to tantalize him, play a game, and provide a distraction from his obvious unsettling boyhood memories, she had jumped overboard, letting the water whirl around her before surfacing. She planned to swim around the boat, come back on board, and end the match. He would be happy that she was safe, offer a towel, and maybe help her dry off. Then they'd laugh about her antics, and he'd kiss her. That was the plan . . . a short-lived plan.

Obviously taking the game seriously, Nick dove in after her, turning the lark into a competition.

Feeling much like a true damsel in distress, she tried to put distance between her and the villain. She wasn't sure the challenge was all fictional, and should have seen this coming. Nick thrived on opposition, whether in business or recreation.

Well, if he wanted a contest, she'd be a worthy opponent.

Stroke after stroke, McCall eased through the water, stretching, gliding, skimming, until she secured a safe margin between them.

As a child, she had spent many hours swimming in the pond behind Granny's house. Riding horses, rounding up cattle, and baling hay left her with strong, powerful limbs.

During her senior year at Kasota Springs High School, all of the good times ended. She'd moved to California due to her parents' health and finished her education. A Texan transferring to a California school ranked somewhere below coming in midterm from a stint in juvie. McCall found comfort in kickboxing and enjoyed the sport as her recreation and a guarantee of self-defense. So what if the distance from the boat to the island was great? So was her strength.

No doubt in her mind, Nick had as much stamina for swimming as he did for everything else in life.

Hitting the beach like the first wave of an assault, McCall felt stimulated and refreshed. However, her legs complained and fought the soft ridges of sand, making her sink into what felt like a bed of wet concrete. Step after step tired, muddled legs sank into the hot gritty pebbles, causing her to stumble, holding her back.

Glancing over her shoulder, she spied Nick rise from the depths below. A bronzed phoenix pushed the water aside with his strapping arms and ascended out of the surf. She needed to make it to the line of trees to continue the game. After all, she had given him consent to torture her, but only if he caught her first. Actually, she'd given the pirate Blackbeard permission, but somehow she doubted Nick saw it that way.

Nick closed the space between them. After swimming God only knew how far, and trudging across the sand, she felt like she'd chased a mirage. Short of breath, heart beating out of control, she fell to her knees.

McCall looked over her shoulder. Dang, wasn't he a remarkable spectacle? Like a copper-toned warrior, forceful strides carried him closer. Stopping to enjoy the devilishly handsome sight cost her time. She dragged upward and set her legs in motion.

Nick's fingers seized one ankle, and she tumbled forward cushioned by the softness of the beach. She scratched and clawed, but came up with nothing to hold on to except a sand dollar that quickly crumbled in her fist. As though caught in an undertow, she couldn't stop being pulled back to him.

She found herself under Nick, eating sand. His chest pressed against her back, crushing her breasts into the beach. She stretched her arms over her head, only to have his huge calloused hands seize her smaller ones. Twisting, she lifted her head up. In a not so ladylike fashion, she dislodged grit from her mouth.

"What in the hell were you trying to do? Kill yourself and take me with you?" he lashed out between labored breaths.

Not giving her a chance to answer, Nick rolled her over and pinned her beneath his full length, keeping her hands above her head. Palm to palm, they locked fingers. Every inch of their bodies melded together like solder on hot red iron.

"Nick, I didn't ask you to come after me. I was only playing with you." She struggled, but he had her pinned too tight. Minute grains of sand clung to her skin, stinging, filling every crevice, creeping under her swimsuit.

"Playing with me is right. Hell, you could have been killed," Nick breathlessly whispered.

"Why do you have to make everything into a competition? You didn't have to save me." She stared at him, feeling exposed and defenseless in the face of his anger.

"Damn it, I thought you were going to drown." He groaned and ignored her question.

"I'm a big girl." McCall struggled to get loose, very conscious of his enticing wet flesh touching hers. "You just can't stand something happening that you can't control, can you?"

"Not when it's someone I care about." Releasing her hands, he anchored long fingers in her wet tresses, clutching a fistful of ringlets. "Do you know how beautiful you are?" Nick moved his thumb, lifted her chin, and ran his fingertips along her jawline. "So very beautiful."

Transported on a wispy, supple cloud, his words sent her thoughts into a whirl. She wanted to squirm from beneath him, away from his words, but she could only breathe.

His warm, moist breath embraced her face, making her heart race.

Resting on one elbow, Nick shifted his weight, pressing her deeper against his hot pulsating body.

Tenderly, he studied her. "You have the eyes of an angel. When you look at me, I can feel it way down in my soul. A place I've never allowed a woman to venture."

"Nick, why do you continue saying these things? I'm not pretty, just an unsophisticated, lanky, country girl that—"

"Don't." Nick's hushed her lips with his finger.

His eyes blazed like glassy volcanic rock as he moved his hand to touch the side of her face. "Don't ever say that. Please, Angel Eyes, don't let me hear those words again." His thumb traced a line to her lip.

His words weren't totally absorbed as she fought the awareness of his body pressed into hers. Blood rushed through her veins like a wild awakening river. Her mind bellowed to resist her urges. But her body did not.

On gossamer wings, the word *beautiful* floated through her mind. She ached to have him repeat the word. The word she had heard little in her life. But if she asked him to do so, it might end the fairy tale. She'd have to return to a clown-like puppet in a box waiting on someone to come along and wind it up, so she could spring to life again.

Feeling wild and daring, she refused to return to her secure, complacent life. The thought of coming out of her private box never to return frightened her. She felt like an inquisitive butterfly that had just escaped its cocoon. "You avoided my question. Why does everything have to be a competition?" she asked.

"I like a challenge, and you sure as hell are one. Never has a woman intrigued me like you, and I like"—he shifted his body—"the feel of your body under mine. Your long, graceful throat." He nudged the hollow of her neck with his nose, running his lips down its length, but never kissing. Only nuzzling. Touching, while his hot breath and the light stubble of his chin caressed her like blades of scrunch grass nestled against forget-me-nots. "I can lose myself when I'm with you. You make me want to be a better person."

Damn. Nick wanted to make her see herself as he did. Kudos for Mother. His pigheadedness had kept him from seeing McCall as a beautiful, exciting woman beneath the layers of self-imposed dowdiness. He wanted to chisel away at the facade until he exposed the true beauty.

"Your breasts . . ." His voice trembled, but his gaze did not. "They're nice." Easing his hand lower, it stilled atop her shoulder for only a moment before moving over her collarbone and settling near the valley between her breasts. "Look at me, Angel Eyes." His lips were so close that he felt the beat of her heart. "They are magnificent, enough to make a man ache. Make him fantasize about how good they would feel in his hands."

Beneath the thin wet fabric of her bathing suit, her nipples stood in rigid knots, exciting him more.

Nick knowingly issued a smile at her responsiveness, her breasts that he longed to touch, taste, enjoy. If only she'd give him permission to explore.

"Nick, you can have any woman you want. Why me?"

"Because you are so down-to-earth and honest. But you still can't see your own beauty. I want to show you. Make you see." He rubbed his cheek down the side of her jaw in a stealthy caress. "Feel it." A throaty groan escaped from deep inside his chest.

"I know I'm not beautiful, but you make me believe that I am." She buried her face against his chest and he took in the intoxicating smell of the ocean mixed with suntan lotion, as he rested his chin on her head.

His fingers slid down to her waist, along curvy hips, and stopped near her firm stomach. With palms tucked beneath her hips, he lifted her against him. Against a very obvious show of desire. He held his breath, waiting for a response, praying he didn't frighten her.

She stiffened, then relaxed, raising her violet-blue eyes to meet his.

"McCall, a blind man could see your beauty. Any man would want you," he whispered. She tilted back her head and arched upward, allowing him access to the cleavage between her breasts.

Slowly, deliberately he maneuvered first one, then two fingers up and down the valley. Covering one breast with a palm, he tortured her nipple with his thumb. God, he wanted to kiss her.

Say it, Angel Eyes . . . give me permission.

Her ragged breathing made her breasts rise and fall, tantalizing him beyond words. She began to soften beneath him, her body supple and warm. He took in her scent. All woman, layered with almond-musk suntan lotion and sea salt. He dipped lower, running his mouth over the upper part of her chest. The salty taste of the ocean lingered on his lips, and he imagined how wonderful it would be to kiss her completely, passionately. He imagined that she breathed only for him.

"Don't do this to me, Nick. Please." Her gaze was clouded with tears. "Please don't . . ."

At her plea, Nick jerked back to reality. The reality that she had zapped every ounce of his willpower when she snuggled her hot, sensual body against him on the boat. Her warm, silken flesh destroyed the self-discipline he had sworn to uphold. Her nearness had driven him crazy. He had let himself lose control and was on the brink of taking what he wanted without asking.

Damn, he had accomplished exactly what he did not intend. Scared her off. He desired her in the worst way, in all the ways a man wants a woman, but he had to keep his word, and could not take her until she was ready. Until she gave him permission. He wanted to kiss her, but she was like a newborn kitten, cuddly and innocent. He had to protect her. But from whom? Him? Nick knew what he had to do.

Drawing to his feet, he grasped McCall's trembling hand and tugged her upward. "You are beautiful, Angel Eyes. Don't ever let anyone make you feel you aren't." He brushed sand from her cheek and stroked a damp curl from her face. "We need to talk about our feelings."

"Yeah, we do," she said warily.

He shot her the most understanding smile he could conjure up, hoping she'd find it sensual as well.

"First, I need the closest thing to a cold shower I can find. Want to come?" He started across the beach. "But, don't expect an apology," he called over his shoulder. "You won't get one."

By hitting the waves, he hoped to clear his hazy mind, quiet the turmoil in his heart, and defuse his full-blown arousal. Then they could talk.

McCall watched the ocean breeze whip Nick's dark hair, making it ruffle from his face in a short crest. He waded through the surf, dove in, and disappeared beneath a breaker.

He had just said he had no intentions of apologizing. Technically he could be right. He hadn't actually kissed her, but she needed to double-check the definition of a kiss. All the elements were there.

His mouth. His lips. His tongue. And her flesh. The key words were mutual touching. A very thin technicality.

Sinking to the ground, McCall hugged her knees. "No, Nick. You can't do what you just did and walk away to, uh, cool off." She didn't want to talk about her feelings, because she couldn't allow him into her heart. Couldn't take a chance on revealing something she didn't want him to know—the part of her personal life she had kept a secret for years and planned to keep that way.

From the tight fit of his swimming trunks, no doubt Nick needed a cold shower. She didn't know how long it took to cool off, but he had been swimming long enough to put out a forest fire.

To give him some privacy and her some time to think through her plan, she decided exploring the island might be a good distraction.

What had happened to her in the last twenty-four hours? She wasn't sure, but was certain she could learn to enjoy the reinvented woman she felt clawing to get loose.

A cool ocean breeze quickly replaced the warmth of the day. Hopefully, he wouldn't be much longer since the sun was slowly sinking over the horizon.

Beyond Nick, she saw the boat. She expected that the captain would send a dinghy for them at sunset. She definitely wasn't up to another strenuous swim. There were not that many backstrokes left in her, not today. Not after the way Nick touched her.

To the west, she spied a rundown shack. Nick motioned for her to join him in the surf, but she waved toward the small hut, indicating she planned to go exploring. The wooden structure overgrown with purple and white vines intrigued her. A dilapidated screen frame hung by one hinge much like someone hanging on for dear life.

As she wandered along the beach her mind soared, swooping around like seagulls attacking anything that moved. Nobody had ever said she was pretty, much less beautiful. Could she tell Nick what his words did to her? How she felt? Deep in her heart, she dug for the answers. Did she dare open up to him and be honest? What would happen if he only spoke the words out of emotion, on an impulse, in the heat of passion? Okay, so maybe heat of passion was a bit strong, but what if . . . what if he actually meant what he said?

The whole idea of getting Nick to break his promise with a kiss had blown up in her face, unraveled as quickly as a bad alibi. Dern his hide for being so resilient, trying to prove his point. Refusing to kiss her had sent her right into a quagmire.

Thinking back to the night of the auction, Nick had said he would have paid more than the thirty thousand dollars to keep her out of the clutches of Anson. She guessed she owed Nick big-time. After all, that was a lot of money, even for Nicodemus Dartmouth.

Last night, she had felt like a rich boy's toy, but today for some reason she didn't feel that way at all. There was something about the attention he bestowed on her. A suaveness she had seen a glimpse of previously covered his rough exterior.

The last thing McCall wanted was to return to the woman she shimmied out of the day before. She liked the new version of the feisty Texan she never knew existed. Out of obligation, she had forfeited the fun side of her life to care for her mother, and suddenly she was ready to see what she had missed.

By dern, that son of a gun wasn't about to force her to go back to that cautious, boring life. She wasn't sure she had ever dealt with a man who was totally honest with her.

Why couldn't she simply settle back and let Nick prove himself?

McCall stopped in front of the hut.

The sand-covered wooden steps to the shack creaked with pain, and brought her back to earth. She stared at footprints leading to the door. Someone had been here and not too long before. Yet, Nick said the island was uninhabited.

Big . . . man-sized footprints.

Who else could be on the island?

She inched forward.

Creak . . . squeak. She slid the old wooden door open, then stepped back in surprise.

Chapter Eight

McCall stood in the threshold of the hut very shaky, but soon the surprise turned to amusement. She had truly let her imagination run wild.

On the table sat an enormous wicker basket topped with towels and a quilt. The shelf-lined walls held cases of water and canned foods. A hot sunbeam illuminated the edge of a stark-white envelope sticking up out of one side.

She leaned down and fingered the elaborate, yet manly, initial *D* embossed parchment paper. "Master Dart? Hmm?" Not the type of paper a simple note is scratched on, but one that cries urgent communiqué. The salutation indicated familiarity, yet formality. Tapping the envelope against her palm, she considered reading the note and putting the envelope back where she'd found it. After all, the envelope wasn't sealed, so it must not be too personal.

But it wasn't hers to read.

She tucked the envelope into the basket right where she got it from, between the fabric lining and the wicker side, and would tell Nick of its existence later.

Within minutes, McCall had toted the items back to the beach, and ventured out to hunt firewood. Thanks to a tin box of matches found in the basket, a campfire soon roared.

Whoever left *Master Dart* the refreshments, and she suspected it was someone from the boat, knew exactly what a woman liked. Champagne packed in ice, chocolate-covered strawberries, and caviar with toast points. The delicacies certainly did not represent a beach bum's idea of beer on the surf. She picked up marshmallows and squeezed the bag.

Perfect for roasting. Perfect. Just plain perfect to work right into her plan.

Digging a hole in the soft sand with her fingers, she screwed in the bottle of chilled champagne.

Looking up, she noticed Nick watching and waved. Thoughts of his roughened chin caressing the valley between her breasts and his thumb stroking her nipple flooded back to her. Double dog dern, if she wasn't having those funny feelings all over again.

"Well Slugger, it's payback time."

Nick flipped over and backstroked away from the beach, keeping his eyes peeled on McCall as she strolled toward the water.

His time in the surf had not only served to cool him off, but also made him do some heartfelt soul-searching. Just the thought of how mouthwatering her skin felt crushed against his, how tempted he had been to ravish her and to hell with the consequences, sent him into a heightened state of excitement. The rushing water quickly dampened the visual effects.

Cutting his eyes sideways, he caught a glimpse of his boat. At sundown, per his explicit instructions to Stanley, he'd have the captain send a rowboat their direction as soon as the campfire died down. But, which fire? The inferno within Nick or the blaze roaring on the beach? Hell, he should have helped her build the campfire but enjoyed watching her domestic side way too much. Domestic? *Damn! That's pretty close to thinking in terms of a commitment, big boy.*

McCall waded his direction, lunged forward, and caught a breaker, letting it draw her under. She surfaced right before his eyes—right between his legs.

Spewing water out of the side of her mouth, she shook her head like a wet cocker spaniel, and cocked a mermaid's smile.

An unexpected mammoth wave from behind caught her off guard, lifting her off her feet. Nick grabbed her around the waist and pulled her against his chest. Her legs locked around his hips for a moment before she dislodged herself and pushed away. Her strength and stamina were at odds with the fluid movement of her body.

"Thanks, Slugger. Saved me again." She smiled and took a deep breath.

Just the feel of her body against his, if only for a fleeting moment, sent a quiver racing through his body. A quiver? No, more like an earthquake.

Pushing wet hair from his face, he flashed his most dazzling smile. "Anytime, ma'am."

"I intended to wash off some of the sand and call you to supper," she hollered over her shoulder. "It's ready. Catch me if you can." Her words could barely be heard over a crashing wave that carried her to shore.

"Hell, she's damn near making this impossible," Nick grunted beneath his breath, as he rose from the water and strolled toward the blanket, where he caught a flying towel with one hand. "Thanks."

"You really are good." Closing her eyes, she patted water from her legs.

"I told you I was good." He dried off first his arms, then moved to his chest. "Need any help?" His eyes never left her face as he watched. He wondered about her thoughts. She seemed to enjoy the toweling off way too much. Meaning? She definitely intended to test his resolve.

"No. I've already told you, I'm a big girl. You're good at everything you do, aren't you?" She pulled the terrycloth around her shoulder and leaned back on her hands. The wind blew her wet disheveled hair into a waterfall of heavy ringlets.

"I'm *very good*. Especially when I put my mind to it." Nick tossed the wet cloth toward her bosom.

"I bet you are." She issued an innocent wide-eyed look, before turning her attention to the bottle of champagne. "If you'll do the honors, I'll get the glasses. Real champagne glasses. Not pimento and cheese spread glasses."

"I see you found the picnic basket Stanley prepared." After filling two flutes, Nick handed her one. "Toast?" He lifted his glass. "To the most beautiful and daring woman I've ever known." His glass kissed hers. "May the remainder of the evening be even more adventurous."

"And, to a very competitive man." She eyed him covetously and took a sip. "And I presume Stanley also left you a note, which I tucked inside the basket. Who is he?"

"One of the people who has worked for Mother for years." Nick gave her a pensive smile. "Stanley has been with Mother since before I was even born."

"I see," she said. "A very thoughtful person. You said you want to talk."

"Yeah, I do. But shucks, Angel Eyes, it's not anything that can't wait until we've eaten."

This bought McCall some time. Time needed to implement her new strategy.

"Okay, I can wait. Do you like marshmallows?" McCall picked up a tree-branch skewer and gingerly slipped on a marshmallow.

"Oh yeah. One of my favorite things in life."

Slowly, she turned the limb from one side to the other over the flames, watching as the outside hardened and turned the shade of vanilla cream. "Did you ever play baseball, or did you buy a farm team just because you wanted one?"

"I played first base in high school, but didn't have any time for it in college. Too busy enjoying the nonscholastic life and learning engineering at UCLA. Then I was much too busy getting the business side of being an engineer pounded into my head at Berkeley." He leaned back on his elbows, stretching his legs out in front of him.

"Guess that's what Madeline calls the softer side of the business?"

"Something like that. How about you?"

"Own a ball club? Naugh! But, if I put all of my CEUs together, I'd have a degree in how to get through college without seeing the campus in daylight." She rolled the stick over again and allowed the marshmallow to darken to the color of caramel. "Unfortunately, I haven't always gotten everything I wanted. You have, though, haven't you?" Without waiting for his answer, she continued, "I can only imagine what Christmas was like at your house."

"It was fun, and I pretty much got whatever I asked Santa for, but I didn't get everything I wanted, believe it or not." His brows knitted together. A look she'd never seen before suddenly shrouded his face, as if the memories were too painful for him to talk about. "There are some things even Santa can't bring a child."

McCall wanted to ask him more, but at the same time wished to respect his privacy.

As if changing the subject, Nick grasped the skewer. "Let me try my hand." He touched the tip to an ember, allowing it to catch fire. Blowing out the flame and cooling the mushroomed sweet concoction, he pulled the crispy shell off and held the treat up to McCall's lips.

"Umm, goood!" She licked her fingers and watched as Nick put the soft inside back into the fire, repeating the process. He ate it before putting two replacements on the stick.

After going through the process a second time, he leaned forward and fed her another toasty delicacy, then popped the gooey sticky center in his mouth. "Now that's what's good."

Roasting marshmallows had turned more sexual than she had envisioned. Nick began to soften much like the gooey centers he roasted. "If you don't quit eating those things, you're going to get soft like . . ." She blinked and shot him a seductive smile. "I mean, your abs will get all soft and, oh gosh, I meant to say—"

"I know what you meant." He pulled another piece of goo off and aimed for his mouth only to have a thin thread of cream form over his lips and run down his chin. His tongue reached to lick it off.

"You've made a mess, and I don't believe your tongue is that long." McCall leaned into him closer and closer until she forced him back on his elbows. Close enough to taste his sweetness. Slowly, deliberately taking full advantage of fate, she licked off the sugared cream. In the process, her glass accidentally tilted until champagne slowly dribbled down onto his chest. The cold liquid ran over his body, pooling near his flat abdomen.

McCall watched Nick's eyes betray his ardor.

"You might be surprised how far my tongue can reach when I want it to." He closed his eyes and let out a soft groan.

Time stopped.

Seagulls quieted.

Palm trees whispered and ruffled their leaves as an ocean breeze picked up. The rolling waves hummed in faint laughter, and the smell of lavender, wild roses, and ocean spray created exquisite perfumes only for Nick and McCall.

Nick broke the silence. "I think you've made a mess of your own." His mouth twitched in amusement. Lightly, he fingered a loose tendril of hair on her cheek. "Wanna clean it up and see for yourself just how hard I really am?"

"By all means." McCall lowered her head and lapped up the droplets of champagne that ran down the center of his chest.

"I mean that my abs are firm."

"I know." Moving lips over his taut skin, through the mass of dark hair, she worked her way back up before kissing each shoulder.

"I believe you're kissing me." He let out a throaty, needy groan and stretched back on the quilt. Closing his eyes, he left no doubt he was savoring the attention she bestowed on him.

McCall eased her gaze upward and watched his features turn from lighthearted teasing to a shadowy pained expression. "I never promised that *I* wouldn't kiss *you*."

Another moan escaped.

Waves of rapture cascaded through her as Nick threaded both hands through her hair and guided her mouth down until her lips touched his chest.

Taking a nipple between her teeth and gently nibbling, she teased it until the tip grew taut. She loved the way he responded, and never realized that a man's nipple could get as hard as a woman's. But then she had very little experience with the romantic side of a sexual encounter.

Only Nick's breathing and the roll of the surf penetrated the fog in her mind as her lips traced a trail of caresses from his chest to his abs.

Kissing one rib, she criss-crossed to the other side. Her breasts dipped and bounced against his arousal as she made her way to the triangle of hair disappearing beneath the waist of his bathing suit. The mere touch of him sent a warming shiver through her, making her slide down a dangerously, slippery slope of passion.

"Whoa, Angel Eyes," Nick said in a thready, hoarse voice. "Don't go any farther unless you mean business."

Ignoring his warning, she lifted her head and in a purely feline fashion ran her chin up and then down his abdomen, stopping only inches from the top of his swimming trunks.

"Enough, Angel Eyes! I'm hollering uncle." He took a deep breath. "Another quarter of an inch, and it's an invitation and, baby, it's coming in loud and clear."

Suddenly, McCall drew upright. "Nick, I don't know what over-came me." She moved away and pulled her knees to her chest. "I, uh"—she bit at her lip and swallowed an apology—"don't know what to say."

She didn't want to apologize. Heavens! What had gotten into her? A hot flush ran across her chest.

What had just happened? Nick had said that she brought out the best in him, yet he seemed to bring out the worst in her. If what she did was bad, then why did it feel so good?

Nick drew out feelings she had tried to ignore. Emotions, desires that a nice girl could only dream of with a handsome tycoon like Nick. She had wanted to do things to him that she had only read about in bodice-rippers and *True Confession* magazines she swiped from beneath her Granny's mattress, then snuggled under her covers on drizzly days in Texas and read until the rain went away.

The wild side of McCall itched to escape, but the Bible-thumping, verse-spouting side of her wasn't quite so willing.

"It's okay, Mac. I'd be a fool to say I wasn't enjoying your attention." Nick eased next to her and dropped his arm around her shoulders. "But, I think I deserve the truth."

"The truth? That I made a fool of myself?"

"No." Nick tucked her into his side. "Tell me how you feel." Nick propped his chin on her head and ran his hands down her arm then back up, stopping on her shoulder. "How I make you feel. About your plan to destroy my resistance, so I'd break my promise, and how it backfired?"

"Why does *everything* have to be a competition with you?" McCall asked for the umpteenth time. Not expecting an answer, she closed her eyes. She had asked for his honesty, but now she was the one not willing to share?

"You were the one that made it that way. I discovered that when you put your hands around me and damn near fondled me," Nick said.

She stiffened and exhaled deeply in exasperation. "Fondled you? You must be kidding. Believe me, you'd know if I fondled you!"

Chapter Nine

Nick tightened his mouth and a muscle in his jaw quivered. He studied the setting sun over the Pacific off to the west, trying to take in her words and not show his frustration. Why couldn't she just tell him the truth? If she wouldn't, he'd confront the issue head-on.

"Call it what you may, but you were way too obvious that you wanted me to make a pass at you, so you could slap my chops, or maybe kickbox my family jewels into the next millennium. Then our deal would be off. Right?" Although he tried to soften his words, he hadn't. Nick had seen his woolliest steelworkers flinch when he spoke to them in the tone he'd just used with McCall.

"Nicodemus Dartmouth, you're just trying my patience." She pulled away, stalked to the fire, and added a log, which quickly caught fire and turned the campfire into an inferno. She rubbed her hands together over the crackling embers. "I just—"

"Just what?" He watched her body straighten with indignity. "Just enjoyed yourself and now don't know what to do about it?"

"Okay. It started out as a plan, but got out of control because of"—she turned to face him, leveling a steely stare—"you!"

"Me? Oh yeah." He rolled his eyes at her.

"It was you. You were just supposed to, uh, well . . . kiss me. You're the man. You should have never let it go that far. You enjoyed it way too much."

"Hell, Mac, it's the twenty-first century. Women take responsibility for their own actions." He exhaled. "Okay, so if I take the blame, where do we go from here?"

"Home! Since I'm supposed to be more of a thoroughly modern

Millie and make my own decisions." She kicked at sand near the fire. "Let's get out of here before I really *modernize* myself and become a woman's libber, and . . . and, oh hell." Another dust devil of sand hit the campfire, sending flames high in the sky.

McCall walked over to a blanket, slid down, and pulled it around her. She closed her eyes.

Taking in what she had said, Nick turned his head east toward the shoreline and watched as the *Porte Bella Princess* moved off in the distance.

Damnation and tarnation!

True to his word, Stanley had taken Nick's instructions to heart. With the sun quickly setting and the flaming campfire, his valet had given the orders to the captain to move back to port until morning. But it sure as hell wasn't a good time to bring the boat's departure to McCall's attention. He had little choice.

"One small problem, Carrie Nation." Nick motioned toward his boat, which appeared about the size of a small yacht. "I think you've got one hell of a swim ahead of you."

Sure enough once she caught sight of the *Porte Bella Princess*, McCall didn't handle being stranded with Nick for the night very well and threw out accusations at the speed of Nick's best pitcher.

Nick hunkered down and stirred the campfire and thought back to her words.

She had not only questioned but flat out made unflattering accusations about his heritage, as well as his legitimacy. Now the quilt-cocooned angelic hellion pretended to sleep like a baby only a few feet away.

A sooted log fell. Gilded, pumpkin-tinged flames shot skyward. He ran his hands up his arms and chased away some of the chill. The breeze off the ocean wasn't all that cold, but compared to the balmy afternoon, the night had become as icy as the tongue-lashing that had belted from the woman nestled in the sand like a clam.

As certain as the tide going back out to sea, he felt the hoodwinking woman's stare on his backside. He'd be damned if he'd give her the privilege of letting her know she bothered him. The safest approach—ignore her. Pretend she didn't exist. As if he could do that.

If it hadn't been enough for them to lock horns like two bulls earlier over the boat leaving them behind, it'd be nothing compared to what was certain to happen once he told her that he planned to exercise his option for an extended date. After all, he'd paid twenty-one thousand dollars over and above his donation.

But why had he decided to make her spend the full week with him that he'd paid for? Maybe it was because she'd proven such a worthy opponent. Or maybe it was because he wanted to see where their relationship might go. At the least, and probably the worst reason he could think of, he had time off and could use the company.

Hell, the real reason might be payback for the torture she'd put him through over the last twenty-four hours. She owed him that much. Didn't she?

Once again his mind dwelled on their argument over being stranded.

Even after producing the envelope from Stanley, she continued to refuse blame, inferring Nick had created the situation by sending the boat back to harbor and planning to trap them on the island all along. She refused to accept any part by stoking the fire time and time again. He even read the note out loud, stating that if the captain saw a roaring fire at sundown that he would return to the harbor.

McCall had continued holding Nick responsible, threatening to swim ashore. Out of sheer stubbornness, she probably would have succeeded.

Nick ambled over to the tree line and found a settling place against an enormous palm. He threw one towel across his thighs, another around his shoulders, and rested his head against the rough bark. He was tired of thinking. Tired of being frustrated with the pretty woman, and tired of wanting something he couldn't have.

A rippled ribbon of moonlight gleamed over the ocean. He stared at the sky, thinking about grabbing a handful of stars, tossing them in a jar like lightning bugs on a summer's night. A peace offering to McCall. His gaze wandered back to the woman lying so near, yet so far away. A longing shot through him worse than a hungry campfire.

Oh hell! What was happening to him? One minute, he wanted to make love to her, and the next, his thoughts turned to giving her a jar of insects! Maybe he was right last night. They were both lost in a rugged sea of loneliness. How could *he* be lonesome? He had everything he wanted, except for one thing . . . someone to truly love. Nick folded his arms across his chest and mumbled under his breath. "A commitment? Right."

A complication was more like it and something he could do without. He grunted and tossed aside the towel from his lap.

Hellfire and brimstone, bring on the matches . . . I'm a goner!

The sexy lady with the eyes of an angel had done him in!

They still needed to talk. Or at least he needed to tell her how he felt. No doubt the spitfire with horns beneath her halo had deep-seated feelings. They had to be intense for her to show such emotion and desire. But he needed to get the hellion to quit thinking everything he did was part of a bigger plan to uproot her emotionally.

Finding mutual ground boiled down to principles. He had paid twenty-one thousand dollars for an extended date. By George, he wouldn't allow her to welsh on the deal! Tomorrow he'd tell her just that. Or maybe he needed to extend an olive branch. After all, he hadn't been completely honest. How could he tell her that he lied about planning to bid on a bachelorette? Let her believe he'd bought her by accident, when he truly wanted to protect her?

McCall lay motionless and took shallow breaths. She kept her eyes peeled on Nick, watching him roam around the campsite, stirring the ashes, restless. She never figured him for the fidgeting type. He seemed to know what he wanted and how to get it, although sometimes resorting to unorthodox methods to achieve his goal.

Suddenly, she realized deep inside he might not be as cool and confident as he appeared on the surface. He had insecurities like anyone else. Like her. Nick just knew how to handle things better. After all, he had been trained in the ways of the bluebloods. He knew how to control his emotions. But then, she had forced him into a prickly position. A situation that needed correcting. Trying to conceal her desires and insecurities by pushing him away wasn't the answer. She must put a stop to the charade. Now!

"Hey, Slugger. Wanna spend the night with me?" She folded back the quilt.

At the sound of McCall's voice, Nick whipped his head up. "I thought you were asleep." He rubbed his neck.

"No. Just thinking. You must be cold."

"Did you forget I spent a frigid night on your porch?"

"It wasn't frigid and wasn't the whole night. It was only a few minutes. I promise I'll be good. I don't like to see you uncomfortable. I'm willing to share the blanket."

"No thanks. It's a bad idea."

"I see."

"That's the problem, Angel Eyes, you don't see. If you did, you'd realize that men and women are different—"

"I'm not a child. I know—"

"You might know about boys, but you certainly don't have a lot of experience with men."

"Then go ahead and fill me in, Mr. Studly."

"We aren't like running tap water, where you can adjust the hot and cold until we're the perfect temperature." His expression stilled and grew serious. "Men are more like drawing water direct from the hot water tank. We come out hot, steamy, and dangerous with no in-between. You can't adjust us to your liking. Can't just turn us off and on to your liking."

"Thanks for the maturation lesson, but this has nothing to do with the difference between men and women. It's to punish me for how I acted earlier. You'd rather punish me and freeze than share a blanket?"

"I'm not interested in punishing you or anybody, but I can't lie next to you and not want you like any man wants a woman. I have needs. Even a pigheaded jerkass has his limits. And Angel Eyes, you pressed me way beyond mine tonight. I can't do it again."

"I'm really sorry. I just never thought, well, I'm kinda, uh—"

"A virgin?"

"No. Not exactly." She pulled the blanket up to her chin.

"Either you are or you're not, and if you don't know the difference, then you've got real problems." The gold in his eyes flickered with interest.

"I know the difference." She lowered her eyes, trying to avoid letting Nick see the shame in them. "Nick, I've had sex, but I've never had a man make—"

"Make love to you?" He kept his eyes locked on hers.

Was he testing the waters? She wasn't sure.

He hesitated before saying, "I see . . ."

"No, you don't." It took all of her courage to tell him the truth. "I've had a man rut around on me like it was his God-given duty to mate."

Nick closed his eyes for a couple seconds, but said nothing.

McCall took a deep breath and continued. "You're the only man I've ever danced with who didn't stay up-close-and-personal with my boobs, slobbering all over them." She pushed aside the quilt and sat up to face him. "Daddy worked at the refinery with rough, tough, hard-working, drinking men. You have no idea what it was like growing up, maturing early, and—"

"I know the kind of man you're talking about. Had plenty working for me over the years."

"Nick, you've known what it's like to have someone besides your family love you, care about you. I never have."

"How do you know so much about my love life? From Josie?"

"No! Nick, I worked with you at the construction business, remember? I saw it. Heard it, and dreamed about it. I mean, I wished—"

"That it was you with me?" His mouth curved into a smile.

"Yeah, but not particularly because it was you—"

"Thanks loads. You know how to deflate a man's ego—"

"I meant . . . I just wanted someone to look at me like I've seen you do with other women. Then one day I saw you watching me in the same way—"

"And I promptly transferred you to the Foundation?" Nick tilted back his head and lifted his eyes to meet hers. A sad expression crept across his face as he slowly shook his head from side to side.

"Yeah. And it hurt. I did a good job for you. But I also realized no matter what I did I'd never be good enough for you. Certainly I'm not socially adept or beautiful, but I still liked the way you looked at me. We had something special, a friendship—"

"I've always valued your friendship, and you know it," he said in almost a whisper.

"I know, and our relationship got back on track when we didn't have to work so close together. Then the gala came along, and your mother made me into one of those women you used to look at. I suddenly saw myself differently. One I liked. All decked out in ivory and beads, with your grandmother's gorgeous necklace around my neck. I thought I just might be pretty enough for you." She found herself studying his profile, searching for the answer. "And then Nick, you know what happened?"

Slowly he shook his head and looked squarely in her eyes.

"You looked at me like I've seen you look at those gorgeous, sexy women . . . like I was one of them."

"Do you know the reason I transferred you?"

"I tried to figure it out for a long time, but finally stopped. I had my answer." McCall shrugged.

"You don't know why. Nobody does. But I'll tell you now. It was because I couldn't work with you day in and day out without touching you . . . because I started seeing you like those other women. And McCall, you deserved better than a man who thinks if he asks a woman out twice she'll want a change of address form from the post office. You didn't deserve that kind of treatment. You're better than that, and I knew it."

"So you didn't transfer me to get rid of me?" She looked up more confused than ever.

"Hell no!" Nick said firmly. "You distracted me. I found myself crawling up twenty stories of red iron, thinking about you. You were as dangerous as going around without my hard hat or safety harness on. You made me lose control, and I began to use poor judgment on the jobs. You were a distraction that I couldn't afford. I did it to save you . . . from me."

"And, you don't want to save me now?"

"Mac, I want you so bad it hurts, but I don't think you're ready for that type of commitment." Nick ran his hands through his hair then took a long audible breath. "You need to be courted."

"Courted? That sounds so old-fashioned."

"I'm just an old-fashioned guy. Anything wrong with that?"

McCall slid off the quilt, crawled over to Nick, and kneeled before him. "Not a thing. I've never been courted." She scooped his face up with her hands. "I want you to romance me. What comes first, Slugger? A kiss?"

And he kissed her. A slow, sincere kiss that rushed through her like a wildfire.

Nick finally released her. "Technically, you are now off the hook for the date."

"Technically, maybe I don't want to be."

"I need to tell you something that might make you change your mind. I gave the thirty-thousand dollars to Mother's foundation as a donation and never planned to buy a date. You or anyone else. I certainly didn't plan to bid on Buffy—or whatever her name is— Armstrong. I was ordering a drink. So, the way I see it, in fairness, although I paid an extra twenty-one thousand for a *weeklong* date, I should let you off the hook—"

"Whoa, Slugger! Weeklong? I thought—"

"I figured you didn't hear the final bid because of the uproar in the crowd, but I outbid Mr. Testosterone with three thousand dollars a night for seven nights. If I hadn't, you'd be spending the night with that, that—"

"Mr. Testosterone, huh? That's what you called him?" She raised a questioning eyebrow. "Then you ended up paying fifty-one thousand dollars for a date?" She raised both eyebrows as her eyes grew wide. "The original thirty thousand donation, plus three thousand dollars a night? Hypothetically, would you really pay that much? Even for a good cause like the foundation?"

"Yes, and I'd pay that much again over, if it'd stop our catfights, give us a chance to really get to know one another, and see where our feelings are headed."

"Then it's a done deal, Slugger. I have a week off, thanks to your mother. All I have to do is make arrangements for someone to deliver my Meals on Wheels and I'm all yours."

"But, I don't have a week off. I didn't read you all of Stanley's note. After we left the boat, he got a call and I have to go up the coast on business by tomorrow. I'm sorry. It sure as hell would have helped if I had known before the *Belle Poule Princess* sailed, but without any telephone reception on the island, there was no way for him to let me know except with the note. It's partly my fault, since I told him I didn't want us to be disturbed for any reason. In the morning, once we're picked up, the captain has to take me over to the Santa Barbara harbor, so I can get my car that Stanley's driving there for me. He can take you back to LA then. Unless you want to—"

"Want to what?"

"Go with me. It's only up to the Bay Area, although I have to make a couple quick stops in the Santa Ynez Valley."

"All I have is a shirt and shorts back on the boat."

"Not that you aren't appealing in that bikini, but . . ."

In a wisp of time, they struck an agreement to sail to Santa Barbara, make an impromptu shopping trek to pick up some clothes and various necessities, and she'd accompany him on the trip.

"McCall, I want to show you that my world isn't all that different from yours, so decide where you want to go. When my business is finished, we'll go there. To Hearst Castle, Winchester Mansion, Lake Tahoe, Vegas. You name it, and it's yours."

"Even go where it's raining and the sun is shining?" she teased.

"And where we can walk to a foreign country? Sure."

"Ever spent any time in Texas?" She slid her arms around his neck.

"Nope, but I think I'm about to." He pulled her tight to his chest.

McCall nuzzled against his corded neck. "Nick, I'm through fighting, but I'm not ready to be your lover. Or anyone else's."

"I'm not asking you to. Just open up your heart and look inside. See if there's room there for me. I'm finished with making demands on you. Next time, it'll be on your terms, but I'm warning you, I won't call uncle again." He thumped the tip of her nose lightly. "Understand?"

"Understood." She kissed him lightly on the lips. "No more secrets between us?"

"Promise. No more secrets."

Chapter Ten

Nick eased his sleek, red Jag convertible along the Pacific Coast Highway in the Santa Ynez Valley. As the sun perched overhead, they topped a hill leading into Lompoc.

McCall let out an audible gasp. "The fields are beautiful."

"I told you that I was going to take the scenic route and the little extra time would be worth it. Now was I right or not?"

Multicolored fields of zinnias, sweet peas, petunias, and a purple blossom he didn't recognize carpeted the vale and swept upward on the hillside. Row after row of grapevines stood at attention in the adjacent vineyards.

"Oh yes. I've seen the strawberry fields around LA, but this is nothing in comparison. I've heard of the flower fields, but I never imagined them to be this beautiful." A smile lightened her face. She turned toward Nick. "And I've never seen a sexier man in all my born days. The way the wind is whipping your hair backwards is kinda like the way the ocean breeze did yesterday. And of course being a Texan, any man in Levi's and boots sets my heart fluttering." An easy smile played at the corners of her mouth.

"Oh shucks, ma'am, you're gonna make me blush." He smiled back at her. "Is that the way they say it in Texas?"

"It'll work."

"When do I get to wear that there Stetson you made me buy?" He motioned toward the backseat with his head.

"Whenever you don't want to chase it for two miles when it blows off." She laughed in a loving way. "Or drive with one hand holding it on and the other on the wheel." Quickly she added, "But I'm enjoying riding with the top down."

Nick knew one thing—if the wind would blow off a ball cap on the open road, he wasn't about to try a cowboy hat to see if there was a difference. No doubt she thought he'd never worn a Stetson, or ridden a horse either, but he'd just keep that knowledge to himself. She seemed relaxed and enjoying herself, so he didn't want to do anything that would mess it up.

He settled back and enjoyed the faint smell of her perfume mingled with the scents of freshly cultivated fields and strawberries wafting in the air.

"I wish we'd had time to locate a thrift store. Hopefully, I didn't max out my credit card, but I had no choice but to purchase a few things or go home." McCall pushed a strand of stray hair that had escaped the Scunci that tied her tumbled curls behind her head.

"You had a choice. I offered to pay, but since your stubbornness wouldn't allow me the pleasure, I'll just have to see that you get a raise to make up for it." Nick sped up to pass a slower moving vehicle.

"No, you won't do anything of the sort. If I get a raise, it'll be because I've worked hard and deserve one, not because you told your mother to give me one. Understand?"

"Understood, but—"

"No buts about it." McCall turned her attention to the roadside.

Nick changed the subject, knowing his efforts were futile. "I hope you kept that cute little black number."

Just the thought of how sensual and exciting she looked twirling around in the slinky gown made him hard in a very delicate place. He shifted his weight to his left hip in an attempt to relieve some of the pressure hugging the zipper of his Levis.

"Yes, but where are we going that requires such a nice dress?"

"I'd planned to surprise you. I made reservations at the Venetian Ballroom of the Fairmont in San Francisco." He twisted again pulling at the leg of his Levi's to loosen their grip. He needed something to draw his attention away from his discomfort. "The flowers are pretty, aren't they?"

"Absolutely beautiful." She shot him a flirtatious smile. "Almost as dazzling as what I've heard about the ballroom."

"I think you'll enjoy it. The plants along here are used for seeds and cut flowers. Big business." He needed a distraction in the worse way. "Along with lettuce. Lots of lettuce. Tons of lettuce. The blue-green fields are cabbage, and, as you know, the ones covered with plastic are strawberries. And horses, lots of horse ranches around here." Nick swallowed. He knew he was rambling, but he had to do something to take his mind off the ache that had forcefully turned into old-fashioned pain below his waist.

He kept his eyes peeled on the winding road. His mind galloped somewhat like the sorrel trotting along the stark-white fence line.

He'd like to give McCall a whole pasture of thoroughbreds, if that was what she wanted.

The knot in Nick's stomach tightened. He fought off his desire to think about the future. One with McCall. He couldn't fall in love with the Texan, but it might already be too late.

If he found himself in love, there would be consequences. His mother would never allow it because she thought every woman he dated was a gold-digger, particularly his ex-fiancée Lauren DePaul. And, she was certainly more affluent and had a tougher shell than McCall.

From the start, Madeline had voiced her disapproval of Lauren. He never should have proposed knowing how his mother felt. He thought he'd eventually win her over. No luck. So, the mini-nuptials ended when Lauren walked out of their engagement party leaving Nick standing with a champagne glass in his hand and a toast on his lips.

Lauren's explanation—he should marry his mother!

Madeline's explanation—Lauren needed a Botox detox program, preferably in San Quentin.

Nick suspected that McCall had heard about his engagement fiasco, but was lady enough not to participate in the gossip. However, he felt sure she didn't know the sordid details.

But as his and McCall's delicate relationship seemed to take on a life of its own, he could take comfort knowing his mother liked McCall. She certainly trusted her, as shown by allowing her to wear a family heirloom necklace. Even taking it home with her. Maddi also seemed to be protective of her, as a mother would nurture her child. Surely, as an employee, not as her son's girlfriend . . . of her daughter-in-law.

Damnation! He had gone from thinking of her as a friend, to a girlfriend, to a lover, and now a wife! That kind of thinking could scare a man, especially one who didn't care to be left standing alone at another engagement party.

Nick wanted to protect the feisty Texan, yet he might be placing her in a position that could potentially hurt her more than anything he could have ever done.

Damn it, he didn't need this distraction. He had a ball team to keep on the road, a construction business to run, that damnable foundation to preside over, and a cussed mother to deal with, not to mention a horse ranch to buy. He couldn't allow McCall to get a stronger grip on his heart, and certainly didn't want to put someone he cared about through the Elliott-Dartmouth scrutiny.

A concerto of chimes called from his iPhone. Seeing who the caller was and not wanting to ruin the moment for McCall, he pulled to the side of the road and answered the phone instead of using the Bluetooth speakers. He touched the pad accepting the call. After taking a deep breath, he said, "Yes, Mother. What can I do for you?"

Glancing toward McCall and seeing her absorbed with the Dodgers' extra-inning game on the radio, he lowered his voice and got out of the car, then walked out of hearing distance. "Damn it, can't I spend a night away from my house without having to report in like I'm still in high school?" He shifted weight to his other hip knowing his mother would issue a severe rebuttal for his coarseness.

Cutting his eyes toward his traveling companion, he watched McCall grab her cell phone as the song "Deep in the Heart of Texas" sounded as a ringtone.

He stepped closer to the car, but continued his own conversation. "Yes, Mother, I'm listening." The truth was he barely heard Madeline while he lent his other ear to McCall's conversation.

Satisfied her call wasn't bad news, he returned his full attention to his mother. Lowering his voice, he said, "Mother, I'm on the way to the ranch, if I ever get off the phone." His gaze never left McCall's face, as he watched her frown deepen. "Remember? You sent me on a vacation to change my attitude. Talk to you later."

Nick disconnected, followed by McCall.

"Madeline." Nick announced. Starting the engine, he revved it up in frustration.

"Josie." McCall frowned and tossed her phone in her purse.

Absorbed in their private thoughts only the breeze disturbed the silence.

Nearing a highway exit, Nick drew her attention back to the scenery. "Look off the road this side of the mountain. That's our next stop, the Triple J Horse Ranch."

"It's gorgeous—so green and those wonderful trees. I love the white fence that seems to go on forever. In the Texas Panhandle, we use mostly barbed wire for the pastures. But some parts of Texas use the white fencing, too."

"I like it here. It smells clean, fresh, like newly mown hay. I could spend the rest of my life here."

"And leave LA?" She seemed genuinely surprised.

"You never can tell. They build things up this way, too."

"Not anything you specialize in."

"If I can construct high-rise buildings, guess I could do fine with low-rise." He laughed, and took a right turn.

"You'd also have more time to spend on your pet project."

"I presume you mean Habitat for Humanity."

McCall nodded. "Yes. It's a worthy cause. I've always been amazed how many of your men volunteer."

"I give them an incentive. Double time and an extra week of paid vacation does the trick."

Waist-high red geraniums and towering pampas grass with showy alabaster feathery plumes guarding the rock entrance to the ranch came into view. A tunnel of ancient Italian stone pines joined overhead and guided them toward the sprawling ranch house and mammoth stables.

McCall gasped at the sight. A chilly shiver ran the length of her spine. "I feel like I've been here before . . . but I haven't, unless it was when I was a child."

"I thought you were raised in Texas."

"I was, but vaguely remember coming out to California on

vacation, but I can't recall where we went. You know that funny feeling you get when you think you've already done something?"

"Everyone has them. There's some explanation about how your unconscious mind works, but it's nothing but a boggling déjà vu in my opinion."

The sleek Jaguar passed the main house and rolled to a stop in front of the first of several stables.

A tall drink of water wearing weathered snakeskin boots and a well-worn Stetson ambled in their direction as Nick unfolded from the car and grabbed his new black Stetson.

"Nick Dartmouth as I live and breathe." The lanky man pulled Nick into a hug as if he were a child's teddy bear. "Ain't you a sight for sore eyes?"

Nick returned the embrace. "Good to see you, ol' man."

"Who you callin' old? And who's this pretty little filly with you?" The gentleman turned to greet McCall.

"McCall, meet Jock Macmurphy, the most cantankerous sidewinder you'll ever meet. There isn't a bronc he can't handle."

"I'm pleased to meet you, Mr. Macmurphy." McCall offered her hand to the grizzled old man, who pumped her arm as though drawing water from a well.

"Everybody just calls me Mac, so I reckon you oughta, too. Name's McCall, right?"

"Yes, sir. McCall Johnson. But I have a question. Won't we get the Mac's mixed up, unless I call you Jock?" A mischievous smile spread across her face.

"Nobody will get an old geezer like me mixed up with a pretty filly like you." He ran the length of his bushy mustache between his fingers. "Name sounds familiar. You ain't one of those movie stars up in Hollywood, are you?"

"Thanks for the compliment, but I work for the Elliott-Dartmouth Foundation."

"Oh yeah, Miz Maddi's mission to keep us old relics up and going on our own. So, folks call you Mac, too?"

"Only two people, and one is standing right here." She motioned toward Nick. "The other was my daddy, but he died a few years back."

"Sorry to hear that, ma'am." The ranch foreman and managing

partner turned to Nick. "I figured you'd be coming up this way as soon as you heard—"

Nick interrupted. "McCall is eyeing that strawberry roan over there, and I bet she's just itching to ride him," Nick interrupted.

"Oh Nick, I haven't ridden for a long time—"

"Missy, it's like a bicycle." It was Jock's turn to interrupt. "Once you've done it you're not likely to forget. If'n you want to take him out for some exercise, I'll get the kid in the stable to saddle him for you."

"Do we have time?" She grabbed Nick's arm and leveled a hopeful glint at him.

He nodded his approval, enjoying the warmth in her touch. "We'll make the time."

"Thanks." McCall smiled at Nick, but addressed Jock. "I can saddle him myself."

"All the tack is there. Holler if you need anything," Jock said. "He's spirited, but an easy one to handle if you're gentle with him."

She patted Nick's arm. "Thanks. Nick, want to come along?"

"Not this time. Enjoy your ride. We have to leave in time to get over Harris Grade before the fog sets in. Jock and I have plenty of uh . . ." Nick hesitated and tried to corral his thoughts. The last thing he wanted was to lie. "Uh, catching up to do."

"I won't be long. I hope he enjoys the exercise as much as I know I will." McCall smiled and strolled off toward the stable.

"I bet Asteroid will like having her on his back, too." Jock wagged a bushy eyebrow.

Nick waited until the lady disappeared into the shadows before replying. "She was raised in Texas and she rode in a couple of LA charity functions. She's rides like a feather balanced in a saddle. No doubt, she can handle any stud thrown at her."

"She's about as spirited as Asteroid. So, why the secrecy about why you're here?"

"No secrecy. She just thinks I get everything I want, one way or another."

"She's a smart one, huh," Jock bantered.

Nick ignored the old buzzard. "So, for the time being, I don't necessarily want her to know I'm buying this ranch."

"It's not like you to care what someone thinks, so then you're tellin' me that you care about that gal?"

"I respect her opinion . . . that's all."

"But you're afraid she'll be thinkin' it's another of your whim-whams? Ain't that what Miz Maddi calls 'em?"

"Don't remind me." Nick removed his Stetson and ran his fingers through his hair. "So until the lawyers find our missing investor and get the papers signed, I'd just as soon not jinx the deal by telling McCall about my plans."

"Sounds like you're wantin' her to hang her bonnet next to your hat."

"Not on your life, you ol' coot. So, tell me about that filly that's standing and ready to breed. Has she been teased with a gelding, yet?"

Jock nodded his head up and down. "No luck yet, but I haven't given up. She'll come around. She just isn't ready." He suddenly changed subjects. "Well, I'll eat my hat, looky out there." Jock motioned toward the pasture. "She rides like she's done it forever. The boy mustva got the saddle and tack for her."

Nick looked up and cocked his head. "She sure seems connected to Asteroid." Pursing his lips, he raised a questioning eyebrow. "About ready to talk about selling me this ranch, you ol' cuss?"

Chapter Eleven

Nick and Jock spent more time than they had anticipated discussing the ranch operation and Nick's pending purchase, while McCall enjoyed a long ride on Asteroid.

After a supper at the Blacksmith Steakhouse in downtown Lompoc consisting of grilled steaks, baked potatoes, and a nice fresh salad, Nick put the top up on the Jag and headed north out of Lompoc toward Harris Grade, a whirligig of weaving curves, tight twisters, and hairpin turns.

On the right, they passed the old Valley Drive-In. Once a haven for young people, the abandoned theater lay silent in a boneyard of memories.

"Haven't seen an outdoor theater in a long time," Nick joshed. "I thought they were history."

"Not in Texas, they aren't."

"Still have those dinosaurs out there?"

"How do you think Kasota Springs grew to a population that topped five hundred?" Her voice was smooth, laced with her lazy Texas drawl.

"I'll bite. How?" He flashed a playful grin.

McCall lowered her voice. No doubt deliberately being mysterious, she said, "Because of all the teenagers that fell in and out of love in the back row of the Kasota Springs Drive-in." She giggled.

"Fell for it." He chuckled in a deep jovial fashion. "You're serious about there still being drive-ins in Texas?"

"Yep, during the summer. Next time you're in Texas, I'll take you to one."

"If we can fall in lust on the back row." He took pleasure in shooting her a seductive grin.

"I said *in love* not in lust," she defiantly corrected, and changed the subject. "The murals on the buildings are breathtaking."

"They are. Lompoc is known for them and is sometimes called the city of murals."

By the time they left the outskirts of the small town, Nick noticed McCall's attention had shifted to a monstrous bank of fog in the distance as the car followed winding curves around the mountain toward a valley cloaked in a mist of darkness and confusion.

McCall continually watched the clock on the dashboard, but said nothing for the longest time. When it turned to ten o'clock, she asked, "Do you think we'll make it all the way down to the valley before the fog gets worse?"

"Got no other choice. There's a lot of curves ahead of us before we come to a fairly long stretch of highway. This road can be very intimidating even in the daylight."

McCall took a deep breath, and Nick suspected to take her mind off the treacherous spell of highway, she joined him in humming a popular tune from the Sirius Top 40 channel.

Without warning, a sudden bombardment of rain pelted the windshield, shattering the serenity of the night.

Already uncomfortable with the foggy conditions, Nick gripped the steering wheel and dropped his speed another ten miles an hour—to a virtual crawl. The wipers swished back and forth in cadence, like soldiers marching off to war. He clutched the wheel even tighter and fought off the knot building between his shoulder blades.

Realizing that he had begun grinding his teeth, Nick watched McCall shift uncomfortably in her seat. He broke the tension. "So, you enjoyed riding today. You seemed to have taken to that roan."

"He was a dream. Fluid, cantered along smooth as silk."

Nick cut his eyes away from the road and caught a glimpse of her face. "How come you felt so drawn to him?"

She frowned as though the question pained her, and pursed her lips. "I'm not sure. I guess you swayed me in his direction when you pointed him out to me."

"I don't think it was that. You seemed like you knew him."

"I just liked him. Maybe it was intuition. A Texas thing." Her words were velvety, edged with steel.

"That could be it." He dodged her comment like she'd thrown a horseshoe. "Did you have any trouble finding tack for the stallion?"

"No. And it was of excellent quality. I had him saddled before Mr. Mcmurphy's ranch hand showed up."

"You said you'd vacationed out here. Did your family fancy horses?"

"We always had horses on Granny's place. Wild mustangs adopted through the Bureau of Land Management, cow ponies—"

"Cow ponies?"

"Yeah, workhorses," she said curtly. "You know, the type that have no pedigree but a purpose beyond making beaucoups of big bucks for some millionaire owner?"

"Oops, that hurt." Nick grabbed his chest as though she'd stabbed him with a dagger. In a way she had, and he felt sure the comment was meant as a prickly message.

"My daddy used to talk about various horses that raced over in New Mexico."

"You said New Mexico. Isn't there horseracing in Texas?"

"Some tracks. One at San Antonio that I know of, but nothing near the Panhandle, where I'm from."

"So your dad liked the fast track?"

"Fast track, fast ponies, fast money. It was all the same to him."

"Did you ever go with him to the racetrack?"

"No, he wouldn't let me, but he'd bring home stories about the jockeys, trainers, and horses." She fidgeted with her blouse collar. "He knew a lot about racing. Even drove over to Amarillo to get tip sheets and racing forms." McCall pulled her cardigan snug over her breasts. "He'd ponder over them for hours and tell me which ponies were a sure bet and which ones were crow bait."

"Do you remember any particular horse he liked?"

"Gosh, it's been a long time, but a couple seemed to intrigue him. He mentioned one horse a lot. He said he spent a lot of money on him. I always presumed he meant he'd *lost* a lot of money on him at the track."

"Remember his name?"

"Don't ask me why it stuck, since I was so young, but I'm sure it was Double Deuce Down or something along that line."

Nick's breath caught in his lungs. "Double Deuce Down?" Shock caused the words to wedge in his throat. He tried desperately to take command over his surprise, but failed miserably.

The roan she had ridden was registered with the AQHA as Double Deuce Down but because he was so fast on the track someone had nicknamed him Asteroid . . . and it stuck.

Nick finally managed to add, "Interesting name."

"Yes. I'm pretty sure, but not one hundred percent, that his sire was one of Granny's stallions. Gigolo, I think, but again, I'm not sure. I was pretty young."

Relief flooded over Nick. He wasn't sure who Double Deuce Down's father was, but knew for certain it wasn't anything like Gigolo. Just a coincidence with the name. On the other side of the coin, he hadn't read the AQHA papers with the lineage on any of the horses on the ranch except for Asteroid. And that was mainly because the horse was unique, with a remarkable number of victories. Nick also trusted Jock's judgment. He knew good stock, and Nick had no reason to question his decisions.

But Nick wouldn't be comfortable until he discussed McCall's father's vices. "Mac, if I'm not prying I have a couple questions about—"

His question was lost in a piercing scream boiling from McCall's lungs.

Nick stomped on the brakes. Barely able to maintain control, the sports car skidded to a stop.

"What in the hell?"

"Oh my God, Nick!" McCall's hands shot to her face, covering her mouth. "You almost hit that woman." She gasped, panting in terror.

"What woman?" Startled, Nick's words riveted like an assault weapon. "You scared the living hell out of me. What are you talking about? What woman?"

"Nick, you must have seen her. You nearly hit the poor lady."

Nick's fists whitened as he clenched the steering wheel. He rested his forehead on the back of his hands and took a deep breath, hoping to settle his racing pulse.

After gaining composure, he lifted his head and looked at the pallid-faced woman beside him. "I don't know what you think you saw—"

"It's not what I *think* I saw, it's what I *know* I saw." She boldly met his stare. "A woman crossed the road right in front of you, and you didn't even slow down."

"Slow down, hell! I didn't see her!"

McCall bolted from the car without regard to the waterfall of rain pounding the pavement.

Nick jammed the Jag into gear and swung it off the road a few yards ahead. Effortless as a thoroughbred, he stepped out of the car and exhaled hot air, prepared to not only face the inclement weather, but also the hellion stomping her way back up the hill. "McCall, you're going to get hit. Get out of the center of the road," he screamed, to no avail.

A sudden gust of wind lashed out, and a wall of rain swooshed against his face, momentarily blinding him.

With long strides, the stubborn woman stalked on.

"You're going to catch your death of foolishness out here in this rain," he yelled, tearing off his jacket.

Once he reached the dripping wet spitfire, he pulled the coat around her shoulders. She didn't seem to notice as she trudged toward an opening near a small gathering of trees.

"This is where she was headed. Toward a sofa sitting on the side of the road." McCall traipsed onward. Nick had to use every ounce of his athletic prowess to stay abreast of her.

Rainwater galloped downhill as though trying to reach the finish line before being boxed out by the fog.

"First a woman. Now there's a sofa on the side of the road. Was it a sleeper or a daybed?" Nick growled and rolled his eyes, glad he was out of her peripheral vision.

Obviously ignoring his sarcasm, she marched onward, like a soldier facing battle. "You probably don't believe I saw ostriches and llamas earlier, either."

"At least they were real. Get over to the side of the road," he commanded.

For the first time since bailing from the car, she followed his orders and stomped off the pavement.

Believing it might be best to appease McCall, since she was so emphatic about what she saw, Nick thought back to the moments just before he heard her scream.

The only thing he recalled, after her talking about her Granny's horse, Double Deuce Down, was a wailing sound. He quickly chalked off the noise as a gust of wind that had accompanied the eerie orb of dense fog passing in front of the headlights.

Damnation, how could he have missed seeing a woman cross the road?

No woman walked through or hid in the mist.

Could this be a distraction to stop his inquiry about McCall's father's familiarity with horses? She was obviously frightened and near hysteria. In fairness, the most accomplished Hollywood actress would have difficulty honing drama to such heights.

"McCall, damn it, was she running?" Nick fought the barrage of rain. "And I didn't hit her."

"You nearly did." She stormed. "She wasn't running, or even walking really fast, just kinda . . . well, not quite a glide, but loped— cantered—and hovering. I couldn't see her feet in the fog, but she moved quickly."

A vicious burst of wind grabbed McCall's ankles and sucked her legs from beneath her.

She tumbled forward.

A stronger blast of air forced her down. She landed within a few feet of the edge of the road overlooking a deep and wide valley.

Nick lunged forward to grab her.

In one quick motion, he caught McCall, pulled her upward, and gathered the shaking woman into his arms. "Damn it, woman!" he barked as though it was her fault she fell.

She crumpled against him and allowed his arms to encircle her. To protect her.

Their hearts beat as one.

"Angel Eyes, I'm sorry I yelled, but you scared the hell out of me." He pushed wet tendrils from her forehead. "I was afraid a car was going to come along and hit you."

Hot tears rolled off her cheeks. Something he had never seen from her. A sucker for a crying woman, Nick pulled her closer and kissed her temple. "Let's get back in the car before we drown or worse yet, finish your trek over the cliff."

"I can't until I find that woman. She might be hurt."

"Baby, don't you think I'd know if we'd hit something?"

"But she might need our help." More tears followed, as she neared hysteria. "Please, Nick, we must go to the sheriff—"

"If it'll settle you down, we'll stop at the *police station* in the next town and report the incident." He choked out the words.

An incident indicated something was wrong, but there was nothing to report. Or was there?

Chapter Twelve

Nick tucked his platinum card back into his wallet and leaned against the pump, waiting for McCall to come out of the restroom. The mini-mart was the only place he found open in the tiny town a few miles from the foot of the mountain. At least they could dry off and fill the gas tank at the same time. Nick hoped he wouldn't have to justify stopping in this little town instead of the larger one to the east. A simple wrong turn in the dark had set their fate. Of course, if he'd turned on the GPS, it might have helped.

"Rain stopped. Feel better?" he asked as she neared.

"Yes. Now are we going to find the sheriff?" She put her hands on her hips, almost as a threat.

"It's a police station. There isn't much to this town after dark. If I pieced together the attendant's waving-arm instructions, we shouldn't have any problem locating it." Nick pressed the trunk lock and dropped her overnight bag inside.

A short time later, he pulled to the curb in front of a weathered building. Like many of the storefronts on Main Street, the antiquated police headquarters needed a coat of paint, a generous shot of air freshener, and a desk sergeant who hadn't tossed out his personality with his Dairy Queen coffee cup.

With jowls that waggled as he spoke, Sergeant Bulldog leaned back in his chair and welcomed the visitors much in the same manner as the federal warden in Lompoc might have received Ted Bundy into his fold.

Nick decided to let McCall handle the veteran lawman.

After listening halfheartedly to her version of the incident, the robust man caught the eye of the radio operator and raised an overgrown eyebrow. He turned back to McCall. "Did he hit her?"

McCall shot a questioning look to Nick, who stood silent, holding up the railing separating the sergeant's desk from the waiting room, decorated with two dilapidated café issue chairs.

"No. Or at least, *he* doesn't think so," she responded.

"Was she hurt or in some kind of trouble?" The police officer folded his arms across his thick middle.

"Not that I could see. And why aren't you writing down what I'm saying?" she demanded.

"No need. It's Agnes. She lives up that way, and is safe as long as nobody runs over her." He leaned back in his chair, pulled out a gigantic cigar, bit off the end, and spit the tip, along with a healthy dose of slobber, in the trash.

"And the sofa?" McCall challenged.

"People dump things up that way all the time. When the fog clears, we'll go up there and look things over," Sergeant Bulldog explained, searching the desk drawer for what Nick presumed to be matches.

"Promise?" McCall's lower lip trembled, and she shot the officer a brutal glare.

"Sure, lady. I'll put it right on top of my stack of urgent files." He patted a clear spot on his desk. "Yes, ma'am, right here with the important investigations." He drawled with mockery.

McCall spun and stalked out of the office, slamming the door behind.

Nick eased up in front of Sergeant Bulldog, placed a hand on each side of the desk, and leaned into him. "Mister, I can promise you haven't seen the last of Miss Johnson, so I'd suggest you get off your lazy butt and take her report seriously." He picked up a box of matches, struck one, and held it up to the officer to light his cigar.

Blowing out the flame, Nick turned on his heels and marched out.

Catching up with McCall, he followed her in a silent trek back to the car. He knew there were times to wake a sleeping dog, and times to let him lie. He swallowed his "I told you so" speech and opened the passenger door for her.

"Did you hear him, Nick?" Not waiting for his reply, she charged on. "He has no more intention of taking my report seriously than you do."

Nick definitely knew when to let a dog sleep, and dodged the comment as he settled into the driver's seat. "Let's see about finding a room for the night."

"You mean two rooms. You don't want to spend the night with a raving lunatic who seems to be the only one of us who actually saw the woman on the road." She locked in her seat belt. "I hope they locate Agnes and she's okay."

Chapter Thirteen

Nick tore back the bedcovers and crawled between sheets as rough as dried cornhusks. "Damn!" He fluffed the pillow with his fist. "Damn it to hell!"

He wasn't sure who he was more angry with, himself or McCall, but he could bet his bottom dollar that he was fighting mad knowing that their shared bullheadedness had landed them in separate rooms at a sleazy no-tell motel straight out of a Stephen King horror movie. Both travelers had been too exhausted to continue on a road where an accident was looking for a place to happen.

To his surprise, once they found the hotel, McCall had bailed from the car, marched in, and asked for two rooms, insisting on paying for her own.

At least she was safe. He had seen to it by placing the Jag's panic button on her bed stand. If she needed help, all she'd have to do was press it. On his way out, he'd made sure that she had locked the door and latched the safety chain behind him.

A passion-laden brain malfunction must have contributed to his dim-witted idea that courting McCall was the right step in his redemption, but no way could he recall celibacy being part of the plan.

The whole "Open up your heart and look inside" philosophy could kill a monk. And Nick was the idiot who'd volunteered to "stop making demands" and give her time to see if she had room in her heart for him.

What a crock of cock crap! One problem, he hadn't been totally honest with her about his feelings because he wanted to see where their relationship might go. What was wrong with him? He'd had many full-blown adult relationships, yet for some reason he let McCall do things to him that he'd drop another woman for even thinking of doing.

But, then he hadn't expected to fall in love with the lady with the eyes of an angel.

Love!

Commitment!

Oh hell, what next—marriage?

Nick closed his eyes.

When the time came, their first union had to be perfect. He planned to be the man McCall thought him to be. Besides, she was nothing like any of his past lovers. McCall was understanding, caring, and loving, yet a voraciously hot, sensual spitfire.

"What do I expect?" he murmured. "It took God six days to create the whole world and I think I can create a lifelong commitment in less time?" Patience, Dartmouth, patience. This courting stuff done right is work. Harder than scaling a twenty-story skeleton of red iron. He'd done that and he could do this, too.

His thoughts wandered back to his mother's telephone calls. Why her sudden interest in McCall's every move? Did Maddi really think the young woman she seemed to trust was a gold-digger only interested in her son because of his wealth?

Resolve washed over Nick. The key to happiness was right in his hands. All he had to do was keep his promise to McCall and try to keep from making a mistake that could cost him the best thing that had ever happened to him: McCall.

To hell with his physical needs. He knew his promise verbatim . . . *and the next time it'll be on your terms.* He could control his urges. Couldn't he?

Vigorous knocking drowned out his musing. He bolted upright and glanced at the clock. Way past bar closing time.

"Let me in, Nick." McCall bellowed. "Now."

Had his prayers been answered? He relaxed and so did the heart-pounding. Her words were demanding, not panicky.

He threw back the covers, combed his hair with his fingers and moseyed to the door. "Sugar, don't be so impatient. Give me a minute to put my pants on." He enjoyed taunting her, knowing he had no intentions of doing any such thing.

"Don't play with me, Nick. Let me in!"

Nick slid off the chain and swung the door open to face the woman standing in his doorway in shorts and a T-shirt. "I'd like to play with you—"

"In your dreams, Slugger." She darted past him.

"You didn't give me time to dress, but . . ." He felt a tightness develop in his white Fruit of the Looms.

McCall peeled off her white tee and dashed to the bathroom, leaving nothing to his imagination from the waist up. "Can I borrow a shirt?" Without waiting for his reply, she slammed the bathroom door.

"There's one hanging just inside," he called. "Under my jeans."

Water spewed in the shower.

Nick stuck his head out the motel room door to make sure someone hadn't chased her into his room.

What in the hell?

The stench of an immensely angry skunk saturated the air. He slammed the door, hoping to trap the smell outside.

While he waited for an explanation of McCall's bizarre behavior, he straightened the bed and turned off the television.

Shortly, McCall appeared looking quite appealing in his white shirt, towel-drying her hair. Nick's gaze roved, boldly appraising her. He cleared his throat, pretending not to be affected by her presence.

"You need these?" She held his jeans in her free hand.

"Might help." He took them and put them on, although he was enjoying the freedom of having on only underwear in a motel room with a sexy half-naked woman.

"Want to explain what kind of burr you got up your—" Nick folded his arms across his chest, to keep from gathering her into his arms.

"My room stinks." She leaned over, wrapped the towel tightly around her tresses and flipped it back over her head.

"Mine isn't exactly a botanical garden."

McCall caught a good view of the easy-on-the-eyes devil leaning against the door, adorned with bountiful fruits beneath noticeably tight looms. Such a handsome man, with rock-solid muscles from head to toe . . . and obviously in between, too.

"Better than mine." She forced her stare upward and caught Nick's approving smile. "I guess you'd like an explanation."

"Your room didn't come with a shower?"

"A polecat's in my room."

"The desk clerk probably just gave him the wrong key. You know how irresponsible polecats are when they've had a few too many." He let out a deep, rich, fun-loving chuckle.

"I'm serious. I heard a noise and opened the door because I thought it was you—"

"You think I'm a skunk?" He playfully frowned, as though her words cut him deep.

"At times," she quipped. "I felt a cat zip past me and all I saw was a ball of black and white fur. It was dark, so I wasn't sure—"

"From the smell, it was a skunk, and you royally pissed him off."

"Do you think I'd have tossed a Coke can under the bed to scare him off if I'd known it was a polecat?" She charged on. "He shot past me and out the door like I'd shoved a firecracker up his butt. Then the stink started. In the fracas, the door closed, locking me out."

"He didn't spray you?" Nick said with a trace of laughter in his voice.

"I was standing behind the door, so I could close it when he got out. I think he missed me, but I wasn't staying around to find out. That's why I needed a shower so fast. Thanks for the use of your shirt."

"No problem, but I think I'd better put on a shirt of some sort. There's a hair dryer if you want to use it. I'll go down to the desk and see if we can get another room." He quirked an eyebrow, as if hoping she'd suggest that she stay with him.

"Thanks."

He pulled a T-shirt from his suitcase, pulled it on, and headed toward the door. Over his shoulder he said, "I'll see if they have a room closer, so I can keep you out of trouble."

McCall attempted to dry her hair, but as luck would have it, within thirty seconds the thing overheated and kicked off.

She heard Nick open the door and stepped around the corner.

"I'm back." He dropped the key on the table, along with a bag of Hershey's Kisses. "They'll fumigate the room and take your things to the office. The night attendant didn't seem too concerned, acted like it was an everyday occurrence."

"But you did get me another room?"

"No room at the inn." Nick pulled a coin from his pocket. "Want to call it?"

"What for? Who gets the bathtub and who gets the bed?"

"Or I could sleep in the car?" He winked at her.

She looked at the clock. Only out of desperation had they taken this motel room, so what made her think there would be another one in town? Plus two more motel rooms would be a waste of good money. But, she couldn't let it go without making a point. "Surely, there's a room somewhere in town."

Nick tossed his extra set of car keys on the table. "If you want to go look for one, go ahead, but I'd suggest you find a store that's open first and get you some drawers to wear under my shirt."

She exhaled in exasperation at the big man, but he was right. She cut her eyes to the bed.

It was inviting.

She was tired.

He was smug.

"Take the bed. I'll sleep in the chair." Nick pulled the bedspread across the floor.

"No, Nick. We're mature responsible adults. There is no reason we can't share. I promise I won't invade your space."

He glanced from the undersized bed back to her. "I'm not sure that'll be possible."

"It'll only be for a few hours." She tugged the musky moth-ridden spread out of his arms and unfurled it over the bed. "Just pretend you're sleeping with your sister." She flounced between the sheets, fluffed her pillow, rolled to her side, and closed her eyes.

Oh, brother!

Nick didn't have a sister, but if he did, he certainly wouldn't have thoughts about her like he was having about the woman burrowed in his bed.

Turning off the light, he slipped in next to her. Only two feet of darkness separated their pounding hearts.

He stared at the back of her slender neck, the soft curves of her shoulders, down her back to shapely hips covered with a sheet. He wanted to touch her. Feel her. Make love to her.

Lying next to the half-naked seductress was a bad idea. A very bad idea.

Before long, he found himself nuzzled against her back, his hand draped over her hips. He kissed her lightly on the delicate slope of her neck, pulled her snugly against him, and shut his eyes.

Nick wanted her to feel secure and safe in his arms, where nothing could harm her.

"Sleep tight, Angel Eyes," he whispered.

McCall eased awake and didn't have to see the clock to know it was still hours until sunrise. She rolled over and watched Nick sleep.

Blinking neon light peeped through a slit in the curtains and cast a band of soft illumination across his face.

What a totally handsome specimen of manhood. She felt secure and protected in his bed, the familiarity of his nearness. All of her life, she had made decisions based on the needs of others. She now knew how it felt to be protected. To have a man look out for her welfare. She liked the feeling, if only for one night.

Tomorrow she would come clean with him. Tell him the truth.

The truth about her deception.

The truth that there would be no more tonights.

She stared at his well-defined features. Bold, chiseled, aristocratic chin with the tiny cleft that formed when he smiled. Chocolate eyes beneath closed lids, inviting a woman into his raw masculinity . . . and him into her dreams.

Curling next to him, McCall rested her hand on his chest. His large calloused fingers covered hers, while his breath settled unruffled in his chest.

She slipped back off to sleep.

White doves veiled in satin led a cascade of orange blossoms through her dreams. The warm, sensual scent of a man wafted the air.

Awakened by her heart hammering against her chest, shivers of delight thundered through her body as she realized she had a magnificent man in her arms. Her eyes blared open, and she held her breath afraid any movement would spoil the moment.

Her and Nick's bodies were entangled like a skein of yarn.

Tangled up beneath her pillow, McCall could not move her arm. Her other was caught between his hand and chest, while he trapped her thigh between his legs, nestled against his . . . and she'd thought *his chest* was the hardest part of his body.

She swallowed and tugged at her leg, but found herself unable to dislodge it. She bit at her lip, fighting an urge to enjoy his nearness. It seemed the most active part of his body was becoming more active with each breath, and bothered her in ways she thought impossible.

Watching his sleeping face, she racked her brain to figure out how to get untangled without disturbing him.

She gingerly twisted her hand. Receiving no resistance, she eased it out of his grasp. Her fingertips halted a breath away from his lips. She wanted to touch them, feel their softness, experience their insatiable hunger, and bask in his nearness.

As much as she wanted him, a fling in a shady motel room not even fit for a hooker wasn't how she pictured their first time together.

She eased away, only to have his hand spring to life and grasp hers. "It's okay to touch me. I want you to." Nick never opened his eyes as he directed her hands to his nipples. Pressing her palms against them, hard peaks formed. His breathing turned ragged, quickened.

Slowly, he guided her downward and clamped his hand over hers, begging her to explore.

A throaty moan came deep from his chest.

McCall quickly moved her hand away. Using his chest for leverage, she dislodged herself and, with one mighty shove, scampered to the edge of her side of the bed.

Thud!

She hit the floor.

Nick managed a triumphant laugh.

"Nicodemus Dartmouth, I can't believe you did that."

"Sugar, I believe it was your knee that invaded my private space."

"Your private—"

"Come back to bed and I'll prove it to you."

"With you? Haw! That's a laugh!"

"Here, you might as well be comfortable." He flipped her pillow over the edge. It bounced off her stomach.

"I'd rather sleep with a rattlesnake." With one heave she pulled the threadbare spread from the bed and pulled it up to her chin. She balled the pillow underneath her head, and reiterated. "A rattlesnake's bite couldn't be any worse than you are, Nicodemus Dartmouth the whatever."

"You want me and you know it."

"When pigs fly." McCall grabbed the first thing she could reach, Hershey's Kisses, shoved herself upright, and threw them at the big man.

He caught the bag in midair. "You could have at least opened the bag for me." He ripped the cellophane apart. "If you ever need a job as a relief pitcher, give me a call."

"Go stick your head in the sand!"

"Tell me a bedtime story. How about the one about the lady I nearly hit up on Harris Grade."

"I guess I didn't make myself clear enough the first time." She took a deep breath and exhaled. "Go to hell! Don't pass Go, and don't collect two hundred dollars."

Chapter Fourteen

The next morning, an amethyst-shadowed sunrise sprang to life as McCall and Nick pulled into the Fairmont Hotel in San Francisco.

The doorman snapped to attention. A stately man appeared and helped McCall from the car, then turned to Nick. "Mr. Dartmouth, so nice to see you again." He flashed a pleasantly starched smile at McCall. "I believe you'll find the penthouse suite to your and your guest's satisfaction."

"Thank you, Samuel. You've never failed me." Nick motioned for McCall to follow the portly concierge, who nodded to a waiting bellhop. She had expected the younger man to click his heels in response. Instead, he efficiently transferred their baggage to a brass luggage carrier.

McCall entered the exquisite, gold-and-ivory-appointed lobby. With its three magnificent domes protecting the rotunda, she had to admit, although she'd been in plenty of fancy hotels in Texas, the Fairmont was probably the ultimate of luxury and beauty. The gilded room reminded her of a massive golden nugget. No doubt the hotel promised to live up to its reputation.

The fragrance of freshly cut flowers filled the massive lobby.

"It's a nice place to stay." Nick touched the middle of her back, guiding her toward the waiting elevator. "I hope you'll like our suite."

Not just a suite, but the penthouse suite, she wanted to correct.

The penthouse door swung open and the sight momentarily took her breath away. It was as though she'd followed a white rabbit through a looking glass into a dreamy wonderland.

Morning sunlight reflected on highly glossed, black-and-white marble floors in the foyer leading to the elegant accommodations that had once been a private residence.

A blaze in the fireplace danced its welcome.

"Mr. Dartmouth, our finest amenities are available to you and your guest. I've advised the valet, maid, and chef of your arrival. The chauffeur and butler are at your disposal. Anything else, sir?" Samuel asked.

"Our accommodations are quite adequate. Thank you, my man." Nick discreetly handed what looked like a hundred-dollar bill to the concierge.

McCall frowned at the thought of such an outrageous gratuity. Granny had always told her that people needed to work for what they got and ask nothing from others. Of course, she tipped, but within the customary range. But Nick handed out tips like they were only pennies. Hadn't anybody told him that a fortune is accrued one dollar at a time? A little frugality never hurt anyone.

Feeling more relaxed and not guilty for enjoying herself, McCall took in the room's elegance. Why ruin Nick's day? After all, he'd taken a lot of pains to make her happy, plus she had carried her tiff far enough. It wasn't just the sleeping conditions last night, but thoughts about the woman on the side of the road that had lingered. Maybe there was no woman. The police seemed unconcerned about the woman she knew only as Agnes. But what if they were wrong?

Plus, how in the world could she stay mad at Nick? He was trying so hard to please her, and she had acted a stubborn mule.

A new beginning. Yes, that's what she'd give Nick. A new beginning.

The oak door closed, jarring McCall back to the moment.

Her gaze followed the railing running around the second-floor library. "Do we flip to see who gets to be on top?"

He wagged a questioning eyebrow. "On top?" His irresistible devilish smile widened, apparently pleased he seemed to be back in her good graces.

"Who sleeps on the sofa and who gets the bed." Ignoring the hidden meaning in his response and his arresting smile, her gaze stopped on the lined bookshelves containing priceless works. "I guess I could sleep up there, if you'll show me where they hid the stairs." Her mood suddenly felt buoyant.

"So you like the library?" Nick tilted his head toward the second floor. "I'll show you the secret spiral stairway later, but I believe you will feel more comfortable in your own room."

Nick guided her toward a bedroom and swung open the door. The fragrance of a half dozen vases of floral arrangements wafted in the air.

"Roses." A soft gasp escaped her. "Nick, how wonderful." She fingered a petal. "And way too extravagant."

"I told you I planned to court you the way you deserve."

A massive canopy bed with rosette-inlay covering was engulfed by the colossal room. McCall looked up from the room's focal point and locked gazes with Nick. "Thanks."

"Yellow roses for a lovely Texan." He smiled that smile that always set her heart fluttering. "Everyone knows the unofficial flower of Texas is the yellow rose, so I thought they'd be fitting. I hope you like them."

"Like them?" She tried to contain her delight at the fact that he truly wanted to see inside her world. A smile trembled over her lips as a warm glow rushed through her body, melting her last ounce of resistance. "Yes, Slugger." She clasped arms around his neck. "I love them. Not just the roses, but everything."

Keeping her eyes locked on his smile, she backed out of his grasp, kicked off her sandals, and unceremoniously flounced spread-eagle on the bed. "I love you for giving me such a wonderful surprise."

Time took in a deep breath.

She froze—half in anticipation, half in dread, and fully torn by conflicting emotions.

His burning eyes held her still as wave after wave of alarm slapped at her soul.

Now she had gone and done it. *Love you!* What in the heck had she said? Had Nick put some kind of spell on her? Yes, that's it. Voodoo. But if it were a hex, she hoped he didn't cast away the magic for a while.

Suddenly Nick's stare turned gentle, understanding, and contained a sensuous flame. No doubt her slip of tongue had not evaded detection by the self-confident rascal.

"I think you'll find everything you need, but if not, dial the concierge's desk. He'll see to your wishes." Nick strolled to the bed, leaned down on one knee, and planted a kiss on her forehead. "Want me to massage your back, so you can relax?"

"No," she whispered. "But, thanks."

She found his touch reassuring, although mentally she pounded her head against the wall for her faux pas.

McCall slipped into his waiting arms.

His lips touched hers like a whisper. "No, thank *you*, ma'am."

His mouth captured hers, demanding. He shifted his embrace and said, "I've got to meet with a lawyer in . . . uh"—not releasing her, Nick glanced over her shoulder at his Rolex—"damn, in thirty minutes. I'm sorry. I've got to go, and it'll take most of the afternoon. Rest up. I have a special evening planned for us, Angel Eyes." He got to his feet, taking her with him.

Closing the door behind him, Nick left the intoxicating scent of musk for her enjoyment.

McCall eased down on the side of the bed and surveyed her surroundings.

Having been to the Texas State Fair and more rodeos than she could count, McCall couldn't recall staying in a hotel as impressive, but then Granny always thought a hotel room was for sleeping and showering. As long as it had those requirements, it was good enough for her and anyone in her entourage.

Now that McCall gave it serious thought, a place like this wouldn't be to the liking of the rough-and-tumble cowboys who usually were part of Granny's traveling troupe. But even Granny would have frowned at last night's lodgings.

A hot bath and nap sounded good. McCall began filling the massive marbled tub and splurged by dousing in extra bathwaters.

When a cloud of bubbles tickled her chin, she closed her eyes, enjoying the tranquility.

She and Nick would be okay, although she still couldn't let go of the images of the woman on the side of the road. Every time she closed her eyes, McCall saw the woman.

Or could Nick be right? It did happen on a rainy, foggy night. Maybe no woman or sofa existed except in McCall's imagination.

After toweling off, she slipped between the luxurious sheets and tried to rest, but a stampede of thoughts kept her from slumber.

Texas waltzed across her mind, led by memories of Granny and McCall's beloved grandfather. Of the good times and bad times. Of staying in the Conrad in Chicago, the Adams Mark, and Adolphus. Of wild rodeo competitions, tough cowboys, and rank bulls with even ranker riders defying death and disfigurement for that eight-second thrill.

Rolling over, she closed her eyes, hoping to round up her memories and corralling them in the recesses of her mind where they belonged. Tonight she must tell Nick the truth about her childhood. About her parents. About Granny.

She and Nick had promised that there'd be no secrets between them, yet she harbored the most deception—the biggest deal breaker of her life.

Finally, she drifted off into a fretful sleep.

Dreams of denim and diamonds, cotillions and honky-tonks, distorted into an apparition of the woman identified as Agnes crossing the road in front of headlights on a misty, foggy night.

Thud!

Head over heels . . . down toward the darkened valley she tumbled. Down . . . down.

Faster and faster.

Farther and farther.

Church bells rang.

McCall startled awake. Perspiration drenched her hair. She pulled to a sitting position and put her face in her hands. Her heart pounded in her ears and her chest felt heavy. She gulped air and the pain eased up.

A dream.

Clamped lips imprisoned a sob.

The ringing stopped. It had to have been the hotel phone.

"McCall, are you awake?" Nick called through her bedroom door.

Her racing heart stilled slightly.

Leaping up, McCall pulled on the lush hotel robe, and swung open the door to face Nick wearing nothing but tight Levi's, a leather belt, and a killer smile.

Deep and sensual, his existence sent a ripple of awareness through her, providing a sense of security she so desperately needed. "I was resting." She stepped into his arms, waiting for the nightmare to evaporate.

"Are you okay?" Nick set her back a step as if checking her out for any wounds. If he only knew the wounds weren't visible.

"I'm fine. The phone just startled me." She awkwardly cleared her throat and adjusted her robe. "I was just glad you got back safely. You could have come on in."

"And invade your space?" His voice turned playful. "Samuel called. We have dinner reservations at seven-thirty." A devilish look came to his eyes as he obviously noticed her state of upheaval. "Is that okay?"

"I'll be ready." She found it impossible to resist his mystique. "Thanks." Sliding her arms around his neck, she buried her fingers in his thick hair, needing his strength to lean on.

"Your heart is racing."

"Being in your arms does that to me."

"I know a cure to make it settle down." Nick's strong fingers found her shoulders and slid the terrycloth robe aside. "Guaranteed to make you relax."

Slowly, boldly his gaze dropped, settling on her exposed breasts. "Eventually . . ."

His touch sent her heart fluttering again, but this time, it had nothing to do with being frightened. He brushed his thumb along her jaw. "I want you, McCall." He stroked her lips with his thumb. "So bad it hurts." Nick pulled her against him.

"I want to make you happy." She trailed a ribbon of kisses through a mat of curly chest hair upward, stopping at his waiting mouth. "I truly do." Was she really prepared to become his lover? Nicodemus Dartmouth was the ultimate thrill. The ultimate danger. But, was she ready?

More than ready, she captured his lips. The kiss that started sensual and soft quickly turned urgent and hungry. A battle between two people in need of a lifesaver in their struggle in a sea of loneliness.

Tonight would change things. No more would they be lost.

Nick's hands roamed over her, and she nestled against his lean, strapping body. The cradle of his hips welcomed her and confirmed his urgency. His kiss began slow and thoughtful, but quickly turned to urgent and needy. The tranquility of being in his arms shattered with the hunger of his kisses. Shivers of desire raced through her.

McCall circled Nick's neck with her arms and took in his freshly showered smell, inching her fingers through his still damp hair. She answered the demands of his lips and tongue, but wanted . . . needed . . . all of him.

Any lingering doubts about whether she wanted Nick to make love to her were pushed aside. The moment was now. She wanted him to embrace her for the rest of her life.

A groan caught in his throat as he pulled away, combing her face with his eyes. "Remember what I said about not being able to stop. Are you sure this is what you want?"

His words were answered with a kiss. Deep, hot, seeking.

Rough, ragged breaths carried his mouth along her throat as his hands slid downward before splaying his large, calloused fingers on her back. Her breasts crushed against his chest, his hard, lean body molded to hers.

When had their friendship caught fire and turned into deep passion? She wasn't sure, but knew she wanted the tough tycoon not for just the day, but for the rest of her life.

"Come to my room," Nick whispered with the certainty of a man who would never be satisfied with only a dream. Pulling her back against him, his arousal made no mistake about his desires. "I'll cancel our dinner reservations. I'd much rather eat in bed." He buried his face against her throat, his lips trailing pleasure upward. "Champagne is chilling."

Damn. Another phone call.

She arched upward until his lips neared her earlobe. "The telephone," she whispered.

"Nothing is that important." He nibbled the words against her neck.

"There might be something wrong. It could be your"—she slipped from his grip—"Mother, so answer the phone. Besides, your five o'clock shadow is nearing ten hours old, and I need to do something." She offered him a small, shy smile. "You know, a girlie thing."

"I'll get rid of whoever it is pretty damn quick, so don't be long." He winked and tossed her the robe.

"You can count on that, Slugger."

For what seemed like a hour, but in reality was probably five minutes, McCall brushed her hair to a shimmer, applied lip gloss, and eyed the hotel robe and house slippers. She remembered she had no seductive lingerie.

Drawing on the robe, she took a long look in the mirror. A pathetic housewife, running late for work.

A towel? Something a man would do.

Nude? Perfect.

She lowered the towel and through awakened eyes studied her body, something she had never done. McCall had nothing to be ashamed of and complimented herself with a hug before rushing across the living area toward Nick's bedroom, butt-naked except for a sheepish grin and goose bumps.

Easing up to the opened door, she saw him sitting at the desk with his back to her still engaged in the telephone conversation.

Relishing his reaction to her nakedness, she waited, hoping the call wouldn't be much longer. Of course, she could go on in and hasten the call along. She knew exactly which of his buttons to push to make sure of it.

She stopped dead still, hobbled by the words resonating through the air.

"That filly is as pretty as a bed of morning glories and just about as hard to tame, but I have no choice. She's been teased and I think she's ready, but the last thing I want is to wear out a perfectly good stud trying to mount her." Nick dropped ice into a glass. "It's a waste of money, not to mention energy. I've got a lot invested in her already."

He stopped and listened to the person on the other end of the line before continuing. "True. She is ripe for the picking, so maybe a feed sack over her head will make it easier." His full-bodied laugh sliced the air. "You know how it is the first time." Nick let out a chuckle and said, "Yelp, courtship. Lots of it, and only a week just isn't enough time for some fillies."

Stopping to listen, Nick took a sip of water, then said, "It isn't anybody's fault. Some just take longer than others."

Stunned and sickened by his words, McCall swallowed the sob that rose in her throat. A sensation of intense disappointment and desolation swept over her. He'd been stringing her along. And she had done something she'd never allowed herself to do, trust a man. Letting her defenses down and caring, even falling in love. She had made an utter fool of herself, all because she listened to her heart instead of her brain.

Nick had turned out to be the uncaring, self-centered jerk she once thought he was. What an actor! He had even fooled her. But to refer to her like she was a standing mare was the most humiliating part of how she felt.

Cowboy up, girl! Pity is for the faint of heart. Pull that shield back around you and let the fury out. Don't wallow around like some schoolgirl finding out her first love isn't for real. Granny hadn't raised a weak-kneed schoolgirl. She was tough, and she'd show Mr. Studly just how tough she could be.

Get mad, girlfriend. Then regroup and even up the score.

She went back to her room where she could allow her fury to be fueled by the thought of being deceived. "Ripe for the picking." She threw on the bathrobe and stalked around the bedroom, slamming drawers, while she tossed her belongings on the bed.

"Teased! That's what he was doing?" She punched her fist into the stack of clothes. "Wear out a perfectly good . . . that's crude, but exactly what I'd expect from the jack ninny."

She halted. Biting the inside of her cheek, she focused on the rather unorthodox solution that had begun to formulate in her mind. "I'll teach that yellow-belly-son-of-slime." She ripped a pillowcase from the bed.

McCall composed herself and draped the case over her arm. Walking lightly through the sitting area, she slipped into his bedroom.

Their eyes met.

"I've been waiting on you." He shot her a seductive smile.

"I'm sure you have." She strolled to the bar, picked up the champagne bucket, and placed it along with the folded pillowcase on the bedside table. She removed the bottle, slowly twisting it between her palms.

"Want me to open that?" His eyes shone bright, eager in the faint light coming from the lamp on the desk.

"No." She set the bottle aside. "I want you."

Her bathrobe dropped to the floor, drawing a manly groan from deep within Nick.

Pinning him to the bed, she lowered her determined body over his and imprisoned him in a web of yielding flesh. "Now, Nick. Right now."

His hands explored her back, waist, and hips.

Although she tried not to respond to his touch, heat rippled beneath her skin and coursed down her entire length as the protective shell she had so carefully rebuilt began to unravel.

Touch by touch.

Kiss by kiss.

"I'll take it slow and will be gentle," he promised, sealed in a slow, drugging kiss. "If I go too fast, let me know."

"I want it fast."

Their lips met with a savage intensity.

McCall pulled away. "Fast and unpredictable. Surprise me, Slugger. I like surprises, don't you?"

Succumbing to his forceful domination of kisses, she felt for the pillowcase and lifted her head, allowing a bemused smile to escape.

"Big surprises," she repeated with staid calmness, while she jerked the pillowslip over his head and pulled it securely around his neck. In one fluid motion, she leaned back, picked up the ice bucket, and watched him struggle to get free.

"Now, Studly, who has a feed sack over his head?"

"Damn it, McCall" he boomed. "This is kinky, and doesn't feel much like fun."

"It's to help you."

"Help me?" He slowed his floundering for a few seconds.

"Yes. To see how it feels to have to wear a sack over your head to have sex."

As quick as lightning, she turned the ice bucket over, allowing the freezing contents to flood his middle, extinguishing any possibilities of lovemaking for a long time.

Hips bucked out of the unexpected ice storm.

"You spitfire." Nick fought for his freedom like a tomcat clawing its way out of a gunnysack. "I don't know what in the hell got into you, but do you know what I should do to you?"

"Charge me a stud fee?"

Chapter Fifteen

"Damn it to hell, McCall, I'm getting tired of your games." Nick slammed his hand against her bedroom door. "Open it or I'll damn well bust it down!" Again, he rammed a fist into the wood and shook his hand profusely to ward off the excruciating pain racing up his arm. "I mean it—now!"

Nick couldn't recall the last time he was as angry with anyone as he was with McCall at the moment. He wanted answers and one way or another, he'd get them.

The lock clicked.

Nick took a deep breath to control his anger, opened the door, and stalked in.

McCall stood in front of the window overlooking Nob Hill. "I'm taking the Amtrak back to Los Angeles." Her voice barely rose above a whisper.

"What was that all about?" Nick shook his leg, and a chunk of ice hit the floor. "You sure as hell know how to take the starch out of a guy's drawers in a hurry." He picked up the ice cube and slung it into the fireplace. On impact, it sizzled, much like Nick. "McCall, all I've done is try to make you happy, but about the time I think I'm making progress, something bites me in the ass and it's usually coming from that shell you always pull back into."

He briefly considered grabbing her by the shoulders and turning her around to make her face him. An odd primitive warning flashed through his brain as he remembered her comment back on the island about being manhandled in her younger days. He resisted. That was the last thing she needed, but he still wanted answers.

When McCall didn't respond to his question, he struggled briefly with the uncertainty her actions had aroused. He knew what his knee-jerk reaction generally would be, but with McCall, all he could say was, "You're beautiful, intelligent, and over the last few days, I've seen a confident Texan I can't keep my hands off of."

"Nick, I wanted this to work, but we're going nowhere. We are just too different." Her voice wavered. "I thought you wanted to make love to me, and then . . ."

"I did. I do." He stepped up behind her.

She whirled. A deep frown etched her normally flawless face. "Sure you did!" She lifted her chin and defiantly locked onto his gaze. "I overheard you talking about me on the telephone like I'm some kind of . . . of . . . some desperate . . . uh . . . hell . . . like a mare in season. No thanks. You're just a . . . a—"

"'Heartless, nasty cad' were the words you used back in LA. If you truly trusted me you would have come in and not eavesdropped—"

"I wasn't eavesdropping. The door was wide open and you invited me to your room. Remember?"

"Yeah, I remember. You led me on just like you did on the island, and baby, your game has worn a bit tiresome. You never intended to let me into your bed—"

"It was *your* bed, and I certainly did—"

"You did not."

"Did, too," She spouted.

Nick called a halt to their bushwhacked exchange. "I'm through with 'I'll show you mine, if you'll show me yours.' All you wanted was to get a rise out of me—"

"And, I did it quite well." She shifted her eyes below his belt. "Yeah, cowpoke, I believe I did a really good job."

"And you didn't enjoy it a bit?"

"Not in the least. Remember it was a *game*?"

"Hell, there is no way to reason with you. If you really want to return to LA, I'll drive you back. But, you are *not* getting on a train with a bunch of strangers." He clenched his jaw. This argument was stupid, not to mention unnecessary. "I never gave any thought to the fact that you could misconstrue what Jock and I were talking about and think we were discussing you."

Suddenly Nick felt like a fool, much like he'd just stepped out of a Tom and Jerry cartoon and been hit over the head with a mallet.

Accentuating her annoyance, she whirled toward the window, revealing a slender leg and hip. Folding her arms across her chest, unyielding, she said, "If you weren't talking about me, then explain yourself."

He watched her reflection in the windowpane as she stared into the dusky evening. Her lips quivered.

Taking his chances on getting frostbitten, he pulled up behind her, slid his hands down her arms, and clasped her body firmly against his chest. "McCall, you need to trust me," he whispered into her ear. "You don't have to take everything I say or do as an attempt to emotionally undermine you." Slowly, his arms wrapped around her midriff. "Jock called to discuss an uncooperative filly that is standing. That means—"

"I know what it means," she said softly, probably feeling as foolish as he did. "My grandfather was a rodeo stock contractor."

"You never told me that. Mac, I'm dead serious about not wanting you to go back to LA. Please stay." Beneath his hands, he felt her erratic breathing settle. "Let's sit down on your couch and talk."

He led her to the loveseat, never letting go of her hand. "I'm so sorry, McCall. I knew you were raised with horses and when I saw your reflection in the picture over the desk—"

"You knew I was there?" Surprise with a tad of shyness laced through her words. "You knew I didn't have any clothes on?"

"Of course. I'm not blind." He tried to soften his presentation. "I thought I'd finish my conversation with Jock, so I could give you my full attention."

"Oh . . ." A minute laugh came from McCall. "I thought when you said seven days, and your bid at the auction was for seven days, that you meant—"

"I know exactly what you thought because a mare only has a good three to eight days to conceive out of their whole cycle. I just thought you'd know that we were talking about a young filly being mated for the first time."

They looked up and their gazes locked. At first, their mutual laughter was low and mellow, but suddenly it turned into a full belly laugh from each of them. Merriment of mutual understanding.

"And you *will not* tell anybody about this, especially Maddi and Josie. Do you understand?" McCall said through a wide spread smile that turned to a chuckle. "I'd be so humiliated. Even more than I am now."

"Hey, remember . . . no secrets between us. Same thing goes with secrets only the two of us can enjoy." He pulled her into his arms and kissed her deeply.

"How about calling and making another dinner reservation?" McCall asked.

"How about calling for room service? I want to get an early start in the morning."

"Why?"

"Because I want to go back and make sure that sorry excuse for a policeman did his job." Nick tucked her deep into his side and figured her temperature had warmed twenty degrees.

"Then you did take me seriously about the lady roaming the mountain?"

"Let's just say I'm taking you seriously. Very seriously." His lips seared a path down her neck, her shoulders, sending deep throbs in the pit of his stomach. "Mucho serious."

"I'm truly sorry that we argued, but Nick, please don't feel you have to hide stuff from me." She shifted her weight and looked squarely into his eyes. "I'm not good at handling that. Daddy left Mother and me in a terrible financial mess because he kept secrets."

"What kind?" He draped his arm around her shoulder, tucking her to his side.

"That's what I've wanted to tell you." Her body quivered. "Dad put all of their savings into some type of business venture, but kept it from Mother. She figured he'd lost it at the racetrack. But after her death, I found some documents that make me believe he may have made a legitimate investment. I think that's the real reason we moved to California, not because of their health."

"You don't have any idea what kind of an undertaking it was or who it was with?"

"No. I ended up having to probate both of their wills, since Mother

never did. I suspect she was scared what she'd find. Or not find."
McCall shifted uneasily. A melancholy frown flitted across her face.
"My lawyer has placed a creditor's notice in a dozen newspapers,
hoping that someone will see it and contact him. It's just an outside
chance we'll hear from anybody, but one I have to take."

"And nobody has come forth?"

"No. But as my lawyer told me, there's little chance, after all of
this time, that anybody will. It's in all the major newspapers in Texas,
a couple in Oklahoma, and several in California. Not to mention
New Mexico. Just about anyplace I could think of where my dad
could have invested. It could be anywhere, but Mother felt strongly
that it was at the racetrack and he didn't want her to know. I think if
it wasn't the racetrack, then it was the oil and gas industry because
of the work he did in Texas."

"Did you look for a safety deposit box or post office box key?"

McCall nodded her head. "No luck. Nothing. No paperwork."

"I'm sorry, Mac. I didn't know, but Mother and I have a team of
lawyers on retainer. Really good ones, too."

"Thanks, but it's something I've got to do for myself. That's the
only way I'll be able to lay to rest my parents' memories. I won't be
happy until I do right by them."

"I understand. I'm having my own problems with lawyers." He
stopped. Now wasn't the time to discuss the horse ranch purchase
when disappointment clouded McCall's mood.

"I know. Josie told me you were buying some land, and it wasn't
going the way you had hoped. I guess since I've known you, you've
always had a dozen deals going at one time."

"That's part of my business, but I don't want to talk about it right
now. You're my priority."

In comparison to McCall's problems, weighted down by her
father's obvious inability to handle business matters, Nick's situation
was inconsequential. She'd think him a bigger cad if he were to
bring up his troubles when they were just barely able to discuss the
ones between them, especially since their problems had one thing
in common. Missing investors.

"I don't mind listening to your business problems. After all,
you've listened to me about mine. I honestly don't mind," McCall

said. "Maybe I can help, unless it's something you'd prefer to keep close to your vest." She smiled up at him. "So, I won't jinx it."

"Angel Eyes, I promise I have no intention of keeping anything from you that will affect our personal relationship. Besides, we've got a lot of miles to cover. I believe you promised to take me to a Texas drive-in."

McCall stared out the window, watching the pavement lap up the miles as they ventured south toward the tiny village near the foot of Harris Grade, the town she hoped held answers about the mysterious woman living on the mountain.

She studied Nick's profile. He stared ahead as though counting the delineator markings in the center of the road.

Chewing on her lower lip, she stole a second look.

No doubt Nick had been patient with her, more than she deserved. Almost like he understood that her need to be stubborn and down right testy at times was a survival skill to shield herself from her own feelings. To keep him at arm's length, so he wouldn't see into her soul. A fear of getting hurt.

So what possessed her to blurt out a crazy thing like "I love you"?

And the almost insulting part? He acted like he hadn't heard her.

As though selecting his words carefully, Nick said. "It's not too far now. I'm about ready for some lunch. Hungry?"

"Famished." Even the one word hung in her throat. She was afraid to say more. Afraid she might tear up. If only he had cussed her out instead of being so patient and understanding.

Although they shared the humor in what she'd overheard and she'd apologized profusely for ruining their evening, her insecurities hovered overhead. She was ashamed of her absurd behavior. Now how could she redeem herself without patronizing the overly confident hunk of testosterone soaked flesh?

Nick's voice broke into her musing. "You haven't had much opportunity for a social life since you came to Los Angeles, have you?"

"Not really. Shortly after we moved to LA, my folks' health turned bad. Caring for them left me with little time for myself, much less a social life." Her words hung heavy as she thought back to the lonely hours spent tending her parents. Of their missing her graduation from high school, then later when she had to decline dinner invitations until one day the invitations stopped coming. "Other than foundation functions, I've been pretty much a social misfit. An evening reading a good novel and drinking a glass of iced tea is a social event to me."

Nick stared ahead making no comment.

"After Daddy died, I was Mother's primary caretaker until she got bad enough for a nurse. After she passed away, I stayed too wrapped up, clinging to her memory, for any fun."

"What got you through the hard times?" he asked in a tender voice.

A knot lodged in her throat, trapping her tears. She dug in the shadows of her heart for the answer. One she wasn't sure she was ready to share. "My personal knight in shining armor."

She felt silly saying the words out loud and quickly changed the subject. "There's the Tadpole Cafe."

"Looks like our best choice. At least three other people think so." Nick nodded toward the quaint diner's near-empty parking lot.

After the only waitress in sight gave them a brusque greeting, she waved them toward a clean table by the window.

Digging under her blouse and adjusting her bra strap, the burly woman sauntered in their direction and slapped down fish-shaped menus. "Today's specials are on the board. Don't suggest the meatloaf, but the tuna salad's okay. Cookie fixed it day before yesterday, so it's still fresh. I'll be back for drinks in a jiff." She strolled away touching her tongue to her pencil tip before jotting on a pad.

Nick alternated between checking out the menu and the blackboard. "Think I'll pass on the tuna. Everything is fried, all greasy."

McCall lowered her voice. "That's why a place like this is called a greasy spoon."

The waitress meandered back. "Whatcha decide on?"

"Hamburger, extra cheese, lots of onions, both sides of the bun grilled, fries, crisp please, and a chocolate malt, extra syrup and lots of whipped cream. And, a slice of coconut cream pie." McCall handed the woman her menu and shot a satisfied smile at her dining partner. "And a diet Coke, please."

"Chef salad, no cheese or croutons, cut the bacon, no egg, with oil and vinegar dressing on the side, and a bottle of water. Penta if you have it." Nick glanced at the frowning waitress. "Please."

The waitress jabbed her hands on ample hips. "Where did your spaceship land?"

"Make the salad dry and I'll have milk. You do have cow's milk, don't you?" His smile faded a bit when it met the waitress's scowl.

"No cow's milk, mister. We milk whales up here."

"And no pie for me," Nick said to the lunch-counter Gestapo, who roamed off, licking her pencil only to make a return trip with two glasses of water.

It appeared McCall and Nick were dead set on getting run out of town without getting any answers about Agnes. So far, on their first visit, McCall had managed to tick off the whole police force, both of them. Now, Nick had succeeded in ruffling the feathers of the only person who stood between them and starvation.

Tired of flipping through the song selections on the table jukebox, McCall broke the tension. "Have you ever truly been in love?"

"Once," he said tersely then but quickly added, "Twice."

"What happened with the woman you were engaged to?"

"I figured office gossip had made its rounds."

"Not really. What made you decide she was the one for you?"

"McCall, any of my, I mean our, prior relationships aren't important now." His jaw clenched, and he unfolded his napkin. "Why talk about what can't be changed?"

"I'm sorry. I didn't mean to pry into your personal life." She studied the vase of plastic flowers.

"No, it isn't that. Everyone has a past and that's why it's called a past . . . over and done with. Like last night. Forgotten." He offered her a smile. "Everybody has them."

Before she could respond, they were distracted by a heated exchange between the waitress and the cook over whether to make a double cheeseburger or a hamburger with extra cheese.

As though being accused of being a troublemaker, McCall lowered her eyes and studied the scratches on the much-used table.

Nick seized his water glass and set it back down without taking a drink. "Her name was Lauren, and she was from old money New Orleans."

"Who?" McCall looked up.

"My near-miss you asked about." He shot her a brief smile.

"Anyway, I had run into her a few times, and now that I think back, she seemed to pop up when I least expected it."

"Isn't that the way love hits a person sometimes?" McCall knew she was referring back to how easily and unexpected her words had flowed when she proclaimed her love for him.

Nick studied the woman sitting across the table. It wasn't her fault they had gotten up on the wrong side of the bed. Hell, from separate beds to boot. She was only making small talk and he acted like she had personally sabotaged his broken nuptials. He had no reason to still be angry with her, although it wasn't every day a man lets a woman blindfold him and douse him with ice water. His words of pasts being pasts for a reason echoed in his head. Everything was cool between him and McCall. Besides, she had said she loved him.

There was no reason he shouldn't explain Lauren and his failed relationship to McCall, especially if she was going to be part of his life. He didn't have to give her all the unpleasant details, just the highlights.

"It just happened. Something I'm not necessarily proud of. I took her home one evening and gave the old 'I'm tired of being alone at night' routine and the next thing I knew she was on the phone telling her mother that I'd proposed."

McCall raised a questioning eyebrow. "So, did you?"

"Not really. But I decided maybe I didn't want to go home alone anymore, and bought her an engagement ring."

A flash of amusement crossed her face. "How did it end?"

"Long story, but let's just say, I have one mother and that's enough." He wiped off his flatware with his napkin. "Plus, Mother thought Lauren's IQ and shoe size were about the same. I'm not holding back anything, either. I honestly don't know what happened. It just did." He shot her a meek grin. "But, I lived to tell about it."

"And the second woman you fell in love with?"

He never answered. The waitress set a bowl of lettuce topped with a paper-thin slice of tomato in front of him.

Maybe Nick wasn't quite ready to discuss the second woman, since he seemingly diverted his attention to McCall's plate and said, "Didn't we just agree that pasts are called pasts for a reason?"

"Does that mean my past is forgiven and I can crawl back into your good graces, Slugger?"

Nick picked up a fork and stabbed at the greens. "I knew you couldn't resist me."

They bantered back and forth, enjoying the sparring.

The waitress sauntered by and dropped two cellophane packages of crumbly crackers beside his bowl.

"Thanks. Ma'am, do you have a minute?"

"Do I look like I do?" the testy woman answered.

"I'll make it worth your time. Know anything about a lady named Agnes who lives up on Harris Grade?"

"Haven't been in town long, but nobody lives up there. If they did, it'd be in a cave." She waddled away and said something to the cook, who let out a belly laugh.

Before McCall finished drowning her fries with ketchup, the cook rounded the counter, and ambled over to their table. "Hi, they call me Cookie around these parts. Heard you're asking about Agnes."

"Do you know about her?" McCall almost shouted in glee.

"About as much as anyone." He set his coffee mug on the table and wiped his hands on a greasy red apron.

With smug delight, she smiled at Nick. "I've, uh, *we've* been concerned ever since *we* saw her on the mountain a couple nights ago. Does she live up that way?"

"You might say she stays in the area."

"See, Nick! There was definitely a woman—"

"The police told us that much." Nick rolled his eyes.

McCall glared at Nick with an expression that reeked of pained tolerance.

"Tell me everything about her." She slid over to make room for the man to join them.

"Was it late on a rainy night and around that old couch?" He slipped his stocky frame into the booth next to McCall.

"Yes. Yes it was," McCall responded.

"Figures. Well, there's a story about ol' Agnes. She's been in these parts for years," the crusty cook began.

"What would she be doing out on a rainy night?"

"Well, missy, legend has it that she usually appears around midnight and likes the fog."

"How old is Agnes?" McCall inquired.

"Let's see." The old man rubbed his chin. "I don't know if we're talking people years or ghost years. Got any idea if there's any difference?" He laughed a full gut-tugging roar.

"A difference?" McCall's eyebrow arched. "I don't understand the comparison." She took a big drink of her malt.

He stopped laughing, and looked squarely at the woman sitting beside him. "Agnes is a ghost."

Chocolate froth spewed like an unleashed water hydrant.

Nick covered his mouth, obviously hiding his amusement, and grabbed for napkins.

"Yes, ma'am. Folklore has it that she lost a child in an accident when her wagon went over the cliff. She's been up there looking for the little one ever since."

"See, Nick. See, I saw a, uh, ghost." McCall dabbed the gooey mess from her lips before wiping up the table top with her napkin.

Cookie drained his coffee. "Truth of the matter, I've heard it's just a story cooked up by the police to keep teenagers off that dangerous stretch of road, but try to explain that to someone who's actually seen ol' Agnes." He stood. "Got to get back to slingin' that hash." He tottered off toward the grill.

"Thanks," Nick said to the man's back and tossed down a tip probably bigger than the whole town's literacy program. "The Dartmouth jet is fueled and waiting for us in Santa Barbara. It's heading for Texas. Surely, I can't get in as much trouble there."

McCall raised an eyebrow. "Don't bet the ranch on it."

"The ranch?" A surprised expression overtook his features.

"You've heard me say it before. It's a Texas saying. One of those Texas things."

Chapter Sixteen

The following morning, the Dartmouth jet flew out of Santa Barbara. The stress of the last few days finally closed in on them. The couple spent most of their time on the plane catching up with the news, then grabbed a couple catnaps.

When the Lear landed at TAC Air in Amarillo, Texas, they were immediately shuttled off the plane and into a waiting car, where they began the last leg of their trip to McCall's granny's.

Following McCall's directions, they passed the exit to Kasota Springs and veered off I-40 about three miles down the interstate before heading the rental car north. To the west, a breathtaking ocher and crimson sunset lay parallel with the road.

Lowering the window, Nick enjoyed the earthy, musky scent of freshly plowed fields.

Rainwater puddled on the road. A field of wind turbines were silhouetted on the horizon, and in the distance a huge communication tower guarded pastures liberally dotted with pumping oil wells.

"How much farther do we have to go?" He glanced down at the dead GPS unit out of habit.

"The main house is up apiece. We'll drop down into the valley first."

"Who does this sweet piece of property belong to?"

"It's all Johnson land."

"So we've been on her land for a while?" He frowned.

"Yeah, it started right where we turned off I-40. Granny's mother was a LeDoux, and they were among the original homesteaders who turned their six hundred and forty acres into a good-sized spread."

Nick studied the land that seemed to go on forever. He had expected to find McCall's grandmother struggling to hold on to a few over-grown acres of mesquite and sagebrush and owning a couple plugs destined for the cannery.

A good-sized spread, indeed! He couldn't help but wonder what McCall considered a serious operation. Recovering from nothing short of sheer shock, he remarked, "We've passed a number of gates that have a 7Bar11 on them."

"That's our brand. The official ranch name is Jacks Bluff, and be-longed to Granny's side of the family. The first gate leads to the east camp. The foreman and his family live there. But there's plenty of room up at the main house."

"Are you sure you don't want to call and let her know you're coming and bringing a guest?"

"I'd rather surprise her."

"I don't know much about Texas customs, but in my family, showing up without an invitation—"

"In Texas, it's called hospitality. They'll put an extra potato in the pot, and another handful of flour in the gravy. One suggestion—"

"If it'll keep me out of trouble, shoot," Nick said with a trace of laughter.

"Just don't ask how many sections she has or how many head of cattle she runs. If you do, you might as well ask for her bank balance."

Nick kept his gaze on the pavement, trying to decide whether McCall was kidding or serious. But the businessman in him screamed she was serious, very serious.

As she promised, the road dropped into a valley, something he didn't think existed in the flatlands of the Texas Panhandle. A rambling two-story ranch house, sprawled beneath century-old cottonwood trees, came into view. A century of majestic grandeur provided the backdrop for the imposing manor.

"McCall, is this your grandmother's house?"

She nodded.

"It makes the Triple J look like a cottage. When was it built?"

"Late eighteen-hundreds."

"And an oil well practically in the front yard?"

"Technically, it's a derrick. It was Granny's first gusher after

Paw-Pa died, and she said they could take all the oil they wanted, but had to replace the rig when they were finished. The well's abandoned, but the derrick is a reminder of her humble beginnings."

Nick pulled to the side of the road and turned to McCall. "Then your family is wealthy?" There was a chilly edge of irony in his voice.

"Well, it depends how you measure wealth."

He narrowed his eyes, and his back went ramrod straight, before he shot her a sideways glance of utter disbelief. He didn't respond, silently challenging her to explain.

She cast her eyes downward and remained silent for what seemed an eternity. "Some people might think of us as, uh, comfortable." Her lower lip quivered as she returned his glower. "Daddy was an only child. Actually, he had an older sister who died, making him an only child. I'm one too, so technically, I guess you could say I'm—"

"You can't even say it, can you, McCall?"

"Yes, if it makes you feel better. Wealthy! Wealthy! Wealthy! Yes! But it isn't mine."

"You barely mentioned ponies and that your grandfather was a livestock contractor, but you didn't say he was also an oil baron and rancher."

"It wasn't important. And Granny was actually the contractor."

"Important, hell!" Nick let out a long, audible breath. "And all of this time, I thought you were just a poor displaced Texan."

"A displaced Texan, yeah. But not exactly a poor one."

"Then you lied to me?" His tone had suddenly turned chilly.

"No. I never said I was poor. You presumed it. Nick, no matter how it appears, I wasn't born with a silver spoon in my mouth."

"Just an oil well!" He accentuated the annoyance he felt with her. "And you live in a rat hole, drive a rattletrap, and drink Mad Dog by choice?"

"I happen to like Mad Dog, my car gets me where I need to go, and I love my little house, thank you. It wouldn't hurt if you'd watch your pennies, either."

"Don't make this about me." He seethed with mounting anger.

"I'm perfectly happy with the way I live. Just because I'm thrifty doesn't mean I eat at soup kitchens." McCall tossed her hair over her shoulders and boldly met his eyes. "I'm a Johnson and proud of it. We were raised to be independent and work for what we have. We don't wait around to inherit the spoils, and don't ask for help from anyone. We take care of our own."

"Is that why you didn't ask for financial help when your mother was sick?" The sharp edge to his voice dulled.

"Nick, I was her only child, and I had a responsibility to take care of her. I'd never . . ." His question had broken through her fragile control. She rigidly held her tears in check. "I could have never put her in a home. As long as I had my job and she had my father's social security we managed. I made it without asking anyone for a penny."

Heaviness sunk in Nick's chest, realizing that her memories tore away at her total being. "Then you lived a frugal lifestyle because your father was a proud man?"

"Daddy earned his master's from Texas A&M, and held a senior position at the petroleum plant, but never forgot he came up through the ranks. He knew someday he'd inherit all this, but was happy to be his own person and didn't ask anything from his parents." McCall said the words proudly. "His worst vices, as I confided in you, were gambling and the horses."

Nick imposed an iron control and studied her for a moment, hoping for more of an explanation.

"Please don't look at me like that." She lowered her eyes as though to say that she had no intention of permitting herself to fall under his spell. "If I had acted like I had money, nobody would have taken me seriously. But even if they had believed me, I could never play the part. It's just not me. It would be like flashing a neon sign, begging some gigolo to try to take advantage of me." She took a deep breath and looked up.

Nick could see the hurt in her eyes.

McCall continued. "After the way Anson acted, I figured he had found out. I'm sure Josie is completely unaware. Nick, all I want is to be accepted for who I am, not what I have or what I'll be worth someday." She shifted in her seat. "I don't need a man to take care of me financially. I want someone to love me." Tears bubbled in her eyes. "I guess you're sorry you wasted time on me—"

"McCall, I don't know how many ways I can ask you to trust me."

There was a faint tremor in his voice as her words touched him deeply. "Do you think it would have made a difference to me?"

"No, but I liked you liking me for me, just the way I was . . . the way I am." She squared her shoulders as though fortifying her courage. "I do trust you, Nick, and never set out to deceive you. My finances were personal. I wanted to tell you many times, but was afraid of what you'd think."

Nick leaned forward, lowered his voice, and spoke with a deep, dusty tone. "Want to know what I think?"

Slowly she looked up and their eyes met. "Yes?"

"I've spent way too many years around women who flaunt their wealth like a Pulitzer Prize. It's refreshing to find someone who has integrity and doesn't want to take the easy way out." His leaned into her. His lips caressed her forehead. "And I love it."

"You honestly love it?"

"No, McCall, I don't love *it* . . . I love you."

Chapter Seventeen

McCall's heart pounded out of control. The words *I love you* echoed in her ears as Nick pulled into the horseshoe driveway in front of Granny's house.

Stopping short of opening the door, McCall turned back to Nick. She cupped his face in her hands, rubbing her thumb along his jaw-line, brushing against a heavy five o'clock shadow. "I love you, too, Nick."

Relieved that she had bared her world to him, she bolted from the car without waiting for a response. Nick had whispered the magical words—"I love you."

Lights flooded the massive veranda. Lola Ruth Hicks flounced down the steps, tying a belt around her chenille robe. "McCall! McCall Johnson, if it isn't my baby girl." She gathered the young woman into her arms in a familiar hug.

Nick rounded the car and stopped behind McCall, who was still locked in an embrace.

"And who is this handsome hunk of horseflesh you're lugging around?" Lola Ruth deposited McCall as though she were a bag of flour and gathered the towering man in a hug.

"Lola Ruth, this is Nicodemus Dartmouth—my best friend." McCall smiled at the overwhelmed man, who looked comparatively small in the grasp of the sassy female. She couldn't tell for sure, but he might have been a bit frightened at the zealous welcome.

"Mrs. Johnson, it's a pleasure to finally meet you," Nick said when she released him. He held out his hand to shake.

"Miz Johnson? Lordie-be, I'm not Miz Johnson. I'm Lola Ruth

Hicks. McCall's, uh, what would you call me, sweetie?" She turned and leveled a questioning look at McCall.

"My everything. Lola Ruth took care of me when I was a baby, bought me my first bra, and told me about the facts of life. She's been Granny's right hand and best friend since before I was born."

Nick smiled. "Well then, Miss Hicks—"

"Oh sweetie, call me Lola Ruth."

"Well, Lola Ruth, you seem to be just the woman I've been looking for. So you can show me pictures of McCall missing her front teeth?" He flashed his best schoolboy smile to Lola Ruth, who in turn slipped her arms around his waist. "And, tell me all about her boyfriends—"

"Nicodemus, those aren't appropriate questions for the first date," McCall squawked, knowing full well that he had suckered Lola Ruth into his wicked web of charisma. She followed the starry-eyed woman as she led McCall's new love up the stairs. "Where's Granny?"

"She's still up at the west camp helping the boys. Should be back tonight. Luther and Colt are branding and cutting. You know how she is about wanting to keep her finger in every piece of the pie."

"Yes, ma'am, I sure do, but I think she likes not having to pay an extra hand more than anything. So, if they're cutting, we'll have mountain oysters tomorrow?"

"If they don't eat 'em up first."

"That's the truth. Where's Mesa?"

"Down at the university teaching a weeklong course on how to handle rescue animals."

"Nick, I told you that my aunt died and Mesa is my only cousin. She runs a horse rescue center on part of the land. We're really proud of what she's doing." McCall smiled at Nick, then turned back to Lola Ruth. "So Granny's out working the roundup?"

"Yep. You know the only thing that will slow her down will be the Good Lord when that time comes."

McCall turned to Nick and smiled again. "They run a calf-cow operation, too. Got any coffee, Lola Ruth?"

As hard as she tried, McCall couldn't help but smile at the memories of the times she went with Granny on roundups and watched her work side by side with the wranglers, not shying away from the nasty business of castrating and branding cattle.

"You know I always have a pot a perkin', girl." Lola Ruth never let go of Nick and hauled him toward the kitchen, planting him in a kitchen chair.

Setting three mugs on the table, the older woman turned to McCall. "What brings you back home?"

"I just had some time off, and wanted to show Nick my little corner of the world. I'm sorry we're going to miss Mesa." She blew on the hot liquid. "Nick, Granny doesn't believe in bottled water. It's a waste of money, and well water tastes better. Can I get you a glass?"

"No thanks. I believe I'll have some of that delicious coffee Miss Hicks—I mean Lola Ruth—was so kind to pour."

"I fried pies this afternoon. You do like pie, don't you Nicodemus?"

"It's just plain ordinary Nick, ma'am." Sugar beets topped with molasses couldn't be as syrupy as his tone. "And, yes, ma'am, I love pie."

"Okay, Nicky, which do you prefer, apple or peach?"

"You choose. If you made them, I know they'll be larruping. I believe that's the right word." When he caught McCall's gaze, he winked.

McCall rolled her eyes. His attempt to sound Texan came off like a mix of Clint Eastwood in *Dirty Harry* and John Wayne. She expected Nick to start calling Lola Ruth "Pilgrim" any minute.

She grabbed his arm as Lola Ruth toddled off toward the pantry. "*Nicky, darling!* I know exactly what you are up to."

"Up to?" His chocolate eyes danced with frolic.

She glared at him. "Nobody gets by with calling you Nicky, not even your own mother. You're sucking up to her."

"Now, why would I want to do that?" He gave her a patronizing pat on her hand.

"Remember? You don't eat anything fried."

"Maybe I'm acquiring a taste for Texas cooking."

The older lady appeared with a tightly wrapped plate brimming with fried pies. After removing the foil, she carefully pressed the wrapping with her hands, folded it, and stored it in a drawer.

"Granny keeps the moo from a heifer," McCall justified the woman's action. "She lived through the war and keeps everything, fearing there might be a shortage some day. I got my frugal ways from her."

"Nothing's wrong with that. Pennies make into dollars." Nick smiled. Pushing away from the table, he meandered over to the cabinet and slipped an arm across Lola Ruth's shoulders. "Those smell delicious." He pinched off part of a fried pie and turned toward the table. "Want some, Angel Eyes?" He tossed the crust in his mouth and licked his lips. "I love good old-fashioned fried pies."

Lola Ruth piped up. "And I don't use any of those new fang-dangled oils, either. It's lard or nothing for me."

A pained expression curtained Nick's face. "And, lard is still made from—"

"Yep, good ol' hog fat."

McCall smiled, knowing that she could bet the ranch on Nick wondering what in the heck he'd gotten himself into. And frankly it seemed fair. After all, he started it back on the boat, trying to make her believe he'd fixed the meal all by his lonesome.

Maybe, just maybe, if they both worked at it they could take the best part of both worlds and make it work.

But it'd be like trying to fit a square peg in a round hole.

Chapter Eighteen

After a good night's sleep in her old bed, complete with one of Granny's quilts, a down comforter, and pillows fluffy enough to hide in, McCall woke fresh and ready to wrestle the world.

She dressed quickly and stepped across the hall to Nick's room. She cracked the door and found him lying spread-eagle in the bed. Letting him sleep, she rushed downstairs to help Lola Ruth prepare breakfast.

Spying Granny's battered Ford F-150 pickup in the drive, McCall shook her head. She'd driven the ol' thing for years and most likely had a brand spankin' new one in the garage reserved for special occasions—weddings and funerals.

McCall smiled and thought back to the last argument Granny and her son had had over her refusing to buy a new pickup. He always knew when Granny had enough because she'd resort to using his full name—Charles Chilcote Johnson.

Impatient to see Granny, McCall rushed to the kitchen. Lola Ruth always was the first up, and today was no exception. Once coffee began perking, she'd begin biscuits. Sausage sizzled unsupervised in a cast-iron skillet, telling McCall that Lola Ruth hadn't ventured off very far. Granny had not come downstairs yet because her favorite mug and a jar of Sanka sat undisturbed on the counter.

McCall headed for the dining room and picked up serving spoons from the huge sideboard and added them to bowls of gravy, fried potatoes, and apple butter on the massive maple table. She heard footsteps coming from the stairwell and glanced up.

Nick appeared in the doorway and surveyed the spread. "What's this? Thanksgiving?" The even whiteness of his smile looked dazzling.

"Nothing but a regular ol' working-day breakfast in Texas. How'd you sleep?"

"Alone." A flicker of a seductive smile tipped the corner of his mouth.

"I heard the screen door slam, so hold on to your hat." She met him halfway, swung him in her arms, and kissed him good morning. "And wipe that smug grin off your face."

The door leading to the kitchen burst open and a troupe of rough-as-a-cob, rip-roaring cowboys entered, led by the feisty, petite matriarch of the Johnson dynasty.

The top of Granny's gray topknot barely reached the chin of the shortest man in the group. The woman wore weathered, full-quill ropers, a white western-cut shirt, and Wrangler jeans that fit her like she was melted and poured into them. A mother-of-pearl and silver squash blossom necklace nearly covered her chest.

Tiny fingers, appearing much too frail to hold up the turquoise rings on her fingers, animated the air as she announced breakfast. "Come and get it or we'll throw it out!" she bellowed in a deep Texas twang contrasting with her delicate features. "And whose rattletrap is out there blocking the whole dang driveway? I couldn't hardly get my pickup parked last night."

"Is that a way to treat a guest?" McCall asked.

Dead silence settled in the air. All heads turned in the direction of McCall and Nick. The cowboys shot to attention at the presence of company, tearing their hats from their heads.

"Jumpin' Jehoshaphat, if it isn't my precious grandchild." Granny crossed the room like a firefly and grasped McCall. Setting the younger woman at arm's length, she raked astute eyes over her, checking for any signs of damage.

"That dern Lola Ruth, dang her hide. She told me I had company, but I had no idea it was you, child." She pulled McCall back into her arms. "I figured it was your Uncle Ralph and some of his rug rats."

Never letting go of her granddaughter, Granny lifted her chin and leveled a stare at Nick. "And who's this handsome son of a gun?"

"Granny, this is Nick Dartmouth."

Nick took her extended hand, lifted it to his lips and kissed it. "My pleasure, ma'am."

"Boys, meet the prettiest thing I've seen since the first time I laid eyes on McCall's Paw-Pa."

Grunted welcomes and prickly mumbles about wasting time on formalities when the wranglers were hungry filled the air.

"The boys are about to head over to the west camp and they're as hungry as a pack of coyotes just gettin' over a toothache." Granny stood beside the chair at the head of the table. "Boys, better take your seats before you all have a conniption fit." She remained standing until Nick pulled out her chair. "Thank you, Nicky."

"You're welcome, ma'am."

"Lola Ruth, you better hurry up. This grub is getting colder than a witch's tit in a brass bra."

"*Nicky*, right here." McCall patted the chair between her and Granny. As he sat down, she leaned into him, and whispered, "Careful, *Nicky*, you're about to run out of suck-up." She pursed her lips into a smile.

Lola Ruth pushed through the swinging door, carrying a platter piled high with bacon, ham, and sausage, and stopped beside Nick. "Nicky, my baby girl told me you don't like a lot of grease, so take those two patties off the top. I sopped them up really good for you."

He looked first to McCall, over to Granny, then up to Lola Ruth. "Thank you, ma'am." He moved the sausage to his plate.

From across the table a young wrangler snickered and accepted the platter. "Miss Lola Ruth, why don't you ever drain our sausages? We'd like that a lot." He raked off a hunk of meat. "Yes, ma'am, we'd like that a *whole* bunch." He passed the tray to the next cowboy.

"Colton Jameson, mind your manners, you boot-lickin' scalawag," Granny scolded. No doubt it wasn't just his verbal manners she referred to. "I should have sent you packin' years ago, but just like your daddy, you can pick out the meanest, roughest stock in a corral even on your worst day."

To change the subject, McCall quickly said, "I was reading the paper last night and I saw that Sheriff Sullivan is running for county sheriff again."

"Yep, he'll never retire. He'll die sitting at his desk waiting for a crime to happen in Kasota Springs. I think the most exciting criminal activity the town has seen was when Bonnie and Clyde drove down Main Street and that was back in the thirties," Granny piped up.

Flashing a smile at McCall, she gazed up at Nick. The action brought an immediate softening to her features. "Nicky, tell us all about yourself."

Nick propped his boot on the lower rail of the corral and with a critical eye watched a broncbuster wrangle a horse. McCall had been with her grandmother since after breakfast and Nick felt about as useful as a saddle on a jackrabbit.

Although she insisted that he stay, he dug deep for an excuse to get away and allow them time together. No doubt the two ladies had plenty to talk about.

"Done any bronc-bustin', Nick . . . it's Nick, isn't it?" Colton joined him along the railing.

"Colton . . . isn't it?" Nick tartly responded.

"Colt to my friends." His eyes became hooded like a hawk. "Colton to you."

Nick tilted back his Stetson with one finger and eyed the young buck. "Well, Colton, I can stay on long enough to beat a horn."

"Yeah, that thousand-dollar pair of crocodile boots don't look like they've seen much cow manure." A stream of tobacco hit the dirt, spraying muck on Nick's boots. "Yep, believe they've seen more of the south side of a northbound bronc than anything else."

Holding raw anger in check, Nick stared across the corral and watched a pair of squealing scrub jays swoop down on their unsuspecting prey. "I take it you don't like me much?"

"You're smarter than you look. This is a working ranch, not some drugstore cowboy's wet dream. Mrs. Johnson raises roughstock. You know, broncs and bulls used on the rodeo circuit. Plus, they rescue horses, so we don't have time to wet-nurse some flannel-mouthed city slicker that's come sniffin' around here like a stud with a hard-on. Want some advice?"

"Not to squat with my spurs on?" Nick wiped off his boot with the edge of the rail. "And, I don't need wet-nursing."

"My advice, take those fancy Lucchese boots back to California . . . or you might just find yourself in a heap of trouble."

"Threatening me?" The muscles in Nick's jaw tightened and he clenched his fist.

"Nope. Makin' a promise." Another stream of tobacco puddled on the ground.

McCall appeared from nowhere. "What's going on?"

"Just spinnin' a yarn with your friend here, *Mac*." Colt slapped Nick on the back.

"Don't call me that." Her eyes blazed azure fire as she cast the words at him like stones. "I'll kindly remind you, I'm McCall to you."

"You used to like it, but then you used to like a lot of things I did." Colt turned to Nick. "Enjoyed jawing the fat with you, cowpoke. Maybe you'll get your chance to beat that horn." Colt bowlegged off toward the bunkhouse.

"Nick, what were you guys talking about?"

"Nothing, Angel Eyes. Not anything I can't handle." He slipped his arms around her and kissed her.

Damn. Nick wanted to ask if Colt was the guy who had hurt McCall so badly, but he didn't have to ask. He could tell by the anger in her eyes. Whether he had been the one or not, she'd made it very clear she didn't appreciate Colton's approach. Nick would respect her look that seemed to plead . . . please don't pry.

"Everything okay with your grandmother?"

"Wonderful. She's a bit more cantankerous than you imagined, isn't she?"

"Let's just say she burst my illusion of a little old mousy lady sitting on the porch, sipping a mint julep. I see where you got your spunk. She calls it like she sees it. I like a woman like that."

"Good, 'cause she's sure smitten with you." McCall returned his kiss. "And, that's no easy task."

"What're our plans for tonight?"

"I've got good news and bad news. The drive-in hasn't opened for the season, but there's a kickin' band over at the Texas Moon Palace in Kasota Springs. Want to go?"

"Sure, if that's what you'd like to do," Nick said.

"Think you can steer clear of trouble long enough to do some boot scootin'?"

"I'll try, but don't bet the ranch on it—"

"Well, Slugger, you're gettin' that Texas thing."

Chapter Nineteen

Nick followed McCall through the Texas Moon Palace doorway into bedlam and thick smoky haze whirling around like dust devils on the open range.

A size-twelve blonde wearing a size-eight sweater, miniskirt, and red ropers escorted them to a table near the dance floor.

"Whatcha gonna have, darlin'?" The barmaid poised her pen over a napkin and cocked a smile at Nick.

"Lone Star," McCall said.

"Ambassador Twenty-Five, neat." Nick glanced at McCall and back to the barmaid. A blank look fell across her face. "That's with no ice, ma'am." He watched a deep frown etch her forehead as though she needed extra time to process his request.

Before he could amend his order, McCall piped up, "Bring him a Black Jack straight up." Then she glanced up at Nick and quickly added, "Make that a double."

The waitress shot her a twisted smile and sashayed toward a party of rowdies.

McCall took up the slack. "It wasn't the neat that bothered her. A place like this doesn't get many orders for three-hundred-dollars-a-bottle Scotch."

Nick shot her a disarming smile before turning his attention to a line of dancers kicking up their heels to "Cotton-Eyed Joe."

"Bull-shit!" sliced the air.

"Whatcha say?" the singer yelled.

"Bull-shit!" the rambunctious crowd shouted even louder.

"Bull-shit?" Nick raised an eyebrow.

"It's a Texas thing." Happiness bubbled in McCall's voice and shone in her eyes.

The waitress returned and set down a longneck bottle of beer and a double shot of Jack Daniel's.

Nick handed her a twenty and said, "Keep the change."

McCall took a hardy sip from the bottle the waitress had placed on the table before saying, "Nick, you've never said much about your father."

"Not much to tell." He picked up his glass. "Mother married him, had me, kicked him out when she was through toying with him, received her share of his fortune, and left me without a father. End of story." Nick downed a slug of the Tennessee whiskey.

"There has to be more to it. Surely Maddi didn't just kick him out—"

"Listen, Mac. I appreciate your concern, but don't go there. I'm not interested in knowing her excuses. I ended up without a father and there is no justification for it." He set his glass down. "I want to be responsible and will never put an innocent child through that, so leave it alone."

"I'm sorry. I didn't mean to bring up bad memories—"

"Let's go enjoy ourselves and scoot those boots." Nick pulled McCall to her feet and guided her toward the dance floor. Drawing her tight against him, he tucked her hand against his heart. A pleasant, lazy look settled across her face. She was obviously very comfortable in her element. He pressed a light kiss to her forehead and winked at her.

"I think you're flirting with me," she said.

"What if I am?"

"Lucky me."

He kissed her again, but this time on her cheek.

The band kicked off George Strait's "Amarillo by Morning." Nick eased her into a comfortable, smooth Texas Two-Step that turned the other dancers' heads.

"I didn't know you could dance Texan." She seemed to be enjoying the attention they were getting.

"There's a lot about me you don't know." Nick effortlessly glided her across the sawdust-covered hardwood.

Hoots and hollers of elbow-to-elbow partygoers gathered around a mechanical bull brought the dancers to a standstill. Nick guided her toward the excitement.

"Ride 'um, cowboy!" A flood of cheerleading came from the tanked-up crowd.

The rider raised his hand high above his head, and yelled, "*Yip-piekiyi yay, get along little doggie!*" Bouncing another couple feet off the saddle, he unceremoniously landed hard on his buttocks, only to be bucked even higher.

A buzzer sounded.

Kerwhallop!

Colton Jameson ate hay and concrete.

Pulling himself up from the dusty floor, Colt slapped his Stetson against his thigh, locked onto a longneck bottle of Lone Star, and pocketed a twenty-dollar bill. "Come on boys, who's the next hard-ass that thinks they can beat my time?" The cowboy chug-a-lugged the cold beer, and scanned the men for takers. His mouth twisted wryly as recognition came to his eyes.

"How about it, cowpoke?" Colt moseyed toward McCall and Nick. "You been braggin' about busting broncs, so put your money where your mouth is. Ride this pretend bull. Ain't much difference."

The rowdy crowd roared and egged on the two adversaries.

McCall grasped Nick's hand. "Don't do it, Nick!" She tugged at his arm. "It isn't as easy as it looks. Colt has a lot of experience."

Nick shucked off her hand. "Tell you what, Colton . . . it's Colton, isn't it?" Nick pulled out a money clip brimming with bills. "Here's what I'm carrying on me, and if it isn't enough, there's more in the bank." He slapped the ante on the table. "Put up or shut up, Jameson."

Colton frowned, his eyes flattened under drawn brows. With a fiery, defiant gaze he accepted the challenge. "Sure, cowpoke, I'll match you. Anytime. Anyplace."

"Not on this contraption." Nick motioned toward the mechanical bull. "Tomorrow. Cut out two of the ranch's toughest broncs." He grabbed his money clip and stuffed it in his pocket. "We'll draw for the ride." He latched onto McCall's hand. "Let's get out of here, Mac."

Nick guided her back to their table, tossed down some bills, and carted her toward the exit.

"Don't be a fool, Nicodemus!" She shook off his hand and took a deep breath. As though dealing with an irresponsible teenager, she adjusted the tone to her voice. "You *will* get hurt. Even killed. Colt knows the stock and he'll make sure you get exactly what you asked for—the worst bad-ass bronc on the ranch." She turned and blindly stumbled to the pickup.

"McCall!" He yelled after her as his gait picked up speed. "Trust me, woman! I know what I'm doing."

She stopped in mid-stride and whirled to face him. "You sure as hell better, because I don't intend to bury someone else I love."

"You have serious trust issues." He took a step forward and attempted to gather her in his arms, but the hurt in her eyes made him stop.

"I don't need to be reminded."

Sleep evaded McCall as she flopped over on her side, fighting with the urge to go to Nick and knock some sense into the bull-headed man. Ego! Male ego bigger than his brain.

Her mind wandered to their parting words, and about the only words spoken on the way home. McCall had so many reasons to have trust issues. More than her share, but she wasn't ready to share them with Nick . . . not at the moment. She couldn't help but think back to the way Nick took to the dance floor. The warmth of his arms was so male, so bracing. McCall smiled to herself. Any cowgirl would be happy to have such a well-endowed, brown-eyed handsome man in tight-fittin' jeans and a Stetson shuffle her around a dance floor.

But what laid heaviest on her mind and heart was Nick's bet with Colt. Sure, Nick was capable of handling himself when faced with a challenge, but riding a rodeo bronc was altogether another thing. He could be hurt, mangled, even killed in an instant. It wasn't like baseball, where he could send in a relief pitcher if the game went into extra innings.

"Oh hell!" She rolled over. "I finally find Mr. Right and he's intent on killing himself trying to prove our worlds aren't that different." Kicking off the covers, she found herself pacing the room.

She shouldn't have shown her anger and stalked out of the honky-tonk and to the car.

Nick was due an apology. An apology, hell! She needed to save him from himself . . . save him from being injured or killed because of his macho ego.

McCall opened her door and saw faint light coming from underneath his, so she knew he was still up.

Stalking across the hall, she knocked lightly, then shoved open the door without considering she was dressed in only boxer shorts and a T-shirt. "Nicodemus Dartmouth, I've had about all of your bullheadedness that I'm going to take." Into the darkness, she shouted, "Nick! I want you . . . now!"

"Hey baby, you don't have to yell," he tormented from the darkened bathroom doorway. "I'm all yours."

McCall whirled and came face-to-face with Nick, who stood broad-shouldered with only a towel around his waist. She forced her eyes from his rock-hard stomach, through a thick coat of flat-ass sexy dark curly hair, until she reached his eyes. Her heart beat in a wild, erratic rhythm. She took a deep breath, savoring the scent of spearmint, musk, and Irish Spring.

His hands gripped the top of the towel that dipped dangerously low over his lean hips. "Sorry, I wasn't expecting company," he taunted in a profoundly sexy drawl. "Want me to get dressed?"

"You're not bothering me." She licked suddenly dry lips. He absolutely was not bothering her. She had seen him in underwear, and that little black job he wore on the boat didn't exactly have a lot of fabric to it, either. So, a towel around his waist wasn't much different. Was it?

Stepping toward her, he tucked the corners of the towel into a makeshift knot, and unhurriedly lifted her hands, pressing them against his chest, letting her feel his unwavering wall of muscles.

"You're bothering me, though." He lazily guided her fingers into slow, sensual circles. "Mucho bothering me."

Her legs rebelled, and her breath caught in her throat. "I, uh, need to talk with you," she whispered.

His chest rose and fell raggedly as he tightened his grip. Pressing her palms flat against his hardened nipples, she felt his thundering heartbeat beneath her hand. He eased his free arm around her waist and pulled her closer. Soft breath caressed her earlobe. "So, talk to me, Mac."

Hushed breeze stirred the curtains at the opened window. Cicadas chirped in the distance. A sliver of moonlight spread a caddy-wampus pattern on the wooden floors.

A whisper of wind disturbed the hair around her temple.

She was afraid to stand so near, afraid of his hot breath, afraid of his tattered breathing. Yet, being in his arms felt natural . . . right where she belonged. His warmth so male, so protective, and so distracting.

His sorrel eyes smoldered like heated lava. Lowering his head, Nick covered her mouth, searing her with a raging, hot, needy kiss. He took full possession of her mouth, opening wide to ravish and pillage with his tongue. Deeper and deeper. Withdrawing long enough to taste her sweetness, he plundered again, drawing her into an inferno of desire, sending wave after wave of molten longing through her until her body spiked with need.

McCall had to remember her mission. Forget flesh against flesh. Man against woman. Dueling tongues.

She finally won the battle with her own rebellious body and scrounged up enough courage to pull away, allowing her hands to linger on his fiery flesh way too long. She lifted her face to find him studying her.

Burning eyes held her still, while he guided her hands to his lean hips. Allowing the towel to drop, he continued down the side of his legs and back up to the naked hips thwarting her resolve somewhere along the way.

Reclaiming her mouth, his lips were forceful and searching. He moaned when she locked her hands behind his neck, instinctively arching into his pulsating body, crushing her breasts against him. She made no protest when he released her long enough to slide her T-shirt over her head, discarding the ribbed fabric on the floor.

Magically, his palm outlined the circle of her breast and tantalized the dusky nipples swollen to their fullest.

"McCall, I can't tell you enough how beautiful you are. So perfect." His tongue explored the rosy peaks.

Softly she moaned an invitation to continue.

Waves of ecstasy exploded within McCall as she struggled back to reality, clawing her way out of her mist of lust. "Nick, I can't do this." She untangled her body from his, and stepped away. "I'm sorry . . ." She whirled, grabbed her shirt, and ran toward the door before turning back to him. "Not here. Not in the house I was raised in. No matter how badly I want you, it wouldn't be right."

Nick stared out into the darkened night, listening to the stillness of Texas. No wonder McCall loved it here. He had acted such a fool. Any full-grown, red-blooded man should have known someone like McCall could never make love under her grandmother's roof. He had been so insensitive, yet she had come to his room and tempted him. Hell, she was too tempting. Like cotton candy melting in his mouth. Dangerous and sinfully sexy, she made him lose his prospective. He wanted her more than ever.

And, the only way? Take her away. Away from both of their worlds. Away to a place where it rains with the sun shining . . . with nary a cloud in the sky.

Tomorrow he would do just that . . . if he was still alive to take her anywhere.

A soft knock came from the door. "Nick, are you still awake?" McCall whispered.

"Yes." He turned at the sound of the door opening.

"Here." She laid a pair of weathered chaps and seasoned leather gloves on the cedar chest. "These were Dad's, and you'll need them." She eased back out of the room and pulled the door closed, only to reappear. "Nick, I really do love you."

"Come here," he said, wanting to hold her, tell her he understood.

She walked slowly to him.

He cradled her in his arms. "Thanks for the riding gear." He lifted her chin. "Angel Eyes, trust me. I know what I'm doing."

"I hope so." She dropped her head onto his muscular shoulder and kissed his warm skin. "Are you sure I can't talk you out of it?"

Nick shook his head. "Mac, I realize you've had trust issues in the past, but please, trust me . . . please."

McCall kissed him lightly and left the room, softly closing the door behind her.

Nick felt like putting his fist through the wall. Something he'd never considered doing before regardless of how mad he had gotten. He wasn't mad at McCall, but at himself for letting Colt goad him into making the bet, but it was too late to back down now. He knew he could best the son of a bitch.

Nick damn well planned to keep his promise to McCall and would not get hurt. He couldn't help but laugh out loud when the thought ran through his head . . . *he could bet the ranch on it.*

Chapter Twenty

One corral over from where Nick stood, a half dozen wild mustangs pounded the dirt, leaving behind long ribbons of dust in their wake. The broncs snorted and bolted as a growing crowd of wranglers turned their attention back to the empty arena waiting for the match between Colton Jameson and Nicodemus Dartmouth to begin.

Spurs jingling, Colt ambled toward Nick, who pulled on his gloves. "Ready, cowpoke?" Colt hollered over his shoulder. "Luther, get 'um in the chutes while we draw for first ride."

"I've been thinking, Jameson. Since I don't know the stock, you'll probably try to screw me over, so this is the way we're going to settle this." Nick rubbed the back of his gloved hand across his chin. "Get two of those ornery devils over there." He tilted his head toward the pen of mustangs. "The first to get his mount saddled up and aboard wins."

"That's suicide, Dartmouth." Colt plunged on carelessly. "But, it's your funeral." He shouted over his shoulder to the ranch hand. "Luther, cut out two of those Slippery Elm stallions."

"Jameson, they just got here and haven't even been evaluated. We haven't even had time to work with them. They're still madder than hell and wild to boot. Mesa is gonna be pissed. I think you should—"

"You don't get paid to think. And I don't give a damn what Mesa thinks. If she cared so much, then she'd have been here when they were delivered. Just get 'em." Colt spoke to the wrangler but eyed Nick suspiciously before addressing him. "Better get outfitted. It's gonna be a long day."

McCall came up from behind Nick and said, "Colton Jameson,

it's gonna be your head when Granny finds out that you're using the land management mustangs for your own agenda." She pointed a finger at him. "I'm warning you. I thought you had enough sense to use horses who are trained to buck, so I'd suggest you'd better call this off or all hell is going to break lose when Mesa finds out. These are her horses, remember."

"You and Mesa are just alike," Colt said.

McCall turned and looked Nick squarely in the eye. "And *you* know how I feel about it." She stalked to the house.

Nick wanted to go after her and make it okay, explain that he was doing what a man had to do. He couldn't turn his back on a challenge—particularly one he could win. He had come too far in his effort to prove he was an ordinary guy capable of existing in McCall's world to turn back now.

The two men headed to the tack room.

After selecting a simple western saddle, along with an array of tack, including a bridle, lariat, and a few short pieces of rope, Nick snatched up a plaid flannel shirt from a peg near the door. He headed back to the corral.

Dropping the saddle and blanket on the ground, he tied the shirt loosely around the saddle horn.

Sizing up their chosen steed, roping and snubbing the stud to a post in order to fit a bridle was the easiest part of the competition.

A grueling, sweating, dusty, nerve-shattering morning commenced as Nick and Colt fought the wild-spirited, raw pieces of horseflesh in their efforts to tame the untamable.

Feet braced, Colt's captured horse plunged wild-eyed against the choking effect of the snubbed lariat. Bawling, the bronc reared and with one ferocious jerk the rope slipped, and the horse broke loose before being bridled, sending his tormentor sprawling in the dirt. Colt grabbed the rope, and began another assault on the frightened animal.

After being tugged around the arena, Nick wrangled his charge into a degree of submission and managed to get the horse bridled and cross-hobbled. None too happy about having his forefeet and one hind hoof linked together with rope and still full of fight, the sorry sunfisher ducked, resisting the saddle.

Not taking time to check on Colt's progress, and breathless from fighting with every ounce of energy in him, Nick considered his next move.

Counting on an old trick Jock had taught him, Nick twisted the ear of the animal and caused enough pain to distract the outlaw until he could heave the blanket over the mustang's back, followed by the forty-pound saddle. Hooking the stirrup over the saddle horn, he scrambled to secure the cinch.

The maneuver worked just as Nick remembered. He pulled loose the hobbling ropes and swung into the saddle. As a natural reaction to the added weight, the bay leaped savagely into the air, trying to send Nick head over teakettle.

Gut-jarring hell broke loose inside Nick's body with every angry jump, while the bronc pitched and bawled, trying to bathe the rider in stars. Pitching a good fifty yards, he smoothed out into a run trying to brush Nick against the fence.

Turning to his last tactic, Nick withdrew the flannel shirt from the saddle horn. "Good night, ears." He quickly pulled the fabric over the horse's head, snuffing out unexpected sounds and motions, while hazing the mustang until he rode to a standstill near the rail.

Grabbing hold of the top railing, Nick vaulted off the stallion, taking the shirt with him.

As mad as a peeled rattler, the testy piece of rawhide bucked off across the pen, fighting the saddle as though Nick had left a porcupine behind.

Nick wiped sweat from his brow, not giving a rusty rat's ass if the ornery bastard spent the rest of his born days sleeping in the gear or not. He wasn't about to unsaddle him.

Looking around, he found McCall standing near the gate, appearing none too happy. Heading her way, he grimaced. His butt burned as though he'd landed in a hornet's nest, and his family jewels felt like they had been used as punching bags. The parts of his body that weren't numb hurt like hell.

"Good ride, Nicodemus." Traces of displeasure remained on her face and he didn't fail to catch the note of sarcasm in the way she used his given name.

Colt approached.

"I'll see you at the house, Nick." McCall directed her statement to Nick, but shot Colt a *go to hell* look before slowly retreating.

As Colt neared, dusting off his Stetson, he spit a stream of mucky tobacco. "Cowpoke, whether I like you or not doesn't matter. You proved yourself, honest to your word." He pulled out a wad of money from his Levi pocket. "How much do I owe you?"

"I don't want your money, Jameson."

Colt hemmed and hawed and shuffled dirt around with the toe of his boot. "I sure as hell don't need your pity or you to think that I don't have the money 'cause I do." He shifted his weight to his other foot. "And, another thing, Dartmouth, if you hurt her, you've got me to deal with." He moved his fingers forward as though offering a handshake, but quickly shoved them into his pocket.

"You got my word." Nick extended his hand, knowing Colt wouldn't shake. "And I want your word that you'll stay away from McCall. I suspect you have something to do with some of the hurt she's still dealing with." He looked Colt squarely in the eyes. "I can promise you if I find out it was you who is responsible for the hurt she carries around, a wild bronc will be the least of your worries." Nick clenched his fist, just itching for his threat to be challenged.

"Dartmouth, you don't know jack about me and Mac." Colton flashed Nick a look of disdain.

Apparently still within hearing distance, McCall turned sharply and returned. Putting her hands on her hips, she said, "Colton Jameson, I've only been home a couple days, and I'm sick and tired of you already."

Then she turned to Nick and with eyes like summer lightning, she said, "You're not my favorite person at the moment, either. Both of you are acting like fool-headed jackaninnies."

McCall stalked to the house.

Colt snickered. "Trust me, greenhorn, she'll cool off and be back in your bed before you know it." He spit in the dirt. "And, she's a damn good lay, too."

Nick's fist connected with the cowboy's chin, sending him butt over shoulders against the corral fence. "I've been waiting for you to prove you're an idiot."

Coming up fighting, Colt took a wild swing at Nick, hitting him just below his left eye.

Hating to make a scene but knowing he couldn't let Colt get in the last punch, Nick took a more calculated uppercut to the cowboy's jaw, sending him over the top rung of the corral. He landed in a fresh pile of horse droppings.

Nick picked his hat from the dirt, dusting it against his thigh. "Next time, think twice before you open your trap, cowpoke. Otherwise, this flannel-mouth will kick your ass from here to the Mexican border and back. And, Colton, ol' pal, don't ever spit chewing tobacco any-where near me again."

Preparing himself for the tongue-lashing he knew he'd get from McCall, Nick took his time walking back to the house.

Chapter Twenty-one

A SWAT team in full riot gear bombarding the kitchen couldn't have shattered the silence any worse than when McCall hit the back door.

Breathe McCall, breathe! She inhaled deeply, swooshing out excess air.

What happened to pasts being pasts? She wasn't ready to discuss the problem between Colton and her with Nick. Not yet. She sure as hell didn't appreciate Nick bringing it up to Colt, either. And now they were duking it out.

To be truly honest with herself, she was more angry with Colton drawing Nick into his dangerous game than a good ol'-fashioned fight between two men. She was glad they'd be gone before her cousin got back home and found out what Colton had pulled. Maybe McCall could do Mesa a favor and kickbox his family jewels all the way up to his head and stuff them into the empty space in his brain he currently wasn't using for a think tank. Make him see the light, in more ways than one.

And she didn't even want to think about how mad Granny would be when she found out. Using trained broncs was one thing, but wild broncs not broke was altogether another. Luther was a loyal hand, so it wouldn't take him long to fill her in on Colt's risky antics.

McCall ripped a ponytail holder from her pocket, pulled her hair back, circled the twisty around the mass, and took a deep breath.

She smelled freshly baked cornbread, cooling in iron skillets.

Lola Ruth slid aside a tiny mountain of green peppers and onion on her cutting board as McCall entered the kitchen. "Who won?"

"The bronc ride or the fight?"

"I know who won the ride." Lola Ruth lifted a questioning brow.

"By the time I got to the mudroom, Colt was sprawled out in a fresh pile of horse dooky."

Taking her attention away from Colt and Nick, the scent of pinto beans seasoned with a healthy hunk of ham hock flitted through the air and provided a sense of comfort, chasing away some of her misgivings.

"Anything you want to talk about?" Lola Ruth asked.

"No. I'll just never understand men," McCall responded before allowing her mind to wander.

Colt had issued the first challenge at the Texas Moon Palace, but why had Nick gone along with the craziness? He obviously knew his way around a horse, otherwise he wouldn't have known some of the tricks of the trade he used to even saddle the bronc, much less ride him.

It was nothing but ego. Unadulterated ego. At least, Nick hadn't killed himself just to prove a point. And the point was? He never loses. Not even in a fistfight!

She'd never understand men. Colt was like a Brahma bull going after a bullfighter . . . again and again until he finally caught him by the horn and tossed him six feet in the air just to show off. But she doubted he thought Nick would throw a punch at him.

Lola Ruth drew a forearm across her brow before wiping her hands on her apron. "Well, Missy, the way I see it, Nicky was only trying to protect you the only way he knows how." She quickly changed the subject. "I'm fixin' your favorites. Barbequed ribs, cornbread, salad, and some of my famous Texas caviar." She laughed as she scooped up a double-handful of peppers and onions, tossing them into a beige crockery bowl half filled with cold, drained black-eyed peas. "Your Granny wouldn't hear of not having a special dinner for you and that gorgeous man of yours."

"He's *not* my man," McCall protested.

"I'm not so sure about that, gal." The older woman shook two hearty dashes of Tabasco into a mixture of vinegar, oil, and sugar. "Don't think you've told your heart that yet."

McCall wanted to put her hands over her ears to drown out the lecture about Nicodemus's virtues from a woman who surely thought that the bottle of burgundy in the liquor cabinet was once water, before Nick turned it into wine.

Resisting the urge to comment, she watched her mentor blend the tangy dressing and drizzle it over the peas. Grabbing a tablespoon, McCall dipped out a serving of the mixture, steering clear of Lola Ruth's fluttering fingers.

"Some things never change. Like you sneaking a taste of my cookin'." Lola Ruth shook her head. "Yep, not much at all has changed, including those scars on your heart."

McCall swallowed a mouthful of peas. "I believe my heart is doing just fine, thank you."

Yeah, if a heart shackled and chained to Nicodemus Dartmouth would be considered *doing just fine*. But Lola Ruth was right. Nick was trying to soothe away the scars on her heart and all she had been doing was fighting him tooth and toenail. She couldn't and she wouldn't allow herself to fall deeper in love with him. But it might already be too late.

Lola Ruth piped up, "If you tell me those scars are healed, guess I'll just have to say it's your story, girl, so stick to it." Apparently, seeing that her point had been made, she switched topics. "In all my born days, I've never seen anything quite like the way Nicky was all over Colton Jameson. Just like stink on a skunk, he was. Yes, ma'am, I saw it all from the kitchen window and your granny's having a conniption fit. She headed for the bunkhouse like she had a hive of bumblebees in her bloomers."

"No doubt Luther beat me to the house." McCall exhaled some of her frustration.

Lola Ruth nodded then split open a jalapeno and scooped out the seeds. "He heard everything that went on at the corral. You know how he is."

"Yeah." The smell of jalapenos waned through the air. "Damn, the last thing I need is to have Granny on Nick's case."

"Oh, she's not put out with *your* Mr. Nicky."

A rich-timbred voice called from the doorway, "Sorry to disappoint you Miss Lola Ruth, but I'm hardly *her* Mr. Nicky at the moment."

"How long have you been standing there?" Cocking her head and scowling, McCall challenged him. "Eavesdropping?"

Nick eased into one of his infectious *If You Only Knew* smiles.

All the frustration she felt rushed back. She walked to the sink and with a louder thud than she had planned her spoon hit porcelain. "I've gotta get some air." Then she turned to Nick and said, "I just need time to think about everything that went on this morning." She took a deep breath, knowing he deserved more of an explanation. "I don't cotton to being talked about behind my back." She took two steps. "Nick, you're welcome to come along, but don't expect much conversation."

"Nicky, don't forget dinner. I'm making homemade ice cream and apple cobbler," Lola Ruth raised her voice two notches.

Boldly stepping out into the screened-in back porch, McCall retrieved a sweat-stained straw hat off a peg.

"Not so fast. I don't know exactly what you heard, but we need to talk," Nick said to McCall's back, then, over his shoulder, he said, "And yes, Miss Lola Ruth, I promise we'll be back by dinner."

A huff that could have staved off a flame-throwing dragon mushroomed from McCall's chest as she took off across the yard. How much of her conversation with Lola Ruth had he heard?

Taking long strides, Nick plowed his way in McCall's direction, closing the distance between them. Reaching her, he gingerly, yet firmly, caught her by the arm.

She pulled out of his grasp, retreating deeper into the shadows of a timeworn cottonwood. "To be hospitable to a guest, I said you could come along, but didn't you hear me say not to expect any conversation?" She glared at him. "I need some air, not conversation. But if it's conversation you want, I'm sure Lola Ruth would love to talk with you."

Fairly quickly, she passed the corral and neared the barn, where she slid through a side door, which she pulled shut behind her.

All six foot three inches of his lean body collided with the barn door.

He wanted to think she didn't know he was behind her still, but he wasn't all that sure about his assumptions.

"Son of a . . ." He thrust the heavy pine door open with his palms in time to see her exit into the sunlight from the opposite end of the tack room. At her side, she swung an antiquated, rust-laden lard can and a short-handled shovel.

What in the hell was McCall up to? Murder crossed his mind. Maybe she planned to dig a grave, bury him, and shovel dirt in his face with the lard can. She wouldn't. Would she?

Chapter Twenty-two

Nick plodded after McCall, stomping across mesquite-dotted, yucca-sprinkled pastures where a herd of Herefords grazed, paying no attention to the couple traipsing through their domain.

She stopped in a low-lying area near a stream, squatted, and raked away the dead vegetation from around a log, before tossing aside a dozen or so rocks.

Standing, she jammed the shovel into the moist ground. A second push with her booted foot, and the sharpshooter sunk halfway down. Nick doubted if even the strongest man on one of his construction crews could have shoved the spade to such a depth with so little effort as the feisty Texan who hadn't even broken a sweat.

Nick leaned against a tree and stuck his thumb in his Levi's pocket. Best to let her work off some of her fury over him punching out Colton, then he'd approach her to have a talk about their feelings.

In the meantime, if she planned to bury him, at least he could enjoy the great view of her butt as she lifted more moist soil from the ground.

Without looking up, she knelt and scooped out the area with her hands. Sorting through the humus carefully, she tossed a clump of something dark and squirmy in the bucket, before topping it with two handfuls of soil.

When finished, she calculatingly thrust the spade erect in the dirt and turned around, facing Nick. "It's your turn, Slugger. Now I can stare at your ass for a while." She retrieved the pail and set out toward the stream.

Nick didn't miss her double meaning of *ass* and yanked the shovel from the ground. Damn, what a shame to break away from such a luscious sight as her behind. What the hell was she digging for? Worms? Big, fat squiggly night crawlers! But that was certainly better than watching her dig his grave.

"Darling, you forgot your broom." Nick let out a triumphant laugh and struck out after her, knowing his words only served to raise her ire. But what did it matter if she was about to murder him anyway?

"Nick, I said you could come, but I didn't want to carry on a conversation," she said firmly. "I'm here for fresh air and to think."

Since she didn't want any conversation, Nick leaned on the sharpshooter and refrained from responding, but just watched the pretty Texan.

She got on her hands and knees near a log beneath the low-hanging branches of the skeleton of a dead cottonwood and retrieved a fishing pole and a metal box.

Marching to the stream, she plopped the tackle down on the bank. Stretching the line taut, she tested for strength, claimed a squiggly worm, and threaded it on the dangling hook at the end of the pole. "Don't stand there like you've never seen a woman put a worm on a hook before. Fish or cut bait. In Texas that means—"

"To either fish or get the hell out of your sight."

"You got it, Slugger."

"I think I'll go back to the house and visit with Miss Lola Ruth. It's very obvious that I'm a distraction you don't want or need right now." He tried to add respect to his voice, but under the current circumstances, most likely he'd failed at that, too.

"Don't trip on the cattle guard as you exit."

Nick turned to retreat, but couldn't resist adding a barb. Over his shoulder he said, "And by the way, that hook is too big, unless you're fishing for barracudas."

Not responding verbally, McCall aggressively whipped the fishing line over her head, preparing to cast out into the water.

"Son of a bitch!" Nick yelped. Pain shot from his hip to his brain and back with lightning speed. As though shackled to the line, he froze in place and squeezed his eyes closed until the initial pain subsided. "What are you trying to do, use me for bait?"

Damn if he wasn't hooked like a big-ass bass in the cheek of his butt. Another half an inch higher and she'd have hit his pocket. But, no, the hook went through denim and cotton to latch onto a hunk of raw flesh. The fishing line arched overhead, ending at McCall's rod.

He slipped his hand down his hip. Oh yeah, good and deep.

"Nick, I'm sorry—so sorry." She dropped the fishing rod.

"I told you the hook was too big." Nick winced in pain.

"It was an accident. Honestly, I didn't mean to—"

"Hey, baby, if you wanted me to stay, all you had to do was say so."

"We need to get that hook out, Nick. Sit down on that log." She motioned toward a tree heavy with branches.

Nick raised a questioning eyebrow.

"I guess that wasn't the brightest idea I've ever had. Lean over. No, on second thought, lay facedown on the grass."

Nick obliged, seeking the comfort of a shady, grassy area protected by a grove of trees.

Tin rattled when she opened the box. He glanced over her shoulder and saw her hold up a pair of needle-nose pliers.

"Oh no, you don't!" He struggled to stand, only to have her push him facedown, kneel above him, and clamp his thighs together with her knees.

"Settle down. I'm going to snip the hook in two, then you can take off your jeans and I'll dig out the remainder—"

"Dig out?"

"Well, that's kinda inaccurate. Not digging really, but cutting it out."

"Maybe I should go to a doctor."

"No. There's nothing to getting a hook out. You can go to a doctor if an infection sets in," she said in a cool, thoughtful voice, but not quite as caring as he would have liked.

She was enjoying this way too much and Nick knew it.

"Hmm, guess I could stitch you up with fishing line."

"No," Nick bellowed, playing along, although the pain was not a laughing matter.

"Then I'd better take you over to Doc Chalmers."

"Does he have an emergency room?"

"No. He's a vet, but I'll be glad to call him, if you'd like. Or better yet, I'll get Lola Ruth to come help. She's a wiz at this kind of thing." A teasing tone came into her voice. "You oughtta see her skin a catfish."

"No, just get to work. Why do you have pliers with you?"

"I just told you. To clean catfish," she answered with a touch of authority.

Nick shivered. He knew how to dress out catfish and it wasn't a pleasant thought. Envisioning McCall ripping off the skin with pliers sent a second tremor through his body.

Snip. The hook separated.

"Now pull down your jeans, so I can get a better look. Guess you'll need to lower your Fruit of the Looms, too. Be careful not to snag the fabric on the pointy part still stuck in your, uh, fanny. As a matter of fact, stand still."

Halfway following orders, he stood up and unzipped his Levi's, only to have McCall insert her hand between his shorts and backside, slowly sliding her palm over his hip, down his buttocks until she found the hook. Even as bad as it stung, the warmth of her soft, helpful fingers searching his sensitive flesh excited him. Carefully, she separated the fabric from the hook and helped him shuck his jeans.

Stepping back a few feet, she issued a cocky smile, openly admiring his shiny heinie exposed to the hot Texas sun.

Making a cushion with his Levi's, Nick laid facedown on the prairie grass and prepared for the inevitable. "Okay, Doc Holliday, go to it."

She ripped open an alcohol pad and dabbed it around the hook, before wiping off her hands and cleaning the nose of the pliers.

"Hold on, Slugger."

Nick latched onto a handful of grass.

McCall latched onto a handful of ass.

She yanked.

He yelped.

The pliers held the metal in a death grip.

She swabbed the bloody wound with a second alcohol pad before applying a Band-Aid on the wound and slapping his unscathed cheek with her free hand. "Good as new. Get your drawers on, Slugger."

"Thanks." Nick pulled on his pants while McCall returned her makeshift medical gear to the tackle box.

Touching his tender buttocks, he offered her a whimsical grin. "You certainly put a different spin on 'turning another cheek.'"

Fate offered him a stroke of genius and a damn good one even if he thought so himself. It had worked on the boat, so how could it fail him now?

"Mac, I feel woozy. I'll feel better if I lie down for a bit." Like a wounded soldier succumbing to a battlefield injury, Nick eased toward a mattress of grass and leaves.

No doubt his plan worked, when he saw concern on her face. McCall helped him down on the earthen pallet. Reaching across to smooth back his hair from his face, one breast rested familiarly against his chest.

"Just lay your head back. It'll be okay." She butterfly-kissed him. "I promise."

Suddenly, McCall found herself under him as he flipped over on her, covering her with his firm, hot, needy body.

"You recovered pretty fast for someone in the throes of death," she whispered.

"Oh yeah. I'm a fast healer." He smothered her lips with demanding mastery.

Her thoughts spun and waned on a soft wispy cloud.

Nick's earlier actions had irritated her, so why did she want to toss out her stash of discount coupons for Double Whoppers and take up escargot when she didn't even like snails? Why was she angry with him in the first place? He was making it hard for her to remember. A few honey-laden words of love and some magical kisses had short-circuited her brain, sending her heart into a fare-thee-well, ring-tailed tooter.

She continued to search her mind trying to recall why she shouldn't thoroughly enjoy his moist, passionate, and very sensual kisses.

Then she remembered.

McCall pressed her hands against his chest, separating their sweltering bodies that neared the boiling point.

They would never be free to explore their true attraction to one another until she had answers. Too many questions hovered around, sucking the life from their relationship.

"Nick, I'm ready to talk."

"You picked one hell of a time to want to start talking." Nick lifted upward, using his elbows for support.

"I know. But sex isn't the answer."

"But . . . it's . . . a . . . good . . . place . . . to . . . start." Between each word he planted kisses on her shoulders, neck, and face. "You have to admit, we've *almost* had some of the best sex of our lives."

Girding herself with resolve, McCall fought off the urge to forget talking and start acting out her passion for Nick. "It's time we get things squared away between us."

"I was thinking of something hard between us but it isn't square."

Nick rolled to his back, tucked his arms behind his head and obviously ignored her scathing look while keeping an eye on the sky.

McCall studied the sky, too. It looked like melted cotton candy swirled over a bed of blueberries, which meant only one thing to her, a storm was brewing somewhere over in the west. She thought more about his statement then said, "You're cute, but why don't we begin by me asking you a question?" This bought her time. She made a silent prayer that when it was his turn he'd steer clear of some of the things she'd prefer not to discuss at the moment.

"To begin with, why are you so scared of commitments? And so competitive, and wanting things you can't have?" McCall asked.

"That's a question. Actually, two questions, not a beginning."

"Good, so you know what a question is. Nick, if you're serious about exploring our relationship, we've got to share our true feelings. If you aren't comfortable discussing them with me, then we really don't have much of a chance to see what comes next with us."

"Okay, we'll share, but isn't that a girlie thing?"

"Either take this seriously or I'm outta here." McCall struggled to her feet.

Before she reached her full stature, Nick grabbed her hand and pulled her down to him. "You deserve answers, but only if I can ask questions, too."

"So, we're back to 'I'll show you mine if you'll show me yours?'"

"No. We're beyond that," he protested. "I've already seen yours and you've seen mine."

"Get serious or I promise I'm gone—"

"Okay. So you think I have issues?" He raked his fingers through his hair and twitched his nose. "Well . . ."

She shot him a weary glare that reeked of *I'm truly sorry I took the hook out of your butt. For all I care, you can stand up the rest of your life.*

"Okay. I admit I was scared of commitments for the same reason that I'm competitive. I can't handle failure. It's a weakness, and I think it all goes back to being raised without a father. Mac, all I wanted while I was growing up was to have a father. I think every successful endeavor was for my dad's benefit. Just in case he ever came back, he'd be proud of me and want me to be his son."

McCall choked back the lump in her throat and imposed willpower to control her tears as she watched the hurt ooze from Nick like a festering wound. She remained silent, touching his cheek, erasing a lone tear with her thumb.

He continued. "After seeing what my mother did to my father, I didn't think I wanted a woman 24/7. That way I'd be protected from hurt and hurting another person. A commitment leads to an engagement, on to marriage, and eventually a family. I couldn't afford to hurt someone else like I'd been hurt. I damn sure didn't want to be responsible for bringing an innocent baby into the world to live like I did—always looking over my shoulder and wondering if any guy who paid attention to me could be my real father."

"And, you want all of this now?"

"Hell, yes. All of a sudden I see things differently. I want to have a kid—kids. I didn't with Lauren."

"Nick, you don't have to tell me about her. I know all I need to know. Like we agreed, pasts are pasts."

"I have to." Nick lifted McCall's chin. "I don't want any secrets between us." He lightly kissed her before releasing her face.

"Mother tried her damnedest to make me into the Pepperdine type, but I was just as determined to be Berkeley. I never fit into her world. Are you familiar with Procrustes?"

"The cruel highwayman from Greek mythology that forced people who passed him to lie on a long bed and then stretched them to fit it?"

"Yeah. I felt a lot like one of his victims."

Lifting up on her elbow, McCall rested her chin on her hand, taking in every one of Nick's expressions. She gave him a questioning look.

"I felt like I couldn't be accepted the way I was, but yet I resisted conforming to society. All I wanted was to be accepted, not stretched to meet another person's expectations."

"Nick, I'm sorry you feel that way. You had everything you needed, a wonderful mother, plenty of money—"

"Everything but what I wanted. A father. Mother saw to that."

"And then I came along and made you feel like you had to conform to my world."

"No. For once, I wanted to do it. To prove to you that I'm just a regular old guy who truly cares for you. I have a confession."

McCall was eager to hear what he had to say. He seemed so serious. "Okay."

"I didn't cook the meal on the boat. Our chef did and then Harold showed me a few things to do to make you believe I did it." He shot her a shy grin. "I don't really even know how to cook."

She smiled and raised an eyebrow as if surprised by his confession, but decided to keep her comments to herself.

"I just care so much about you that I wanted you to think I can do anything I set my mind to."

"Do you really care about me, Nick?"

"I didn't think you'd have to ask that. I've always cared, but don't know when I realized just how much. Suddenly, I began thinking about building a life with you. Hell, I even had little Dartmouth ankle-biters playing in the front yard surrounded by a white picket fence, neighborhood barbeques, and picking out curtains for the kitchen."

"Then why didn't you tell me that we'd gone from *I love you* to a true desire to be one?"

"Because I didn't know myself for a long time. Suddenly, I began experiencing something unfamiliar. I think that infection has set in, and I'm on the verge of delirium. That's the reason I'm spilling my guts to you now."

"You'll be okay. Why did you take Colt's challenge so seriously?" She smiled at him, then added, "Other than male ego."

"Mainly because I knew I could beat him. One thing I didn't tell you about Jock and the ranch is that I spent most of my summers up there on the Triple J with Jock and his father. That's where I learned to be a man. It certainly wasn't swashbuckling with a doting man-servant who I could twist around my little finger and who still calls me Master Dart." He touched her cheek tenderly.

"I didn't know how it came about, but I figured out when I saw you ride that you knew your way around a horse and weren't trying to show up Colt." She couldn't resist smiling as she thought back to the look on Colt's face when he landed in a pile of horse droppings. "And, I was glad you slugged the jerk."

"I was trying to put him in his place because I knew what I was doing, but when he mouthed off, I had no choice but to hit him. A man never allows another man to talk trash about someone they love. All I've wanted since the day I realized how I felt about you is to make you happy. Make you want me as much as I want you."

"Oh Nick, you didn't have to try that hard, because you've made me very happy. In the last week, I've learned more about myself than I thought possible. You made me see myself differently. Made me face my own feelings and fears." She fought back tears that clung in her throat.

Somewhere during the conversation, Lauren, along with Nick's intentions to tell McCall about the Triple J acquisition vanished. His business problem could wait. McCall could not.

"Back in LA, I asked you about the hurt in your life. You made it very clear you didn't plan to discuss it. I respect that, but please re-member, I'll always be here and have a big shoulder," Nick said.

"Thanks. I like big shoulders." She nestled up to his side. "Nick, you've earned the right to know what I'm scared of, too."

"Mac, you don't have to—"

"Yes, I do. I'm scared of rattlesnakes. I hate to throw up. And the worst, I'm horrified of getting one of those viruses that get under your toenails. You know the type you see on TV where the little ogre-looking thingy lifts up a toenail and looks at the yuck under it?"

Nick chuckled and rolled toward her. "Now tell me what your heart is scared of."

"It's terrified of the thought of losing you like I've done every-body in my life. Paw-Pa, Daddy, and then Mother. All the people I ever loved, except for Granny and Lola Ruth. And, yes, I was afraid of you, too. Of my feelings. I think that's why I acted like I did on the island. I wanted you to go away, so then I wouldn't take the chance of getting close, of feeling, of loving you." McCall peered up into his eyes. "I was afraid I'd run you off, if I got too close."

"I'm not going anywhere, Angel Eyes." He slipped his hand behind her head and pulled her down to him. "How do you figure it's your fault that you lost your parents and grandfather? That's a big burden to carry for a young woman."

"I should have been able to do something to help them stay safe. Make Daddy take better care of himself. Make Mother strong enough to stop smoking and save her from being ravaged with cancer. And to stop Paw-Pa from tangling with that stallion the day he got trampled to death. I should have been able to do something. I guess that was why I was so angry at you for taking such a risk in the corral. I was so mesmerized by your talent that I couldn't leave, but knew you could end up dying in the dirt and there wasn't a damn thing I could do about it."

"That was beyond your control, Mac. You don't have to save the whole world. I'll be here to shoulder some of your burden. And there's one thing for sure, you can't get rid of me that easy. I'll be there for you."

"I'm glad. Where do we go now?"

"To a place where it rains while the sun shines. Do you have your passport?"

"Yes. I don't know what possessed me, but when I found out we were going out in the Pacific on your boat, I put it in my bag."

"Good. I always have mine with me. Can you be packed by morning? I'll have the jet readied."

She nodded and settled her head on his broad chest. "But we still have a lot to talk about. I want to know about the land deal you're working on, what is going on with your construction firm, have you scouted for a new pitcher?"

"We have a lifetime to talk." He grew silent and pulled her closer to him. "Right now I want to focus on us. Business comes second to you."

"I know you spend a lot of time on your iPhone," she said. "Are you sure we don't need to go back to LA?"

"No. That's why I have the best managers money can buy running my businesses. Plus half the calls are from Mother. I hate to admit it, but if she continues checking up on me, I'm going to begin ignoring her calls."

"Shame on you, but okay. No more questions for the time being."

Together they gazed into the sky, feeling closer to the heartbeat of the universe than they'd ever felt.

The stillness of the prairie settled around them as they lay cocooned in one another's arms, in their own universe, far, far away from the pressures of the world. Far away from the clouds that churned in the west like boiled Armageddon.

McCall snuggled closer to Nick and they watched as ominous clouds erased the sun.

"Slugger, as much as I'm enjoying our outing, we'd better head for the house." She motioned her head toward the west.

They sprang to their feet when random jolts of wind lashed against their faces. Lightning danced across the soundstage of the sky as throbbing green-black clouds threatened and coursed their way toward them. A wagonload of thunder rumbled.

Forgetting the fishing pole and tackle box, they raced through the pasture, trying to outrun a wall of rain.

Feeding heifers raised their heads as though checking the severity of the storm and formed a single file, ambling toward shelter.

"Damn it, McCall, hurry." Nick grabbed her hand and pulled her close to his side.

"This isn't much of a storm. It'll pass in a bit and you'll see the most gorgeous Texas sunset you've ever seen."

"It isn't the storm I'm worried about. I promised Lola Ruth that we'd be back by dinner. Don't want to miss her homemade ice cream. And I'll be the judge of whether it's the best sunset I've ever seen."

Chapter Twenty-three

The next afternoon, the turn and descent of the Learjet woke McCall. She looked out the plane's window as it approached the Niagara Falls International Airport. Within what seemed like only minutes after landing, a car shuttled them to their hotel.

And now, McCall felt safe and secure with Nick's arm around her shoulder as they stood in the gleaming sunshine of Niagara Falls. They enjoyed the tapestry of turbulent waves and billowy foam when the river thundered over the spectacular waterfalls. The allure of the town known for romance, coupled with the mystery of the cascading falls, washed away any remaining misgivings the couple had about their relationship. They were in love and eager to explore their future.

"Come sit with me." Nick guided her to a park bench. "Did your Grandmother really fire Colt?"

"Oh yeah. She's wanted to send him packing for years because of his attitude, but she had promised his dying father that she'd see after the kid. He was lucky and had inherited his dad's gift for recognizing rank stock, which made the ranch a lot of money."

"Then it wasn't all because of our altercation?"

"No. Granny didn't have a problem with a good ol'-fashioned buckin' competition, but would have preferred it with trained rodeo stock. I think deep inside she was happy that you sent Colt over the top rail of the corral, but of course, she couldn't admit it." McCall laid her hand on Nick's thigh. "It's been a while since there's been a good ol'-fashioned fistfight on the Jacks Bluff. But when she discovered that Colt put you both in danger by foolishly using Mesa's wild mustangs, Granny had had enough. She won't let anyone put the ranch in jeopardy for any reason." McCall patted his leg. "I just wish I'd seen more of the fight."

"Glad you didn't. There were three blows, two of them mine." He smiled shyly and tucked her closer to his side. "Sure wasn't my finest hour."

"Nick, I'm happy he's gone." She reached up and caressed his knuckles. "It was time, and thanks for defending my honor."

"You're welcome, ma'am. Insulting a woman in Texas is purt near a hangin' offense, I heard."

She nodded and smiled. "You've been reading the book on Texa-sisms, huh?"

A sheepish smile crossed his lips. "Yep. Trust me, ma'am . . . it was the Texas thing to do."

"Just as long as he drew first."

"In a manner of speaking, he did. I wouldn't be much of a man if I'd ignored him."

"Nick, I need to clear up a misconception about Colt."

"I told you before, Mac, you don't owe me any explanations. Re-member, our pasts are our pasts."

"I think you have the idea that Colt hurt me, and he didn't. He's just a natural born idiot and blowhard who wanted to get your goat. Honestly, if anything, he was a bit protective of me. We never had anything going, but it wasn't because he didn't try." Her heart beat out of control while she scrounged up the courage to confront the demon of her past, and tell Nick the secret she'd kept buried in the cemetery of her past. She continued. "This isn't easy. It's something I've told nobody, especially Granny. She'd probably have gone for her Winchester if she'd known what happened."

Nick looked at her questioningly. His brow creased with obvious concern, and he took her hand.

"I was touched inappropriately. No, I wasn't just touched. I was raped when I was eight." She looked up at Nick and fought for the courage to continue. Telling him the truth was much harder than she ever imagined. "And, yes, I told my mother, but she didn't believe me."

Miserable, utter chaos exploded within Nick. His temples pounded and his throat constricted in anger. A primeval instinct to protect the woman he loved wrestled with rationality; he knew that he must remain calm. Words formed on his lips but seemed unable to come forth.

McCall hushed his response with her fingers. "Please, don't say anything. This is hard enough. Nick, I don't want sympathy, but you need to know why I seem to have a need to sabotage things every time you get too close."

Tight-jawed and trembling, Nick fought for control. Angry with his inadequacy to comfort her—to say the right thing, to make it all right—he listened.

Yesterday's clouds hung heavily over today's sunshine as McCall told about being stalked by a refinery worker who her father called a friend. One night, after one of her dad's weekly poker games, the man followed her to the barn. Instead of leaving the ranch for home, he attacked her.

Nick struggled to hold his temper and his tongue in check while something rancid and wrong swathed his heart.

Just telling Nick that much had unraveled her courage to a single hair-like strand of steel, but she continued digging through the hostile valleys of her memories, feeling naked and exposed. A patchwork of humiliation and frenzied emotions brought tears to McCall's eyes. They mingled with relief that she had finally uttered the words kept hidden in her soul way too long. She could now release herself from a self-imposed sentence of shame.

Shrinking back into her past, she told Nick about the secret she harbored, the guilt deep inside, and how she'd tried to figure out what she had done to provoke the attack.

For weeks after the incident, she had withdrawn from her family members, feeling insecure and shameful. After weeks of turmoil, she tried to talk to her mother—seek guidance from the one person who would protect her. But her mother refused to listen, telling McCall that accusations of that sort would ruin her father's career and that she would tell *nobody*. McCall had retreated from the house and for weeks spent every spare moment fishing or riding, wondering what she had done wrong. Each night she climbed in bed carrying a burden of guilt that no child should have to. The word *nobody* repeated itself daily. Nobody, no doubt, meant her grandmother and teachers, but especially her father.

Being so young, McCall didn't understand the judicial system, but years later she always thought that if her own mother wouldn't believe her, then why would anyone else? She swore to keep her secret . . . and had done so, until today.

Determined to turn her back on the past, McCall said, "Now I know he'd groomed me. Made me think he was my friend. Took me to town for ice cream. He'd go riding with me and always told me how much he loved me when he'd hug me." Humiliation and embarrassment shrouded her being. "The worst part—my own mother hadn't believed me. I had been violated, lost my innocence, yet I was the one to feel the shame. I asked myself for years—if my own mother didn't believe me, then why would anybody else?"

"I believe you, baby. I truly do." Nick's expression was a mask of stone. Anger seethed in his eyes.

"Nick, you have no idea how it makes me feel to have this burden lifted. Of knowing that I told the truth and somebody believes me." She snuggled deep against his shoulder. The cursed past was behind her and she could applaud the future. "You have brought me full circle."

Nick didn't say anything for a while, but from the look on his face he was trying to put his own feelings into words, digging deep inside to find the right ones. "Rape is an act of power and dominance. Survival depended on compliance and submission. You were too young to understand, but it's never, never a victim's fault, McCall. Never." She felt sure by his responses that her story disturbed him because he only whispered, "I love you, McCall. I truly do. I won't push you into an intimate relationship until you're ready." He looked deeply in her eyes. "I promise to be here when you are."

"You have no idea how much I've prayed for this day, and with your understanding, I know I can learn to love, give of myself completely." She kissed him. "I know one thing. I will never feel unprotected ever again. I'm free, Nick. Truly free for the first time in my life." McCall looked into his eyes.

She should have felt spent and exhausted, but instead it was as though she had been freed from the guilt and shame just by having someone believe her.

Breaking loose, she pulled off her raincoat, tossing the heavy cloth in the air. Shaking out her hair, she lifted her face to the sky and let the mist from the falls pepper down on her.

"Isn't the mystique of the rapids awesome? Come play with me," she said.

"Oh yeah, I'll come play with you." Following suit, Nick dumped his slicker and joined in. "Look across to the farthest brink. It's twenty-five hundred feet wide and way over there is the Canadian side."

"Oh Nick, you really did bring me to a place where it rains while the sun is shining—and I can see a foreign country at the same time." McCall smoothed his hair with her fingers, and loved him with her eyes. "Thanks."

He smiled a thank-you and winked. "This is nothing. Come on." He grabbed their raincoats, took her hand, and pulled her toward the trolley stop.

After a short ride around Goat Island, across the bridge over the American Rapids, and through the Great Lakes Garden, they exited the trolley.

Still holding her hand, Nick half dragged McCall down the winding path toward the Rainbow Bridge. "Come on, hurry."

He threw back his head and laughed as McCall stopped to catch her breath. "I thought you were in better shape than that," he said.

"I'll show you who's in shape." She darted to the bridge entrance and slowly picked up speed, battling the uphill walkway. A few feet ahead, she stopped and looked behind to see Nick's long legs eating up the concrete.

McCall halted, leaned over with her hands on her knees and inhaled deeply.

"Back up about three feet and face me," he ordered when he caught up with her.

She complied. "Now what?"

"Take one big step forward."

She did.

Nick stepped in front of her and took both hands in his. "Angel Eyes, you're standing in Canada and I am in the United States. My heart is pounding like the six billion pounds of water rushing under this bridge a minute. I have a dilemma."

"A dilemma? You're scaring me." McCall swallowed, her heart pounding at four billion pounds a minute.

"I don't know whether to ask you to marry me in Canada or the United States." The warmth of his smile echoed in his voice.

She tilted her head and caught the look in his eyes. "Come here."

Nick stepped forward. "Will you marry me, McCall Elise Johnson?"

He took one step back, bringing McCall forward one step.

"Yes, I'll marry you, Nicodemus Dartmouth."

Nick asked her to marry him in Canada, she accepted in the United States. They bound together in an international kiss.

In disbelief, two hours later, McCall disconnected from her iPhone, after talking briefly with her lawyer's paralegal.

Wave after wave of shock slapped at her. *A horse ranch!* The words were barely audible over the pounding of her heart. "Daddy really did make an investment and didn't lose everything on gambling." She sat at the desk in their hotel suite and took a deep breath trying to settle her racing pulse.

She walked to the window and stood hugging herself, trying to absorb the news. For months—no, years—she had questioned her father's business venture. Now it had come to fruition. She had been so astounded at the news she failed to ask where the ranch was located or who owned it.

Think McCall! Think! What did the lawyer's assistant say? The best she could recall, in all of her excitement, someone had seen the creditor's notice and come forth, notifying her parents' estate through her attorney that they held money in her father's name. She was so caught off guard that she didn't even ask where the ranch was located or even how much money was involved. It could be a few dollars or a million.

And there was already someone who wanted to buy her out.

Everything hadn't been lost after all. With Nick in her life, she had someone to love and cherish, and could finally lay the loss of her parents to rest.

McCall thought back to her and Nick's visit to the Triple J when he told her that he'd like to relocate from LA and buy a ranch. He had certainly proven his prowess on a horse.

Now she could give him the perfect wedding gift. His own horse ranch . . . wherever it might be.

McCall stopped and listened for any stirring in Nick's bedroom. All quiet. Apparently, he was still soothing his bronc-busting aches, bruises, and a fishing hook mishap.

Capitalizing on her privacy, she redialed her attorney's office. Excited at the possibility of surprising Nick, she impatiently tapped her fingers on the desk while she waited for an answer. After being told her lawyer was in a deposition, she held a brief conversation with the same woman as before. McCall disconnected, smiling outwardly.

She had left instructions for her lawyer to inform the buyers that she'd reconsidered and did not wish to sell her share. "Dang it—" She snapped her fingers. She was so excited. Once again, she'd failed to ask where the ranch was located. As long as it was a ranch of some sort it'd be the prefect wedding present for the man who got everything he wanted.

Her excitement could no longer be contained. She slipped into Nick's bedroom.

In the hearth, burnished cinnabar and umber-tinged flames blazed from crackling logs, taking the chill out of the air, making the hotel room cozy. She fed the fire another log. Hissing, tiny blazing embers shot forth.

Two half-empty glasses of Dom Pérignon sat on the table, reminders of their afternoon together making plans for their future.

The excitement still churned in her being. She could wait to tell him the good news that she could finally settle her parents' estate, but tonight . . . tonight she planned to make Nick make love to her until he hollered uncle.

Nick lay on the sofa with hands tucked behind his head, breathing evenly.

Tiptoeing across the room, she stopped and stood over the sleeping man. As much as she wanted . . . no, needed to wake her knight in shining armor, it would be best if she let him rest. She reached across the back of the sofa for a blanket to cover him.

Without warning, he masterfully caught her behind the knees and she buckled down on top of him. Grabbing her by the waist, he pulled her tight to him. As she settled against his body of steel, they shared a heartbeat.

Hands met hands.

Lips met lips.

Caresses met caresses . . . seeking, yielding, plunging . . . hot and wet.

"You're making this hard on me," Nick growled and rolled, taking her with him, pressing her between his body and the back of the sofa.

"I hope so."

"I'll show you hard . . ."

In one fluid motion, Nick stood, wrapped her in his arms, and carried her to the bed. Gently, he eased her down.

Breathlessly, shedding her remaining clothing, she watched Nick stand over her, unbuckle his belt, and step out of his Levi's.

McCall reached out and helped him disrobe.

Nick kicked his jockey shorts into a pile of white cotton and denim.

Standing before her, he wore nothing but a tiny chin cleft entrenched in a devilish smile.

She forced her gaze upward. "You're so—"

"So what?" Laughter rumbled deep in his chest. "Ready?" He lowered himself to her, bracing his weight with his arms.

"Oh yeah, that's the word. Ready." She touched his face, running her fingers along his rough unshaven jaw. "Nick, I've waited so long for this, but I want to tell you something." Her fingertip traced his lower lip. "News that will make you happy."

"It can wait," he whispered in a hoarse voice. "I can't." His voice was impatient, rough, and wildly thrilling.

"Neither can I."

Greedily, Nick sought her mouth. "I love you, Angel Eyes." His kiss ravished her. Demanding, hard, conquering. Wild with need, she responded with the same urgency . . . sizzling passion. Her body quaked at the promise of ecstasy that racked her, when she felt the hot shove of his tongue as it entered her mouth again and again.

Their lips, tongues, mouths played out an uninhibited fantasy.

"I want to touch you," she whispered, light and breathy as a sea breeze.

"You can touch me all you want. I'm all yours. Just touch me."

He groaned deep in his chest when she found his raging ridge of arousal. Delicate tapered fingers closed in on his hardness and fed his hunger, while her thumb drew soft lithe circles near the top.

Hurled against the point of no return, untamed flames of desire burned within them.

Later in the evening, they lay in the magical afterglow of love-making. Nick held her quaking body in the crook of his arm, brushed away damp ringlets from her forehead, and kissed her temple. "I love you, Mac," he said in a husky whisper.

"I love you, Nicodemus. I truly love you," she managed in a soft willowy voice.

"You have no idea how wonderful that sounds. Know something?" He draped a leg over her thigh.

Her only reply was a soft groan.

"I'm glad I didn't take advantage of you on the island." Slowly, preciously, he lifted his knee and applied pressure on her love-swollen flesh.

"You're glad?" She made little circles with her fingertips in chest hair.

"Yeah, because if I had, I may not have ever gotten to know you well enough to fall in love."

"You don't regret waiting?" She slid her hand down to the inside of his thigh.

"I can assure you of one thing, Angel Eyes." He rolled on top of her, shielding her legs with his, and dipped down to meet her. "I plan to make up for lost time."

Chapter Twenty-four

Midday sun filtered through the vertical blinds in the hotel suite, creating diagonal patterns on the carpet.

"Damn it to hell," Nick slammed down his iPhone. "Son of a bitch." His fist hit the desk.

Nick wanted the Triple J as bad as anything he'd ever wanted in his life with the exception of McCall. Seeing how happy she was when she first saw the ranch only increased his desire to obtain it. It wasn't one of his famous whim-whams. It was a true dream. A dream not only for him but for McCall.

He couldn't believe that the investor first said he'd be willing to take his share of the investment and sign the ranch over to the remaining investors, who of course he wouldn't have known were Nick and Jock. Then suddenly, the elusive investor changed his mind, making it necessary for Nick's lawyer to file suit to clear the title showing that the investor had been a silent partner and had not participated in any improvements or operations of the Triple J. Once cleared, Jock planned to sell his share to Nick, making him sole owner. The suit would be settled quickly, according to his lawyer, because the owner couldn't show they'd been involved in the day-to-day operations and the amount of money held in trust for them would be enough to make the most aggressive investor accept an out-of-court settlement.

Nick flopped down on the sofa more frustrated than he could ever remember being. And that was saying a lot, just thinking about the years waiting for the silent partner to appear. Now only hours away from finalizing the sale, the backer had suddenly come forth and wanted to take an active part in its operation.

His lawyer said it'd take a couple hours, but he'd fax the first draft of the petition to Nick in care of the hotel. Nick called the concierge desk to have the papers delivered to his suite as soon as they arrived.

Nick let out another string of profanities. Damn J.J. Macmurphy, Jock's father, for taking on a backer and not keeping the records more secure. It wasn't his fault they were destroyed in a fire, but it wouldn't have happened if he'd kept the partnership papers in a safety deposit box. When J.J. died, he took the true identity of the silent partner or partners with him.

Not until Jock decided to retire and let Nick buy out his part of the ranch did the search for the other owner begin in earnest. After all these months, they had finally gotten a lead and the jerkass changed his mind and didn't want to sell.

At first, Nick wanted full ownership as an investment and as someplace to get away from the city. He'd even rejected his mother's suggestion that they buy the property under the umbrella of one of their businesses, which made her mad. Nick and Maddi never spoke of his purchase again.

After visiting the Triple J and spending time with McCall in Texas, he realized the main reason he desired the land had to do with the memories of some of the best times of his life. As a young man, most of his summers were spent on the Triple J learning about horses, helping J.J. and Jock, while learning how to be a man's man.

After seeing the look on McCall's face when she first saw the Triple J, his reasons had changed. He wanted it for her. To please her. He knew they'd be happy living there.

"To hell with it," Nick spat out. There are other ranches, but none quite like the Triple J.

He needed some fresh air. He glanced at his watch. McCall wasn't due back from the spa and beauty salon for a while. He'd have plenty of time to take a breather, reconcile some of his anger and return to the hotel in time to meet with the jeweler the concierge had arranged for—bringing his best engagement rings for Nick to choose from.

Nick grabbed his phone and stuck it in his pocket. "Missing Investor, I don't know who in the hell you are or where you've been, but the suit to clear title should bring you out of the woodwork."

After jotting a quick note to let McCall know he'd be gone for a while, Nick stalked out the door.

One way or another, he'd gain control of the Triple J ranch. Nothing would get in his way . . . nothing!

Three hours later, McCall opened the hotel suite door to eerie silence. She dropped her purse on the sofa and checked both bedrooms. She saw Nick's note on the desk and wondered what had drawn him away so unexpectedly.

A knock on the door drew her attention away from Nick's note and when she answered a young woman wearing a hotel uniform asked, "Is Mr. Dartmouth in?"

"No, but he'll be back soon." McCall noticed the papers in the woman's hand. "Is there something I can do for you?"

"Mr. Dartmouth asked that this fax be delivered to his suite as soon as it arrived."

McCall took the papers the woman extended to her. "Thank you. I'll see that he gets them. Just a moment, please."

After grabbing her pocketbook, McCall handed the woman five dollars. "Thank you so much." She closed the door and laid the papers on the desk.

The hotel phone rang and she talked briefly to the concierge, assuring him that the faxed pages had been received.

McCall glanced down at the documents. She gasped and raised her hands to cover her month as she read again the words . . . *Estate of Charles Chilcote Johnson.*

"Oh my God!" Trembling fingers touched the page as though the words could feel her caress. She took in each word, letter by letter, trying to grasp their meaning.

In Re: Nicodemus B. Dartmouth, et al. vs. Estate of Charles Chilcote Johnson.

Her knees buckled. She slipped onto the chair and read the pleadings.

"Nick is suing me," she whispered.

Her heart pounded out of control and chills ran throughout her body as though she had suddenly taken ill. She tried to swallow, but couldn't. Grabbing her stomach to hold down bile fighting for release, she attempted to sort out what she had read. Nick and others were suing her father's estate . . . suing *her*.

Gaining a semblance of composure, she picked up the petition. She shook so wildly that she had to use both hands to hold the piece still long enough to finish reading it.

Slowly, McCall turned back to the first page and laid the pleadings aside. Nick was suing her for control of the Triple J Horse Ranch . . . and she didn't even know she owned it.

Hot tears ran down her cheeks. "It was a game all along." For the first time since she was a child she cried not from anger or fright, but from a hurt so deep there was no bottom. "He didn't expect me to see these papers and I wouldn't have if my appointment had been longer. Nick doesn't love me. He loved the game. He wanted the ranch, and the only way he could gain control was to court me, make me think he was in love with me . . ." She folded over and grabbed her knees. "He was willing to marry me to get what he wanted." She rocked backward and forward. "Or did he ever plan on marrying me? Or was he just talking about the future and asking me to marry him to throw me off base?"

Raising her hands to her face, she couldn't help but think that she'd bared her soul to him, told him her most intimate secrets, and for what? To be worked, so Nick could get what he wanted.

How long had Nick known of her father's involvement in the ranch? When had he decided to become interested in it? Before or after the auction? Before he professed his love for her?

The news that her father had actually made an investment and not wasted the money at the track had consoled McCall, as well as excited her, since she could give Nick something he wanted so badly. But, now everything had changed.

Nick might be accustomed to getting everything he wanted, and this would be no exception. He'd get his ranch. Regardless of her hurt and anger, she loved him too much to deny him the one thing that he wanted so bad that he'd asked her to marry him to gain it. She'd step out of the picture and enter into an agreement for him to purchase the property. All of this could be done through their lawyers without either of them ever having to speak to one another again.

But why hurt her by suing her when all he had to do was ask? The words *trust me* flooded back.

Between gathering her belongings and packing, McCall made two calls.

The first was to her attorney, directing him to negotiate a settlement with Nick.

The second, to the hotel concierge arranging transportation to the airport.

The displaced Texan was going back home.

Back to Texas.

Back to a world where she belonged.

As Nick stepped off the elevator, his hand automatically checked his pocket to make sure his purchase was secure. He had looked at a dozen stones before he found a truly colorless, flawless pear-shaped diamond encircled with baguettes. If McCall didn't like the five-carat stone, he'd buy her as many as it took to give her the perfect engagement ring.

Not only had his outing ended up with him buying the engagement ring, but also it gave him time to think about the problems with the sale of the Triple J.

For some unknown reason the mystery seller was more intent on keeping his share of the ranch than Nick was in acquiring it. Nick wasn't a man to give up easily, but maybe the good Lord had played a bigger hand in the dealings than Nick had given Him credit for. Maybe it wasn't meant for Nick to own the ranch.

While in Texas he had felt good, liked having a family, and realized what he had been missing . . . a real home.

Stanley taking him fishing and the Macmurphys teaching him horsemanship wasn't the same as having a real family. Nick liked the idea of having someone to come home to.

He had stopped and called his lawyer, who was in a meeting and couldn't be disturbed. Nick left word with his paralegal that he was no longer interested in the property and to stop litigation.

Maybe his energy would be much better spent on finding that house with the white picket fence and raising that houseful of ankle-biters.

"Hell's bells!" Nick rubbed his forehead. "First, it was a wife, and now, I'm serious about children. I can't win for losing with that spitfire." He unlocked the penthouse suite.

"McCall, I'm home," he teased, letting the words slip off his tongue as though they were natural.

No response. No music. No television. No McCall.

Maybe she had gone downstairs to one of the gift shops.

The telephone rang. Nick snatched up the phone, thinking it might be McCall.

"Mr. Dartmouth," the concierge began. "I'm sorry to bother you, but Miss Johnson left a package in the limousine when the driver took her to the airport."

"The airport?" Nick's heart sank to his knees.

"Yes, sir, about an hour ago. She barely got there in time to get her flight. Sir, what should I—"

"Thank you." Nick returned the receiver to the hook and eased down in the chair. "Why would she leave without telling me?" He stared into space, feeling his heart being ripped from his chest.

What had he done to make her fly home without letting him know? He racked his brain, but when she left for the spa she was excited because she'd arranged a special night for them. He distinctly remembered her saying she had something very exciting to tell him. She'd kissed him and even turned back and gave him a second one before leaving.

What had gone wrong? Could she have been kidnapped? Did she have second thoughts about their being intimate the night before? Maybe he'd asked too much of her too soon?

Nothing seemed to fit.

With one surge of anger, Nick swiped his arm across the desk, sending everything crashing to the floor. He looked down at the page staring back. *Estate of Charles Chilcote Johnson by and through his next of kin and executrix, McCall Elise Johnson.*

"Christ Almighty, McCall! Chili Johnson was your father!"

Chapter Twenty-five

The flight from Niagara Falls to Texas had been long and uncomfortable for Nick, but not as unpleasant as the mess he had made of his relationship with McCall. The worst part was he hadn't even known it was happening.

A half dozen telephone calls gave him no hint of her whereabouts. If Josie knew, she wasn't telling. She suddenly knew little about anything, not even his mother's schedule. The lack of knowledge about where McCall had gone only confirmed his suspicions. She would have retreated to the only place that gave her comfort . . . Texas.

No wonder Mother thought him inept at taking care of matters of the heart. For the first time in his life, he had found something he wanted more than anything. McCall had changed him in ways he never thought possible. Hell, he had had nary a sip of Ambassador Twenty-Five for days, but had chug-a-lugged enough Lone Star longnecks to have a vested interest in the brewery. He'd learned the Cotton-Eyed Joe, fell in love with Texas, and had been literally hooked by the feisty Texan.

But now he was afraid McCall was as unattainable as the jar of stars he had wanted to give her back on the beach.

Nick pulled the rental car to the side of the road and stared into the sunset, then turned his attention to the great house. The oil derrick towered over the grounds like a sentry. Lights flooded the yard. He could almost smell Lola Ruth's sweet, fried pies and taste her stout coffee.

Suck it up, man!

If McCall were half the woman he knew she was, she would accept his explanation about the Triple J. But why had she kept her involvement a secret? She had hinted when they were at the ranch that she felt comfortable, almost as if a familiar feeling had overcame her, but he'd blown it off. Looking back, he realized he shouldn't have. The answer . . . she didn't know. That was the only reason. She was much too honest to play him a fool. He knew her and loved her for that very reason. He had to make it okay and hated that he had jumped to conclusions about her reasons for not divulging her involvement with the ranch.

She had certainly told him on more than one occasion that neither she nor her mother thought her father had made an investment, but if he had it would have been in the oil and gas industry, which made total sense to Nick as he thought through the whole issue. There was no reason for either of them to think her father was involved with the Triple J.

If he was a smart man, maybe Nick should turn around and head back to California and put the spitfire, with the eyes of an angel, and the whole Johnson fiasco out of his mind. But then, he had never been known for being all that smart when it came to his heart. Not to mention he loved McCall and wouldn't let her go so easily . . . and he wanted that damn ranch for *them* not just him.

Nick started the engine and as quietly as possible parked behind Granny's weathered, mangy F-150 pickup that had obviously seen its odometer turn zero more than once.

A shadow moved near the corral. A tall, lanky, yet beautiful and sexy, Texan held tight to a post and rested her booted foot on the lower railing.

Quiet as a prairie dog, Nick walked toward her. Easing up behind McCall, he shuffled a foot so as not to scare her. She never moved, only clung to the post as though it were a life preserver.

Cicadas droned.

Frogs croaked.

Horses neighed.

Hearts pounded.

"What do you want, Nick?" Her words were weak, yet silky.

"We need to talk."

She never looked up, just said, "Why is it that every time you get your back to the wall your only solution is to want to talk?" Not waiting for his response, she continued. "I think our lawyers have already done the talking for us."

He took her shoulders and turned her around to face him.

She twisted away. "Haven't you done enough? I trusted you, and then you used me like this—"

"I used you!" He wheeled around to stare at her, trying not to let his frustrations show. "Used you—" He stopped and calculated his words. "All you had to do was tell me you owned an interest in the Triple J."

"I didn't know until yesterday." Her tone was relatively civil in spite of her obvious fury.

"Yesterday? Why didn't you tell me then?"

"I wanted to surprise you. Remember, right before we had sex—"

"Made love," Nick corrected.

"I told you that I had something to tell you. A surprise? Then again this morning when I told you I'd planned a special dinner and a surprise. But I guess I was the one that got surprised. Sued, that is."

He ran his fingers through his hair. "Jeez! Do you believe I would have let my lawyers start litigation if I'd known you were the owner? Honestly?"

"I—" She shook her head. "Not really."

"Why would I need to trick you into selling me the ranch? As far as I knew, you were desperate for money. All I would have had to do was ask you to sell it to me. It would have been a simple business transaction."

"Exactly, Nick. If I'd known you wanted it and knew I owned the dang thing, I would have moved heaven and hell to give it to you." She took a deep breath. "But you have full ownership now. I told my lawyer to draw up settlement papers. All I want is whatever money my father invested." She looked him squarely in the eyes. "All I ever wanted was to have someone love me, *for me,* not for money, but for me. I thought I'd found him—"

"You did. I love you, McCall." Nick caught her by the arm and gently pulled her toward him. "Knowing how happy you were at the Triple J, I told my attorney to do whatever was necessary to get it for you . . . *for us*. I didn't know you were involved until after I saw the fax."

"You did? But, Nick, once I saw the papers, I instructed my lawyer to go ahead and let you have the ranch. If it was that important to you, I love you too much to stand in your way."

"You still love me?" He offered a mischievous smile. "McCall, I have another question." He dropped to one knee and took her hand. "If I promise to steer clear of trouble, will you try to teach me the Texas thing for the rest of our lives?" He pulled a ring from his pocket and slid it on her finger.

McCall pulled him to his feet. "Yes!" She threw her arms around his neck. "Yes, Nick, I'll still marry you, but—"

"Why am I not surprised that you have to add a *but*?" He smiled down at her.

"But you promise you won't come near a stove, and I'll do all the cooking."

He nodded in agreement. "And I'll do the fishing."

"And you'll keep your opinion to yourself about the table decorations at your mother's next fund-raiser. And you'll stop coming up with those whim-whams you're so famous for."

"All of them?" He deliberately twisted his lips into a pout.

"Well, maybe you can do one every now and again."

"Two?"

"Don't push your luck." She chided then smiled. "Okay, two."

He pulled her into his arms. "And, we are both through with jumping to conclusions. So, who do we tell first?"

"Granny," they said in unison.

As though on cue, Granny's voice bore through the evening like a sudden thunderclap. "McCall Elise Johnson! I want you in here right now!"

"And you too, Nicodemus Beauregard Dartmouth!" Each word was punctuated with Madeline's best boarding-school English.

"Mother!" Nick exclaimed. "What is she doing here?"

"Beauregard?" McCall shrugged her shoulders as if she didn't know, then marched toward the house. "You must be kidding. Beauregard?" She laughed out loud.

"It's better than her first choice. Archibald!" Nick stalked behind.

McCall slowed down and Nick caught up. When he got close enough, he grabbed her by the waist and spun her to him. She slipped her arms over his shoulders and kissed him, whispering, "I think we're about to face our first challenge as a couple. Stick together?"

He quirked an eyebrow.

She raised her arm and met his palm with a high five.

The two entered the kitchen as though being called before a disciplinary board. Nick skidded to a stop.

Madeline Elliott-Dartmouth and Granny Johnson sat at the kitchen table looking as though they had just returned from a week-long cattle drive.

He wasn't sure but thought he smelled something resembling what he'd raked off his boots. "Mother, what are you doing here?"

Madeline propped her elbows on the table, something he'd never seen her do before. She exchanged looks with her son.

"Nicky, darling, I understand we have a problem." She popped a stuffed jalapeno into her mouth. "You should try these. And those." She motioned to a plate of calf fries. "Since you've given everyone else permission to call you Nicky, I presume I can also."

"You never answered me, Mother. What are you doing here? You look like—"

"What? Like I just came off the range?" Not waiting for a reply, she continued. "McCall's grandmother showed me all around their lovely ranch."

"Tell me why you're here. And why you're dressed like Annie Oakley." He shrugged at McCall and turned back to two pair of eyes scrutinizing his every move. "What in the hell is going on?"

McCall leaned against the cabinet and studied Nick's reaction before speaking. "Can't you see? Your mother isn't Annie Oakley, she's Superman and has come to save the day." McCall folded her arms across her chest and a bemused smile took over.

Nick shook his head and faced his mother. "This is none of your business, Mother. Stay out of it. McCall and I can work out our problems without your interference. You don't have to control everything and everybody."

It was Granny's turn to speak. She pulled all four feet ten inches from her chair and caught Nick's stunned look with eyes that blazed in anger. He half expected her to lay her sidearm on the table.

"Watch your mouth, young man. That's your mother you're talking to. We are having a family intervention. That's what," she said in a steely Texas twang.

"We're not all one family, Granny," McCall said.

"Not yet we aren't, but if we have anything to do with it, we will be," Granny barked.

"Oh, Jeez!" Nick ran his hands through his hair.

Madeline followed Granny's example by standing and slapping her hands on her hips. "Nico . . . Nicky, I think we need some privacy to talk."

"No!" Nick snapped without thinking. "I want McCall to hear whatever you have to say. There will be no more secrets between us." He raised an eyebrow at McCall, who winked back. He continued. "Because I've asked her to—"

"Marry you," Madeline finished.

Granny nodded in agreement.

"Guess you both have taken up spying," interjected McCall with a smile kissing the corner of her mouth.

"Just looking out of the curtains was all," Granny stated. "Can't help what we see."

"Okay, Nick, if you want McCall to know everything." Maddi wiped her hands on a napkin. "First, neither one of you knew about the other's part in the Triple J transaction. It wasn't until your lawyer called that I knew anything about it. If you'd taken my calls this could have been avoided." She gave Nick the look she always gave him when she was truly irritated with him. "And before you ask. When McCall called to resign, I saw the caller ID was in Texas, since she didn't use her cell phone. Once I got here, it was easy to find the ranch, since everybody in Kasota Springs knows where the ranch headquarters are. I presumed you were here."

Nick rolled his eyes at her.

"By the way, you owe me for airfare from LAX to Amarillo, since you had the jet." She rubbed her rump. "Anyway, when I got here, Mrs. Johnson and I were able to talk and the facts came out."

"You and Mrs. Johnson have been conniving behind our backs?"

Nick asked, only to have Granny Johnson shoot him a reprimand similar to the one she had given Colton at breakfast only a few days before. "I thought Josie was your only partner in crime."

"We had to do something. You have loved McCall for a long time. You two belong together. Josie and I worked too hard to make sure it happened—"

"So you rigged the auction." Nick said with cool disapproval. "I should have known when you allowed McCall to wear Grandmother's diamond necklace. But to rig—"

"That's a bit harsh, darling. There was no duplicity. We simply had to, let's just say, encourage McCall to participate and make sure you won her and not that Anson fellow. You can't trust an actor—"

"I thought he was a model," Nick interjected.

Mrs. Dartmouth glared at her son. "A model. An actor. What's the difference? I paid him the same."

"So you hired Anson?" McCall entered the fracas. "I can't believe it. You staged everything, Madeline."

"I admit it, but he was a, you know . . ." Madeline turned to Nick. "By the way, don't forget that you owe the foundation another twenty-one thousand dollars." She shrugged her shoulders and waved her hand through the air. "Now, the two of us"—she motioned toward Granny—"don't plan to let you throw away what we've all worked so hard to make happen because of a little spat."

"You manipulated this relationship just like you did mine and Lauren's." Happiness and frustration mingled in Nick's heart.

"Since you insist on bringing *her* up, it's time you know the truth. You want McCall to know everything, then everything she will know." Maddi rounded the kitchen table with Granny as her backup. Butch Cassidy and the Sundance Kid on a roll.

Granny piped up, "I'll leave you all alone."

"No. If we're going to be family, we'll keep no secrets," Maddi said to Granny, then turned back to face Nick. "Lauren wasn't what she seemed. She was truly after your money. I hired a private investigator—"

"Private investigator? How cold and calculating."

"I did it for your own good. She was a fraud, and I caught her stealing jewelry from the house. She wasn't from the New Orleans

DeBose. Her name wasn't even DeBose. Honey, if she'd been from Podunk, I would have accepted her if you truly loved the woman, but you didn't and she was taking you for a ride." Maddi stopped and looked directly at Nick. "I couldn't stand to have you be mistreated like . . ."

"Like you did to my father?" He jerked his head in his mother's direction.

"No." She hesitated then drew in a deep breath. "Like me. I didn't want you to suffer the disappointments and hurt that I felt with your father. I chose to let you believe that I kicked him out, toyed with him until I didn't need him any longer. But the truth was that he was an adulterous gigolo who was only after my money. When he learned that I wouldn't inherit the Elliott trust until I turned thirty-five, his patience wore thin and he walked out, probably never giving any thought to what he was doing to his son. Three days later, he was found dead of an overdose in a hotel room with a prostitute, leaving me alone and with a precious little boy." Tears bubbled in her eyes. "You're the only good thing that came of our relationship, Nick. That's why I was so protective of you. Too protective, I know."

A war of emotions raged within Nick, coiling in his body like a hissing, angry snake. He was numb with increasing fury and shock. He had always thought his father was the wealthy one, and his mother had inherited his riches.

An air of calm suddenly engulfed him.

He studied his mother.

Realization shrouded Nick . . . the father he had waited on for so many years was never coming home. And it was okay.

For the first time, he viewed his mother in a different light. Her only transgression . . . trying to keep the son she loved from following in her footsteps where love was concerned.

Nick fought through the cobwebs that seemed to tangle up his thoughts to ask, "And Lauren?"

"She gladly took a check to disappear, so I wouldn't press charges for stealing. I'd hoped you'd never know, but I realize now, I should have told you the truth from the start and not tried to handle the problem for you. You're a good, honest man and would have done the right thing. I just thought I had to take charge, but I've learned my lesson. And you are right. I can't control everything and everybody."

"But you turned right around and got involved with the Triple J sale." A muscle in Nick's jaw quivered.

"I backed off just like you asked until yesterday when Jock called. He was in LA and saw the legal notice in the paper. He phoned me and in turn I called and gave the information to your lawyer. I thought I was doing you a favor." She shifted her weight from one hip to the other. "However, if you had taken my calls you would have known—"

"If you'd let my business alone, McCall and I could have had a good laugh over the coincidence, instead . . ."

McCall looked up at the mention of her name. She ached inside for Nick.

His eyes caught and held hers. In their depths was a smoldering plea to help him understand, and a play of emotion on his face.

She studied him thoughtfully. Too much was being slapped at him at once.

They shared a moment.

No words were needed.

McCall slid next to him, touched his face with her fingers to let him know she understood. McCall turned back to the two ladies, both standing with hands on their hips as though waiting for a decision. "Ladies, I should be furious as hell with both of you, and believe me, neither of you are off the hook yet." She stood tall and authoritative. "Madeline, I can't be angry with you. Josie told me that someday, I'd thank you both. So"—McCall stepped toward the Dartmouth monarch and pondered her next move—"Thank you." She felt a bottomless peace and satisfaction as the older woman issued a warm smile and opened her arms. A genuine bond formed between the unlikely pair.

"Welcome to our family," Madeline said as more tears found their way to her eyes. "I knew he couldn't stay pigheaded all his life."

McCall gave her a second embrace, then quickly turned to her grandmother. "And, Granny, I could never be mad at you. But I want the truth. Nick's mother told her side of the story, but why didn't I know about Daddy's involvement?"

The crusty woman defiantly lifted her chin and glared at her granddaughter like she was about to peel the hide off a Gila monster.

"Because you never asked," she answered indignantly. "All you had to do was ask and I would have told you everything," she snapped. "Your mother didn't care for this life or the horses. Professed to be too frail to be subjected to the elements as she called them. Pooh! Smoking and being scared too much to enjoy life made her that way."

McCall shot her a look of disbelief that she'd be talking so poorly of the dead. But suddenly the missing pieces of her parents' life had been added to the puzzle. She saw it clearly, and understood. She continued to stare at her grandmother.

"Don't look at me that way, missy," Granny shot. "Your mother was a wonderful person, but tried to rule my son. She was too needy and insecure to tame his devil-may-care goings-on."

"What does that have to do with the ranch?"

"When you were pretty young, your father took your mother to California to see if she wanted to live there. She hated it, so he came back. Along the way he met J.J. Macmurphy. I think Jock was off at college during those days. They formed a friendship and before long your dad was a partner in the ranch. He didn't want your mama to know, so he kept it all from her and ultimately from you."

"That's why I felt so comfortable at the Triple J."

"Yes. You loved the time you stayed out there. We had a stud, Triple D Figero. Your daddy and J.J. were convinced that if one of the Triple J mares, Double Deuce Down, and our stallion got together they'd produce a winner. Sure enough, Double Down Figero won them all."

"Now I understand why I was so connected with that particular horse," McCall said. "Because one of the Jack Bluff stallions is in his lineage."

Nick spoke up. "Then McCall had no way of knowing she was part owner of the ranch. All she knew was that the Triple J roan was named Asteroid. There'd be no way for her to connect the horses without their AQHA registered name."

Granny sat down, but continued. "I think you two young'ns need time alone to work things out. Maddi and I haven't finished our supper." She dished up a bowl of red beans.

McCall looked at Nick and watched a smile creep in the corner of his lips.

Chin set, Nick turned back to McCall. "I understand why you

wouldn't have known I was the buyer, but why were you so unwilling to sell one minute and then suddenly changed your mind?" A smile ruffled his lips.

"I told you." McCall moved closer until she faced him shoulder to shoulder. Heart to heart. "I planned to surprise you. I didn't even know where my ranch was located, certainly had no idea it was the Triple J." She was disarmed by the smile she looked into, swallowed to settle her wild heartbeat, and continued. "I wanted it as my wedding gift to you."

Reluctantly, they parted a few inches. "Why were you so insistent on buying it?" she challenged.

"For you . . . because you were so happy at the Triple J."

With one simple sentence, he unlocked her heart and soul and she made room for him once again.

"One more question." He looked squarely at Maddi, who seemed to be engrossed in replenishing her plate of mountain oysters. "Mother, is that manure on your shirt?"

"No, Nicodemus, *darling*." She picked up a jalapeno and used it to scoop beans on her fork. "I think the proper term is horseshit. It isn't manure until it's dried."

The stunned look on Nick's face coupled with the shock of such an uncouth statement coming from the aristocratic mouth of Madeline Elliott-Dartmouth set the stage for gaiety.

Nick tossed back his head and roared, deep and jovial.

Unable to keep her amusement under control, McCall burst into a choking laugh.

The room rocked like revelers as Madeline and Granny looked at one another in amazement, and then bent over in mirth, not stopping until tears rolled down their cheeks.

Like a Dreamsicle forgotten in the heat, McCall's willpower melted away and didn't even ask her heart for permission. When the dust settled, she threw her arms around Nick's neck and kissed him. Leaning back, looking deep into his eyes with a cocky smile, she asked, "Now, will the ranch be named Johnson and Dartmouth or Dartmouth and Johnson?"

"Well, the Texas thing to do would be name it Dartmouth and Dartmouth and call it the Double D."

Author's Note

For those who wonder about Agnes, my story is true to the urban legend that on rainy nights she roams the hillside on Harris Grade between Lompoc and Santa Maria, California, trying to locate a child she lost when her carriage rolled off the side of the mountain. Whether it is a story made up by law enforcement to keep the kids off the treacherous road or not is uncertain, but try explaining that to those who have witnessed Agnes on the road.

I took creative liberty in moving Lompoc's stand of Italian stone pines that shade a path between H Street and Locust Street and placing them at the fictional Triple J Ranch.

The Texas Moon Palace was a real Texas honky-tonk in Amarillo, Texas.

And it does rain with the sun shining in Niagara Falls.

Dear Readers,

If you got a hankering for Miss Lola Ruth's Texas Caviar, I thought you'd like to have it for yourself. I hope you enjoy the Texas favorite as much as McCall, Granny, and Maddi did.

Texas Caviar

1 pound black-eyed peas (dried)
½ cup finely chopped jalapenos
2-ounce jar diced pimentos, drained
1 cup finely chopped green onions
2 cups diced green peppers
1 tablespoon finely chopped garlic
1½ cups diced sweet onion

For the dressing:

½ cup vinegar
½ cup olive oil
⅓ cup sugar
½ teaspoon garlic powder
½ cup cilantro, chopped
½ teaspoon celery seed
Salt and pepper to taste

Soak peas in enough water to cover for six hours or overnight. Drain well. Transfer peas to saucepan. Add enough water to cover. Place over high heat and bring to boil until tender (approximately one hour). Drain peas well. Transfer to large bowl.

Blend all dressing ingredients, then mix into warm peas. Allow to cool before adding in all remaining ingredients and mix well. For best results, refrigerate overnight.

Serve on a bed of lettuce.

In a hurry? Substitute homemade oil and vinegar dressing with 2 cups Zesty Italian salad dressing.

Makes 10–12 servings.

ABOUT THE AUTHOR

A native Texan, *New York Times* and *USA Today* bestselling author Phyliss Miranda still believes in the Code of the Old West and loves to share her love for antiques, the lost art of quilting, and the Wild West.

Visit her at phylissmiranda.com.

www.ingramcontent.com/pod-product-compliance
Lightning Source LLC
Chambersburg PA
CBHW031426250626
47155CB00004B/1641